A Simon Kirby-Jones Mystery

POSTED
TO
DEATH

Dean James

KENSINGTON BOOKS
http://www.kensingtonbooks.com

KENSINGTON BOOKS are published by

Kensington Publishing Corp.
850 Third Avenue
New York, NY 10022

Library of Congress Card Catalogue Number: 2001092973
ISBN 1-57566-885-8

First Printing: April 2002
10 9 8 7 6 5 4 3 2 1

Printed in the United States of America

To Joan Lowery Nixon

Ever the epitome of generosity,
never too busy to encourage an aspiring writer,
Joan is the kind of mentor any writer dreams about.
Thank you, Joan, for all your support and
enthusiasm over the years.

Acknowledgments

First, a special thanks to Elizabeth Foxwell and Sharyn McCrumb, who gave Simon and me our first opportunity to break into print together.

Second, to my agent, Nancy Yost, for doing her best with the strange things I send her to read.

Third, to John Scognamiglio, Laurie Parkin and the fine folk at Kensington Publishing, for believing in the book and being willing to give it a chane; your support and enthusiasm means more than you can ever know.

Finally, to Patricia R. Orr, Megan Bladen-Blinkoff, Julie Wray Herman, Deborah Adams, Dorothy Cannell, Susan Rogers Cooper, and Charlaine Harris, the best cheerleading squad a vampire ever had. Your encouragement made all the difference in the world!

POSTED
TO
DEATH

Chapter One

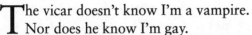

The vicar doesn't know I'm a vampire.

Nor does he know I'm gay.

If he knew either of these facts about me, I'm not sure which would cause his no-doubt-fatal heart attack. The Reverend Neville Butler-Melville is just a tad old-fashioned, shall we say? Having a vampire—and a gay one, mind you— on the committee to raise money for the church fabric wouldn't sit well with the bishop, of course, and dear Neville might find himself forcibly retired from the church.

Drearily conventional as he may be, Neville is rather scrumptious looking in his ecclesiastical kit. This was my third visit to the vicarage, and I braced myself for a sip of the hideous bargain-basement tea that Letty Butler-Melville served, in the interest of economy, I supposed. As I raised the teacup, I let my eyes linger on Neville, who was more than enough compensation for the awful tea. Neville's shiny black priest's togs complemented his pale good looks: jet black hair with a touch of gray at the temples, an aquiline nose, full, sensuous lips, and a muscular frame well suited to the cover of a romance novel. Dear Neville at forty is quite a dish. Although I'm not a regular churchgoer, I took one look at those deep emerald eyes of his and said, "Yes" when he approached me yesterday afternoon to serve on a parish committee.

Regardless of what you may have read in all those trashy vampire novels, we *can* set foot in churches without horrible things happening to us, and the sight of a cross has no effect. Unless, of course, it's cheap and vulgar, and then I promise you I'd shudder at the very least.

But more of that later. Right now I was more interested in the composition of the vicar's tea party. Having lived in the village of Snupperton Mumsley for a scant month, I still had not met many of the leading citizens, though I had glimpsed them on the odd ramble through the village. Another reason that I decided to join the committee: I needed to get to know my neighbors. We vampires no longer fade into the woodwork, as we once did, and being visible in the community is a good way to allay the suspicions of anyone who might otherwise think we're odd.

Letty Butler-Melville bent toward me to offer a plate of buns. "My very own recipe," she whispered with pride. "Garlic buns. So good for the heart, they say." I recoiled in horror. I do *not* like garlic, which is deadly to a vampire.

Puzzled at my reaction, Letty Butler-Melville whispered in concern, "Is something wrong, Dr. Kirby-Jones?"

I shook my head, relieved at my narrow escape. "It's just that I'm allergic to garlic," I whispered back. "Makes me have quite nasty hives." A small bit of garlic wouldn't be all that toxic, but if her tea was anything to judge by, the buns were probably oozing with garlic. Better safe than writhing on the floor in agony.

She gave me an odd look, but that seemed to satisfy her as she continued offering the plate of buns around to the assembled company. Apparently, the others were well acquainted with Mrs. Butler-Melville's culinary gifts, for they all declined to partake.

I surveyed the assembled company once more. Beside her husband, Letty Butler-Melville seemed oddly colorless. Whereas Neville had dramatic good looks, Letty tended to fade in one's memory. Almost as tall as her husband, with a physique not much different from his, she wore a bulky, ill-fitting dress that emphasized her drabness. Apparently the Fashion Sense Fairy had taken one look at her and run away screaming.

In addition to the vicar and Letty, our little party included Lady Prunella Blitherington and her snobby son, Giles, the matriarch and scion of the "first family" of the village. The other guests were an older woman named Jane Hardwick, who lived in a cottage near the church, across the lane from me, and a horsey-looking individual named Abigail Winterton (female, though it was hard to tell from the way the creature dressed and the state of its hair), evidently the postmistress and proprietress of the village shop.

Dear Lady Prunella Blitherington (God *does* have a sense of humor, after all) was holding forth, yet again, on something. I had, only moments after meeting her, discovered that tuning out a voice that sounded like unrefined felines in the throes of passion a matter of dire necessity. My senses are, as you might imagine, preternaturally acute, and hearing Lady Blitherington live up to her name is excruciating. I tuned in briefly; I had to pay attention at some point or they'd think I was completely brainless.

"Dear Vicar," she squealed, "naturally one would dearly *love* to donate the *entire* sum which dear St. Ethelwold's *needs* to restore it to all its glory"—here the snooty Giles began to look alarmed—"but of course one simply *cannot* these days, thanks to the depredations of the Inland Revenue." She babbled on in the same vein, and Giles relaxed. It's a pity he has such a snotty look about him, otherwise he could be quite tempting. About twenty-five, he has curly auburn hair, deep blue eyes, and creamy skin that many a debutante would kill for. He's also six feet three or so and built like a linebacker. With the cranky disposition he seems to have, I wouldn't want to make him angry. He looks like he could bench-press his mother (who must weigh close to three hundred pounds) and still have a hand free to crush something, like my head.

My eyes roved around the room. The furnishings, like the clothes the Melville-Butlers wore, were slightly tatty. Well worn, showing signs of age, but obviously well cared for. After all, they would have to do for quite a while. I imagined that there were many other vicarages around England that looked very much like this one. The Church Temporal no doubt could use an infusion of pounds sterling. Despite the air of genteel poverty that the room exuded, Letty Melville-Butler had made it warm, comfortable, and inviting. I decided to forgive her for the tea and the poisonous buns, poor woman.

That *voice* broke through my thoughts once again.

"No, no, no, my *dear* Letty," Lady Blitherington intoned, "one simply *cannot* approve the notion of putting on some *terribly* old-fashioned play like Shakespeare or Oscar Wilde." At the latter name she seemed to give a delicate shudder. "We *must* look to the *future* and our up-and-coming writers for inspiration. One *must* insist that the Snupperton Mumsley Amateur Dramatic Society try something *new*. I am the chairwoman of the board of directors, after all, and I do believe that I speak for the *entire* board when I say that a completely *new* play is most *assuredly* the ticket." She paused for a sip of her tea. "In fact, if I might be so *bold* as to suggest, I daresay that we might put on *dear* Giles's little play. It's a thriller, isn't it, darling? And you *know* how audiences love that *silly* Christie play, *The Mousetrap*. After all, Giles is *just* as clever as Dame Agatha ever *dared* to be, and I'm certain that a production of *Who Murdered Mater?* would bring audiences simply *pouring* in."

I coughed a mouthful of tea back into my cup. Curiously

enough, the same thing had happened to most of the others in the room at approximately the same time. Giles Blitherington turned rather an interesting shade of pink as we all stared at him.

"Mummy," he said in a surprisingly pleasant tenor, "naturally I'd be *thrilled* if SMADS chose my play, but perhaps other members of this committee might have more worthy suggestions."

False modesty will get you nowhere, boyo, I thought to myself.

Abigail Winterton seemed skeptical as well. "Nonsense, Prunella," she trumpeted in a voice about an octave lower than my own baritone, and those nostrils flared in a good imitation of Secretariat. "Giles got sent down from Oxford after one term, and Cambridge wouldn't have him. Boy can't get a degree, how can we assume he can write?" She slapped her teacup down with such force I thought it would shatter.

"*Really,* Abigail," Lady Blitherington responded, injured pride oozing from every syllable. "Just because one doesn't have a university *degree* doesn't mean one isn't *intelligent,* after all. There are *some* minds which are simply *too* brilliant for the mundane requirements of the present educational system. Don't *you* agree, Dr. Kirby-Jones?"

Thus appealed to, I had little choice. "My *dear* Lady Blitherington, that would *certainly* be the case in the American educational system, with which I am most familiar, as you no doubt know." Frankly, I'm surprised she would deign to ask the opinion of a mere American. "In my own experience, I encountered any number of bright and articulate students who nevertheless had difficulties complying with the routine demands of the educational system. *Some* of them persevered, some did not." I gave Giles a rather superior smile, and he sulked back at me. Pity the boy was so determined to be unpleasant.

"Rather," Lady Blitherington replied, uncertain whether I

had upheld her or made Giles look even more foolish. "Well, quite, um, yes. After all, my dear Abigail, I'm not certain that a mere *shopkeeper* is qualified to pass judgment on the *literary* merits of a play. I'm sure the *rest* of the board will be able to see the merits of Giles's play even if *you* are prejudiced against him."

Abigail Winterton sniffed loudly and derisively. "If the only thing you're worried about is saving the board money, my *dear* Prunella," she mocked her adversary, "then you needn't worry. I know of another author who has written a play *perfectly* suited for our needs, and this person would be absolutely *delighted* to grant SMADS the right to perform it for *no* remuneration whatsoever."

"What type of play is it?" Lady Prunella demanded, icicles practically hanging from every word. In the last few minutes, I had begun to think that village life was going to be vastly entertaining. "One presumes that you know *something* about it?"

Miss Winterton chuckled smugly. "Oh, most assuredly, I do. In fact, I have read it *several* times." For a moment, her mirth nearly overcame her. "Everyone in the village would find it *most* amusing. Not to say, enlightening. The author is a local who, I assure you, is most au courant with village affairs." She looked slowly, one by one, at everyone in the room except me.

Was it my imagination, or had Letty Butler-Melville turned even pastier than usual? The vicar took a big gulp of his tea, while Lady Prunella seemed at an uncharacteristic loss for words. Jane Hardwick evinced only amusement. Her eyes caught mine briefly, then flickered away. Giles Blitherington made an intense study of his fingernails.

Lady Prunella finally found her voice. "I suppose, Abigail, if you *insist,* the board must needs *consider* this play. Can you arrange to have a copy of it at the board meeting?"

Miss Winterton nodded.

"We shall consider the play, then," Lady Prunella said. "But I have *little* doubt that it will prove *vastly* inferior to Giles's work. I suppose, however, one *must* give the nod to notions of *democracy* in this situation." She glared at Miss Winterton, perhaps in retribution for having to use the word "democracy" in public.

Abigail Winterton turned red, and I feared for a moment that she would rear up and let fly. But I suppose she had gained whatever it was she wanted, for the moment. Round two would come later, I shouldn't be surprised. Lady Blitherington swept on, paying no more attention to Abigail Winterton. "As I was saying *before,* Giles has written a simply *marvelous* thriller which I think it would behoove the SMADS to consider, but that is a decision we must apparently postpone."

"I've no doubt that the board will choose the most prudent course of action," Jane Hardwick said into the brief silence that had followed Lady Prunella's words. There were definitely undercurrents here of which I was completely ignorant. But perhaps someone in the village could enlighten me. Whom should I ask? I eyed Jane Hardwick speculatively. She had distinct possibilities. Her sardonic smile seemed to indicate that she knew where plenty of the village's skeletons were hidden. There was something naggingly familiar about her, anyway, and I decided I should get to know her better. I had already observed her, on several occasions, working in her garden alone or directing a couple of workmen who seemed to be doing some heavy digging for her in her back garden. No doubt she kept an eye on the goings-on in the village.

Miss Hardwick continued in her smoothly cultured voice. "I propose that we postpone further discussion of the activities of the Snupperton Mumsley Amateur Dramatic Society. This committee is really *not* the proper venue for such a decision, since only the two of you are members of the board of the society. We, as members of the Church Restoration Fund Committee, may express our interest, since the society has so graciously agreed to aid us in our efforts, but we simply cannot dictate the choice of plays."

"Quite right," Neville Butler-Melville added, his voice light, determined to spread the proverbial oil. "When two committees unite for a common goal, we must endeavor to work well together. After all, our goal is such a worthy one, the restoration of our beloved St. Ethelwold's, that we must not injure our efforts with the hint of dissension."

"Yes, of course, *dear* Vicar," gushed Lady Blitherington, though she cast a steely glance at both Abigail Winterton and Jane Hardwick. "We must *all* pull together for the sake of *dear* St. Ethelwold's. Dear Jane," she continued, "always *so* sensible. And so, *so* democratic." In Lady Blitherington's mouth, the word again sounded like an insult. Which, no doubt, it was intended to be. Jane Hardwick smiled graciously in return.

Giles stood up, smiling at the rest of us. I blinked at the change in his features. Oh, my. "Mummy, I'm afraid we ought to be going. Remember that you wanted to be home in time to supervise Alsatia's riding lesson with Dirk." From the odd tone of his voice, I rather got the impression that if Lady Blitherington were not present, the aforementioned Dirk might be giving Alsatia something other than a riding lesson.

At the reminder, Lady Prunella practically hopped up from her chair. "Oh, yes, Giles, dear. Thanks for reminding Mummy. I'm sure you will all excuse us. We shall continue our discussion tomorrow evening." She headed for the front door of the vicarage without waiting for anyone else even to acknowledge her farewell.

Abigail Winterton spoke up. "I'm afraid I, too, must be going, Vicar, Letty dear. This is the day my assistant leaves early, and I have to get back to close the shop." She stood.

The vicar rose from his chair. "Thank you all for coming

today. I know with your dedication to the project, we are bound to succeed in our goals of raising money for the restoration of the church fabric. And"—here he turned to beam in my direction—"we are certainly most delighted to have the assistance of so distinguished a young historian as Dr. Kirby-Jones. I am pleased to welcome you to the committee and, indeed, to Snupperton Mumsley, as, I'm sure, are we all."

"Thank you, Vicar," I responded modestly. "It really is good of you to invite a stranger to take part in village life. I knew from the first moment that I set eyes upon it that Snupperton Mumsley was the home in England for which I had always longed. I trust I will be able to make my contributions to the life of the village." I can smarm with the best of them, in case you hadn't noticed already. And I'm sure the potential size of my bank balance had as much to do with my presence here today as my charming personality.

"Oh, well said, well said." The vicar continued beaming at me. "Now, all of you, I'll expect to see you tomorrow night at our joint meeting with the board of directors of the dramatic society, what?"

After assuring him that we would all be there and thanking Letty Butler-Melville for the insipid tea, we all made our way down the cramped and dim hall of the vicarage to the front door, retrieving hats and other accoutrements as we went. Lady Blitherington, Giles trailing in her wake, was already marching off down the lane toward the ancestral manor, Blitherington Hall, which stood on extensive grounds just outside the village. Abigail Winterton snorted her goodbyes and loped off toward the post office. Jane Hardwick paused to speak to me.

Out in the sunlight of the late August afternoon, I had my first really good look at Jane Hardwick. She could be anywhere between forty and sixty, with neatly cut and styled gray hair, the standard twin set and pearls, sensible shoes, and a capacious handbag. Her bright eyes sparkled with intelligence, mischief, and humor. She looked like anyone's favorite maiden aunt or a slightly junior version of Miss Maud Silver.

"If you wouldn't mind, Dr. Kirby-Jones," she said, "I think there are a few things we should discuss. Things that would be of mutual benefit."

"Certainly," I said, gallantly offering her my arm. "I had been hoping to further our acquaintance." As we talked, she led me across the lane to her cottage.

"Thank you," she said, glancing up demurely into my face. "After all, our kind should stick together, don't you think?"

Chapter Two

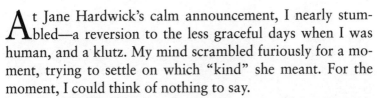

At Jane Hardwick's calm announcement, I nearly stumbled—a reversion to the less graceful days when I was human, and a klutz. My mind scrambled furiously for a moment, trying to settle on which "kind" she meant. For the moment, I could think of nothing to say.

With a serene smile at my momentary speechlessness, Miss Hardwick directed our footsteps toward her gate, fifty yards or so down the lane from the vicarage. My own cottage stood another few yards down, at the north end of the village.

As the gate closed behind us, Jane broke the silence. "I'm not a lesbian, Dr. Kirby-Jones."

"How did you know, then?" I demanded, my voice rougher than I intended. While waiting for her reply, I observed her garden with interest. Her garden had well repaid the time and care she had evidently lavished upon it, to judge by the elaborate and extensive beds of flowers. The colorful profusion dazzled my eyes and made me ruefully aware of my own neglected garden.

Jane Hardwick unlocked her front door and motioned me

inside. Before answering, she took my hat and placed it on an ornate stand near the front door. She then glided through the narrow hallway into what I presumed was her sitting room. I found a seat on a plush high-backed sofa near her chair while she arranged herself comfortably, regarding me quietly all the while.

"How could you tell?" I asked her, impatiently breaking the silence. "I mean, I thought there was something oddly familiar about you, but I didn't know what."

"You are rather new at this, aren't you?" Jane inquired, and I nodded. She laughed, a bit patronizingly, I thought. "Mainly it's the skin tone. Once you've been around as long as I have, you can spot another vampire just from the skin alone. But there are other things," she told me. "The eyes, for one. I can always tell by looking into someone's eyes. You'll understand what I mean in time." She laughed again, and I rankled slightly at the sound. "And the other clue, I must admit, was the fact that you are living in Tristan Lovelace's cottage."

I sighed, relaxing a bit. "I might have known." Tristan Lovelace, that dashing, gorgeous vampire, who also just happened to be my dissertation advisor in graduate school, had given me the cottage a few months ago. As far as anyone in the village knew, however, I had bought the cottage from Tris. He had told me about the cottage itself, but he had neglected to tell me anything about Jane Hardwick or the other folk in the village. He simply had assured me that I'd enjoy Snupperton Mumsley immensely. I thought I was beginning to see what he had meant.

"Yes, dear Tristan," Jane said, grinning wickedly. "When I heard his cottage had been sold, I was expecting someone like you. Tristan's outstanding good taste never falters."

I blushed. (Yes, we actually can, though it's not as noticeable.)

POSTED TO DEATH   13

"At some point, we should have quite a long talk about Tristan," Jane continued. "He and I have much in common, including our taste in men."

"Thank you," I said. "I think."

Jane laughed. "You must call me Jane, and I'll call you Simon. No need to be formal, I think." She inclined her head toward me, and I nodded.

"Have you spoken to Tristan lately, Simon?" she went on. "I've not heard from him in simply ages."

"No," I said, "Tris and I aren't that close any longer. We rarely talk these days." No need to go into all *that* with Jane, no matter how well she knew Tris.

"A pity." She smiled, a bit wolfishly. I was momentarily taken aback. "There is one thing I must ask you right away, however," she continued.

I forestalled the question. "No need. I don't follow the old ways." I shuddered at the thought.

"No," Jane said. "I thought not. Nor do I." She paused. "Usually." I had a terrifying glimpse, only the briefest flash, of another Jane, and I shuddered again.

By now, no doubt, you are wondering about vampires who walk around in the daytime and partake of tea at the vicarage, no less. The secret lies, you see, in some very special medication. The budget-watchers in Congress back home would have a fit if they knew about it, but there's one laboratory at the National Institutes of Health in Bethesda in which all of the scientists are vampires. They took research on a failed drug for hemophilia discarded by scientists in another unit and, on the sly, came up with something that has completely changed vampire life. Thanks to their ingenuity, via the marvelous little pills I take twice a day, I no longer have to hide at the first hint of daylight.

The pills are quite a decent substitute for all that nasty bloodsucking vampires used to have to do, and the fact that I don't have to spend roughly half of every twenty-four hours hidden away certainly increases my literary productivity. Vampires also don't need much sleep, you see. Two or three hours in any twenty-four are more than sufficient for my needs.

Mind you, there are those vampires who cling stubbornly to the old ways. Attacking mortals, sucking their blood, then scurrying away to bury themselves in mausoleums or hide themselves in dank, dark cemeteries at light of day. But there are groups within our ranks to take care of rogue vampires who become too destructive, thankfully.

I think all that's a bit disgusting, myself, but you know how stubborn people can be when they cling to traditional values. Afraid to try anything new. In my own case, I can heartily testify to the fact that the pills have made my life in death that much more enjoyable.

Since I don't have to worry about finding my daily ration of blood, I can give thought to other matters. Instead of haring around, looking for a tempting neck to bite (or, horror of horrors, making do with the nearest cat, dog, bunny, or cow), I can spend my "hunting" time in more pleasurable ends. Another myth you may have heard is that vampires can't have "relations," shall we say, in the accustomed human manner. Total bunk, I'm quite happy to report. I wouldn't have given *that* up, let me tell you!

Jane Hardwick was apparently one of the New Age vampires like me. Which was just as well. Those bloodsuckers make me nervous.

"Snupperton Mumsley is, on the whole, a quiet village, and I would rather see it stay that way," Jane said. "Before"—and I knew she meant before the advent of our little pills—"I used to lead such a rackety existence, and the folk here thought I was more than a little eccentric. But the last ten years have been marvelous, and I've been able to take part in so many more village activities."

"The Church Restoration Fund, no less," I said, my voice dry.

Jane laughed merrily. "Exactly. No doubt there are those in the village who believe I must have had some sort of conversion experience when, after living here a decade, I suddenly became an assiduous churchgoer and indefatigable worker for all sorts of causes."

"A blinding light on the road to Bedford?" Bedford was the nearest town of importance, only a few miles away. Jane affected not to notice the tone of subtle mockery in my voice.

"You should have little trouble fitting into village life," Jane said. "As long as you're discreet, that is. There are some rather nosy folk in this village." She smiled again. This time I took it as a warning. "After tea at the vicarage today, no doubt you could see how clueless our vicar is—I believe that is the correct American expression, is it not?—and poor Letty, as you witnessed, sees little beyond the vicar and her own good works about the parish. Prunella Blitherington is so massively self-absorbed that she notices only that in others which might have some effect upon her and hers."

"That reminds me. *What* is the story between her and the unfortunate person who runs the village store?" Now perhaps we could get to the really good stuff.

"Ah, yes, dear Abigail," Jane purred. "Once upon a time, Abigail Winterton and Prunella Ragsbottom (and, yes, that was really her name) were the best of friends. All through childhood, school, and so on. Both were the daughters of tradesmen, though Prunella always glosses over that fact. Mr. Ragsbottom was a greengrocer with pretensions, and Abigail's father ran the shop before her. You might not be able to imagine it now, but years ago, the two of them were quite lovely young women. Lovely enough, that is, to attract the dubious charms of the only son of the local baronet. The late Sir Bosworth Blitherington fancied himself a ladies' man, as men of that class unfortunately are wont to do at the slightest encouragement, and ever with an eye to the main chance, Prunella waged an all-out campaign to become the eventual Lady Blitherington. Abigail, who actually might have loved the poor old sod, rather bitterly had to concede defeat in the matrimonial stakes, and the two have been enemies ever since. Poor Bosworth Blitherington never had a chance, once Prunella set her cap at him."

"The mind boggles," I responded weakly, warding off visions of the youthful Prunella and Abigail. "That must have been thirty years ago or more," I reasoned. "Were you already living in the village?" My own discreet way of pumping Jane for a bit of her history.

Ah, but she was much too fly for such a simple ruse. "My dear Simon, one thing you should learn right away. Be direct with me. Knowing Tristan, he never even mentioned my name. I'm sure he wanted to surprise you." She smiled again, and I squirmed in my chair. She was a bit terrifying. The steel magnolias I had grown up with had nothing on Jane. "Don't pussyfoot around with me. I really don't mind answering a direct question. At least not for you."

I pondered this for a moment. "All right, then, just how old are you?"

Jane laughed. "If I tell you I was first presented at the court of Elizabeth Tudor, what would you say?"

"Absolutely smashing!" I said before I could stop myself. Good Queen Bess had ever been one of my favorites, and the chance to talk to someone who had actually seen her in the flesh thrilled me no end. Not to mention the details I could glean for my next historical romance.

"To go back to your previous question," Jane said, smiling at my enthusiasm, "I've lived in Snupperton Mumsley for about twenty years. Though I was unfortunately not present to witness the matrimonial campaign, I have my sources among those who did. Suffice it to say, Prunella was every bit as shrewd as dear Bess was when it came to manipulating men."

"My dear Jane," I said happily. "We're going to be great friends."

"Yes, Simon," she replied, staring intently at me, "I do believe we are."

What was it that Alice Roosevelt Longworth was reputed to have said? "Come and sit by me, if you've got any good dirt, that is." Oh, yes, Jane and I would get along like houses afire.

"Now, tell me," I said, reverting to an earlier subject, "more about Prunella and Abigail. Do they often . . . *erupt* like they did today at the vicarage?"

Jane frowned. "No, actually, they don't. That was a bit odd, now that I think of it. Most of the time they simply ignore each other as much as possible and speak in icily polite tones when they can't avoid talking. Something must have happened to upset their nasty little acid balance." She looked thoughtful. "Frankly, I'm surprised that neither of them has been murdered before now. They're both unpleasant. Prunella tries to interfere in everyone's business, but she does it openly. Abigail, on the other hand, is rather sly and prying. They battle constantly over the running of village affairs, while Letty Butler-Melville tries to keep the peace and does most of the actual work." She laughed. "But that's life in the village for you. Snupperton Mumsley, at any rate."

"It certainly sounds to me like there's something brewing over the choice of a play. Do they get this worked up over everything?"

"Unfortunately, they nearly always do." Jane frowned, thinking. "But I'm rather surprised that Abigail is being so coy about the author of the play she wants us to stage. There is most definitely something afoot, and I'll have to rely on you to give me all the details after the meeting tomorrow evening. I have a previous engagement, so I won't be able to attend the joint meeting."

After assuring Jane that I would be delighted to report back to her, I soon took my leave and meandered down the lane, to my cottage. Though it was now going on six P.M., the sun was still hanging high in the sky. Ah, summer in England!

I pushed open my gate and walked up the path to my front door. My front door, I thought. *My* front door! I still couldn't quite believe that the cottage was mine, that I was really here in England. I reached out a hand and touched the reddish brown brick in wonder. I had seen similar brick farther east, along the coast of East Anglia, where Flemish influence in building was strong. In the evening sun the brick glowed with warmth.

"Cottage" was actually something of a misnomer for this building, because it had once upon a time been two laborers' cottages. Sometime in the late nineteenth century the two cottages had been knocked together and the whole renovated extensively to turn it into Laurel Cottage, a suitable country residence for a Victorian gentleman of ample means. The brick had been added then, as had a kitchen and pantry across the back, and the roof covered with pantiles. During his ownership (and I had never asked him just how long he had owned it) Tristan Lovelace had updated the plumbing and electricity. I had lots of Olde World charm but with few of the inconveniences.

While fiddling in a pocket for the latchkey, I glanced around the garden. I definitely needed someone to take care of the grounds. Jane Hardwick's garden put mine to shame.

As I let myself into the cool dimness of the cottage, I flicked on the lights in the small hallway. I hung up my hat, then proceeded upstairs to the bathroom. It was time for my medication, and I didn't like to miss a dose. The complications could be a bit uncomfortable.

I downed my magic little pill with a glass of water and glared at my reflection in the mirror. (Sorry to shatter another illusion.) If I grimaced just right, I could see my fangs. I think they give me rather a rakish look. Ordinarily I'm not a vain person, but I have to admit that I make a distinguished appearance. Dark hair, dark eyes, and a dark, short-trimmed beard give me an encingly mysterious look, I think. And one other good thing about being a vampire—I no longer have to worry about a weight problem. Though I do eat and drink, the amounts are minimal compared to what I used to consume when I was alive.

Back in my bedroom, I stripped out of my tea-party duds and got comfortable in a worn T-shirt and a pair of jogging pants. I had quite a bit of work ahead of me tonight, and I might as well be comfortable in front of the computer.

Downstairs, in my study-cum-office, ignoring the stacks and piles of papers and boxes that needed attention, I turned on the lamps, got the computer started, then plopped myself down in front of the screen. I had to finish the final chapter of the latest magnum opus by Daphne Deepwood. When I last left them, the hero and heroine of *Passion in Peru* were about to be thrown over a cliff by the bad guys, they of the Shining Path, and I had to devise some way to get them out of this dilemma. My loyal readers, who had made my previous three novels huge best-sellers, would expect something dazzling and original, no doubt.

The world knows me as Dr. Simon Kirby-Jones, historian and well-respected biographer. I could make a decent living (pardon the irony here) turning out popular history, but I make absolute scads of lolly churning out popular fiction as Daphne Deepwood (historical romance) and Dorinda Darlington (hard-boiled-female-private-eye novels). Besides, Daphne and Dorinda are a heck of a lot more fun than the semistuffy Simon. Who, by the way, was actually born about thirty-five years ago as one Sam Jones in Pleasant Springs, Mississippi. But that's a whole 'nother story.

For the moment, I was having trouble getting myself interested in the perils of my characters in *Passion in Peru*. Lisette insisted on squealing rather loudly, and Thorne was more interested in combing his hair than escaping from Shining Path guerrillas. Characters can be quite tiresome. I was tempted to let them both jump off a cliff into a pit of alligators and be done with the whole thing, but I knew my readers expected better of me. And, frankly, so did I. More than enough time to concentrate on the job at hand; the intrigues of Snupperton Mumsley could wait till later.

Sometime in the wee small hours of the morning, I shut off the computer, satisfied that the ending of *Passion in Peru* was exactly what I wanted. I could ship off the manuscript tomorrow to my agent in London and relax a bit before launching into the new Dorinda Darlington. I turned off the lamps in my office and moved over to the window to look out on the sleeping village.

The moon shed a beguiling glow over the lane outside my window. Nothing moved. Ah, the peace of a quiet English village, I thought. I could make myself quite at home here, immersing myself in writing and taking part in village life as I chose.

As I watched, something moved in the shadows cast by the trees along the lane. I focused my gaze, and as the thing moved closer, I could see that it was a person. Who on earth was out walking the village at this time of night?

The figure paused for a moment at the gate of the house next to Jane Hardwick's, then slipped inside. Fascinated, I continued to watch as whoever it was wandered through the garden and around the house, emerging back into view a couple of minutes later. Back out into the lane it came, then through the gate at Jane Hardwick's. Once again, the same procedure—a circuit around the cottage. Puzzled, I wondered for a moment whether it was the village bobby making late-night rounds to ensure that all was well.

Then the figure approached my own gate, and I could see, finally, who it was. What on earth was Abigail Winterton doing prowling through the village in the dead of night?

Chapter Three

I t took death to make me a morning person.
That's one of the many ironies of my existence as a vampire. When I was mortal, I hated worse than anything having to get up before at least ten A.M. Now that I need so little sleep to keep me bouncing along like that annoying bunny in the television commercials, I can get up quite happily at the crack of dawn. Those magic pills really do make a difference. Disgusting, isn't it?

I had a luxurious shower. Tristan's cottage—now mine, I reminded myself—might look like something out of Jane Austen, but inside it was thoroughly modern. Ever the sybarite Tristan had made sure of that. The heat of the water on my skin refreshed me. I know you're disappointed to find out that vampires do something as mundane as bathe, but we do sweat a little, after all.

After drying off and dressing, I wandered about downstairs, waiting for the water to boil for my morning tea. While I waited, I turned on the computer and started printing out the final chapter of *Passion in Peru*. The post office opened at nine, and I wanted to be there when it opened to get the manuscript off my hands and into the Royal Mail.

I sat and sipped my tea as the laser printer spit out page after page of my deathless prose. I think I am one writer who can use that adjective with some justification. Thanks to the speed of the printer, I had the pages I needed in less than twenty minutes. I bundled them together with the rest of the manuscript, quickly composed and printed a cover letter for my agent, then put it all in a box.

Wrapping paper, I thought. Where is it? I glanced around the room, wondering which box held what I needed. Sorry to disappoint you yet again, but I have no X-ray vision. I had to open the boxes by hand and shuffle through the contents until I found what I needed. What I really needed, I decided, was someone to organize this mess. And preferably not me.

Eventually, I had everything in order, and I was ready to head out the door a few minutes before nine. I stuck my head out the door. Clear and hot already. I retrieved my hat and my sunglasses from the hat stand in the hallway, clasped my parcel under my arm, and set out.

Though I had, in theory, resided in Snupperton Mumsley for all of a month, I had, in practice, spent very little time here until the past few days. Upon arriving in England, I had spent much of my time in London, taking care of various matters. There is quite a bit of red tape involved for any American who wants to live in England, and though Snupperton Mumsley is located conveniently near a stop on the Thameslink line north of London, I figured it would be much simpler to hang around in London until everything was sorted out. I had been given the cottage furnished, sight unseen, by Tristan Lovelace and had my books and other personal items shipped there. I had been down once to check that all my things had arrived, but the rest of the time I had been mostly in London, with the occasional short weekend visit to the cottage to start putting things in order. I do adore London, but by the time I got all the paperwork taken care of, I was ready to settle for a while amidst the pastoral plea-sures of village life in Snupperton Mumsley.

All of the foregoing being, of course, a rather long-winded explanation of why I had as yet not set foot in the village store–cum–post office.

I paused at my gate. A warm, fragrant breeze eddied around me, carrying with it the myriad scents of an August morning in England. I sniffed deeply the heady smell of freshly mown hay from the farm down the lane from me. Memories of my childhood and youth in Mississippi tumbled in my head, triggered by that smell.

I ambled down the lane—it was the main road through the village, actually, but it was such a minor thoroughfare, it was hard to find it on any map, and I didn't worry much about being run over by a car or lorry. I strolled past Jane Hard-wick's cottage, past the church, and on into the "business" section of the village, enjoying the shade of all the trees along the way. When I walked up to the door of the post office, Abigail Winterton was just unlocking it.

"Good morning, Dr. Kirby-Jones." The greeting was grudging, offered in a sour tone that belied the adjective. No doubt lack of sleep, thanks to her late-night ramble, made her less than gracious this morning.

"Good morning, Miss Winterton," I responded with my most gratuitously American bonhomie. I even tipped my hat to her. "How *are* you this morning? It was *so* delightful to meet you yesterday at the vicarage! Living in this charming village is going to be *such* a thrill for me, you know. I've loved England for so *many* years, and here I am, living *right* in the middle of a lifelong dream. And you have *such* a de-lightful shop!"

Babbling on, I poured it on so thick, my accent becoming ever-so-slightly more southern with each syllable, that I had her simpering with superiority before it was over. By the time

I was done, she knew I was just another one of those potty Americans who wanted to be more English than the queen herself.

I handed her my parcel to be weighed, then passed over money for the appropriate postage, and Abigail Winterton condescended to indulge my curiosity about the Snupperton Mumsley Amateur Dramatic Society. "The society goes back over one hundred years, you know. It was originally founded by the late baronet's great-grandfather"—how carefully she avoided mentioning the Blitherington name—"and we have had great success with our programs for many, many years." She paused to size me up. "Are you interested in trying out for a part?" Her eyes gleamed for a moment, and I wondered what scheme she had in mind.

"Sorry," I replied, hanging my head in shame, "but I have absolutely no dramatic skills whatsoever. I'm afraid that what talent I have lies with the written word." I am shameless, of course, but why not be? I'm so good at it.

Miss Winterton frowned at that, considering. But then she brightened. "Well, we are always interested in new writing talent, of course. Have you written any plays, or considered writing one? After all, if a brainless wonder like Giles Blitherington can turn out one, surely a man of your education could do the same." The spite in her tone amused me, and the expression of hatred on her face, fleeting though it was, was a wonder to behold. If I were Prunella Blitherington, I'd watch my back.

Once again I had to express my regrets. The last thing I wanted to do was get involved in writing plays for an amateur dramatic group, no matter how august they might be. And I certainly was going to reserve judgment on that!

Abigail Winterton barely heard my regrets, however. "This year, fortunately, we won't have to use some drivel written by an overgrown schoolboy." For a moment, I thought she was referring to me, but then I realized that Giles Blitherington was her target. I was beginning to have some sympathy for him.

"Oh, yes," I said politely. "You mentioned last evening that you knew of a suitable play."

Miss Winterton simpered. I don't believe I had ever seen an adult female actually simper, but Miss Winterton could have given Shirley Temple lessons. "Why, yes, I do." She laughed. Horses for miles around probably perked up their ears. "This play would be just the thing for our group. The village would never, *ever*, forget it!"

She seemed privy to some source of mirth that escaped me completely. She rocked silently back and forth, gripping her sides in a most unladylike manner.

"That bodes well for the Church Restoration Fund, I suppose," I said. "Have I perchance *met* the author of this astonishing work of drama?" I even batted my eyelashes at her, but to no avail.

She turned coy. "Now, that would be telling, you *naughty* man." She was actually flirting with me. "I don't believe I shall tell you, even though you asked *so* prettily. No, I do believe I shall share the good news with everyone tonight, at the meeting, when we're all gathered together."

"I shall look forward to it," I responded politely.

"It will be a night Snupperton Mumsley might never forget," she chortled.

I decided to take a chance. "Yes, nights can be rather interesting here. I'm something of a night owl myself, you know, and one can observe the most *interesting* things just by peeking out the window in the dead of night."

Miss Winterton had been reaching for something under the counter, but she hesitated, glancing at me through a fringe of the unkempt hair hanging over her eyes.

"Such a peaceful time to be taking a walk, don't you think?" I continued.

She straightened, watching me uncertainly.

"One can see such interesting things, I suppose."

"I suppose," she finally spoke, "if one *were* walking about at such a time of night, one *might* observe something out of the ordinary. A village like this has many little secrets just waiting to be discovered." Her face took on a vulpine look, and I thought for a moment that she had forgotten me.

"My goodness," she finally said. "Where is my head this morning! I'm sure you'd like to have your mail, now, wouldn't you?"

"Certainly. Thank you very much," I said as she handed me a small bundle of letters.

The door opened then with a jingle, preventing me from the further probing of Miss Winterton. The morning sun accompanied the woman who entered, wrapping her head in a halo that made her thick blond hair seem to glow. Then the door shut, and the sun receded, leaving me blinking. I pulled on my dark glasses, and the world came back into view.

She wore one of those outfits that looks so simple, yet so elegant, that it probably cost as much as the advance on my first novel. She moved with an assured grace, confident that nothing and no one would stand in her way. Her face had a serene beauty that seemed out of character with what I had observed thus far of the inhabitants of Snupperton Mumsley. I thought she might be in her late thirties, but she could be a very well preserved fifty. What on earth was she doing here? I wondered.

"Good morning, Mrs. Stevens," Abigail Winterton cooed at her. "How are you this fine day?"

Miss Winterton's voice was so sweet I could tell that she was either terrified of the other woman or detested her. Or both.

"Good morning, Miss Winterton. I am exceedingly well, thank you. And you?" Mrs. Stevens paused to give me a thorough going-over, paying no attention whatsoever to the state of Abigail Winterton's health.

Once the X ray was complete, Mrs. Stevens turned back to Abigail Winterton. "Won't you introduce us, Miss Winterton?" The formality of the tone rebuked the postmistress for her breach of etiquette, and the poor woman flushed a terribly unbecoming shade of puce. At least it drew attention away from the unfortunate state of her hair. What on earth did she fix it with to get it to look like that? An eggbeater?

"Forgive me," Miss Winterton stuttered. "I don't know where my manners are this morning." *Ah,* I thought, *but I do know where you'd like to put your knife.*

"Mrs. Stevens, may I introduce Dr. Simon Kirby-Jones? Dr. Kirby-Jones, Mrs. Samantha Stevens. Dr. Kirby-Jones has just moved here from America." As I took the proffered hand, I restrained myself from asking where Darrin might be or whether Endora might pop in any moment. I doubted either one of them would have known what I meant, anyway.

"Very pleased to meet you, Mrs. Stevens," I said, clasping her hand. She inclined her head, coolly. She had already cataloged me as attractive but unavailable, and her interest was merely intellectual, no longer hormonal.

"Welcome to Snupperton Mumsley, Dr. Kirby-Jones," she said. "What, may I ask, brings an American to such a backwater as this?"

I was a bit surprised that she would ask such a question directly. I had thought finesse would be one of her strong suits, but perhaps she was in a hurry.

"I'm a historian and a biographer with a lifelong interest in English history, and when the chance came to live in England, I simply couldn't resist." I smiled my most charming smile and was rewarded with a brief twitch of the lips.

"Then you must be, of course, the person who has bought Tristan Lovelace's cottage." The slight emphasis on Tris's name said it all. Suspicions confirmed, it said. Might make an entertaining dinner companion or decorating consultant but little else.

She was definitely built to be a man-killer. You might say it takes one to know one, if you'll pardon the feeble (and mostly inaccurate) joke. Again, I wondered what *she* was doing in this little village, but I restrained my curiosity—for the moment.

"And how is *dear* Mr. Stevens?" Abigail Winterton purred. "All recovered from that nasty *accident* he had while you were on holiday last week?"

I looked at Samantha Stevens with renewed interest. By the tone of Abigail Winterton's voice, I was convinced that Mrs. Stevens had somehow contrived her husband's accident. A merry widow in the making, perhaps?

"He's recovering quite nicely, thank you, Miss Winterton. The poor dear"—she turned again to me—"simply cannot be convinced that he's a little past the age to do certain things. You know how men are." Her gaze challenged me.

"Yes, I know just what you mean," I responded.

Abigail Winterton hadn't quite got it all figured out yet. Someone would have to take her aside and explain rather carefully that I was one of those nasty poofters her parents had whispered about. The poor dear seemed a bit slow on the uptake on certain matters.

"Well, I'm so delighted," Miss Winterton continued, blithely, "that Mr. Stevens is doing so well. After all, he has so many *obligations*, doesn't he? I mean, he is so busy with all his investments. One wouldn't like to think he was losing any of his *own* money." Whatever could she mean by that? I wondered.

She rattled on. "We've all been so happy that a man so eminent in the City should choose Snupperton Mumsley for his retirement. I do hope, though," she added maliciously, "that no little accidents deprive us of him anytime soon. What a shame it would be if something happened to him before he could see to his various responsibilities."

I was a bit taken aback by that one, but Samantha Stevens didn't twitch so much as a nostril. "It behooves us *all*," she said, "to be very, *very* careful, doesn't it?" She stared straight at Miss Winterton, who paled a bit and took a step back from the counter. Wish I could have seen Samantha Stevens's face just then.

"Yes, of course," Miss Winterton mumbled. "Quite right, quite right."

I thought it a good time to make my exit. Then, if either one of them was so inclined, she could commit homicide without yours truly as a witness.

"It was a pleasure to meet you, Mrs. Stevens," I said, bowing slightly in her direction. "Miss Winterton, I believe I'll see you again this evening at the meeting."

Abigail Winterton tittered. "Of course, Dr. Kirby-Jones, and Mrs. Stevens as well. Didn't you know, she's a member of the board of SMADS?"

"No, I didn't know," I responded faintly. I could imagine the combination of Winterton, Stevens, and Blitherington. Tonight would be fun—or a bloodbath. "I'll see you this evening, then." Clutching my mail, I walked briskly out of the post office.

And literally right into a very attractive man.

Chapter Four

"**D**o forgive me!" I said, dropping everything as I reached out a steadying arm to my unwitting target. I had cannoned right into him, not paying the least attention to what—or who—might be on the other side of the post-office door. I bent quickly to retrieve my mail from the pavement.

"It's quite all right," he assured me, looking up into my eyes and smiling. He stood several inches shorter than my own lanky six feet three. His chestnut hair and neatly trimmed beard, highlighted with gray, framed a strong face, and dark blue eyes sparkled at me. Closer to forty than thirty, I reckoned. He stepped back. "I don't believe we've met, but I'm Trevor Chase. I own the bookshop here in the village."

"I do beg your pardon once again." I smiled. "I'm Simon Kirby-Jones, and I've just moved here. I promise you that I don't run over people deliberately."

"I'm sure you don't." He returned my smile. "I was on my way to my shop. I don't open the doors to the public until ten, but I'd be delighted if you'd consider having a cup of tea with me."

At the very least, I told myself as I stood admiring his

lithely muscled body. He was built like a teddy bear, but a teddy bear who could mow down a defensive line if need be. Just my type. "I'd like that very much, thank you." I grinned back at him, not quite baring the fangs but nevertheless giving the impression—so I hoped—that he looked good enough to nibble on.

My reward was another smile. "Then come with me," he said. His bookshop was only a few doors down from the post office, past a small combination bakery-tearoom and a lawyer's office. The Book Chase was emblazoned in gold letters across the windows, with Trevor's name more discreetly printed near the bottom. "Catchy name," I commented as I waited for Trevor to unlock the door.

"Thank you, Simon, but I actually can't take credit for it. Believe it or not, that was already the name of the business when I bought it about six years ago," he said as he opened the door. "I hope you don't mind if I call you Simon upon such limited acquaintance?" The door swung open, and Trevor Chase motioned me in.

"Not at all, Trevor, not at all," I assured him. He closed the door behind us, then reached for a light switch. The lights sprang on, and I inhaled deeply one of my favorite scents—books. The shop consisted of one large main room, from what I could see, with lots of shelves and nooks here and there where one could browse to one's heart's content. I wandered around while Trevor locked the door behind us and quickly found the section where Daphne Deepwood was shelved. I was relieved to find several copies of each title. Now, what about Dorinda Darlington? Was there a separate section for mysteries? I didn't want to be too obvious, but I can never resist looking for my books in any bookstore I run across.

Trevor stood and watched for a moment while I hunted in vain for good ol' Dorinda; then he motioned for me to follow

him. He pointed out the section where my biographies were
shelved. "I really did admire your biography of Eleanor of
Aquitaine," he said. "Not only was the research impeccable,
but the writing style was lively and eminently readable."

Oh, dear, if he keeps this up, I thought, *I really will be in
love.* "Thank you very much," I replied modestly. "I had
enormous fun with that book. I'm glad you liked it."

We passed through a doorway at the back of the main
room into a small hallway. A set of stairs led up to the second
floor, and a discreet sign advertised that the second floor held
out-of-print and collectible books. I had thought Trevor
would show me upstairs, but apparently he was ready for his
tea. He led me on to a small office in the back, where he bus-
ied himself with filling a teapot at the small sink. Soon he had
the teapot settled on a small gas ring, and we got comfortable, Trevor seated behind his desk and I ensconced in a comfortably overstuffed armchair across from him.

"My, this is cozy," I said cleverly. There were posters
around the walls, most of them advertizing various books, a
couple displaying the attractions of art exhibits. A sofa stood
against one wall, and it looked like a pleasant place for an afternoon nap, with colorful pillows scattered along it. The
usual office paraphernalia was there, too: filing cabinets, letter trays, a computer, and so on.

"I find it a comfortable place to work," Trevor agreed. He
pulled a pipe and tobacco pouch out of his jacket pocket.
"Would you mind?" he asked, his voice polite.

"Not at all," I replied with some enthusiasm.

"One never knows with Americans these days," Trevor
said, smiling as he prepared his pipe. "So many that I've encountered are so rabidly antismoking that I never presume
these days."

I made a face, and he laughed. "Please don't get me started
on American obsessions. Antismoking has become a religion

back there, as has anti–just about everything else. Those are only some of the reasons that I'm happy to be living in England for now."

"I can understand that, Simon," Trevor agreed. "I've traveled a bit in the States and encountered enough of those obsessions to last me for the rest of my days. On the other hand, at least in some areas, the atmosphere is much less oppressive with regard to certain matters than it can be in a small village like this."

He wasn't quite sure of me yet, perhaps. I thought I had given him enough signals so that he couldn't possibly mistake the nature of my interest. But caution is not a bad thing.

"I can imagine that Snupperton Mumsley isn't exactly the center of the British gay rights effort." I laughed, and Trevor grinned around the stem of his pipe. Fragrant smoke billowed around us in the office, and I sniffed appreciatively. "But I see no reason why two consenting adults"—I gave him the full benefit of my dark gaze—"can't enjoy themselves behind closed doors as much as they want, despite what the matrons of Snupperton Mumsley might think."

Trevor took the pipe out of his mouth and laughed aloud. The teakettle began to sing, adding to the merriment. "Ah, Simon"—he stood up to fix our tea—"I do think Snupperton Mumsley has suddenly become a much more interesting place to live."

"I'll drink to that," I said, moving to help him with the tea things. A few minutes later, we raised our teacups to each other in a silent toast.

"I've been in London most of the past month," I explained, setting my teacup aside for the moment, "getting through all the paperwork which allows me to live here, which explains why I hadn't discovered your shop before now. I never dreamed there could be such . . . amenities when I decided to move here."

Trevor puffed at his pipe. "I had wondered why you hadn't

been seen much in the village before. We all heard, oh, at least six weeks ago, that someone had bought Tristan Lovelace's cottage and would be moving in. Rumor was rampant, of course, about who it might be." He grinned at me. "I never really knew the infamous Professor Lovelace, though I got an earful from various sources. I'm quite pleased to see that, in certain respects, my informant was spot on."

"To the effect that the queer quotient at Laurel Cottage remains as high as ever?" I responded dryly.

He laughed again. "Spot on, my dear chap, as I said."

I had to laugh, too. Tristan was the only person who had ever called me "my dear chap." I suddenly felt terribly English. "I suppose it's useful, in a way, to have one's reputation established even before one moves in."

"Don't worry about it," Trevor advised. "There's bound to be a certain amount of gossip, especially in a small place like this. But in six years I've had very little trouble. Some are like the delightfully oblivious Neville Butler-Melville and simply don't have a clue. Others figure out quite quickly, but as long as you're discreet, there's no mention made of anything so vulgar as one's sexual preference."

"Sounds like where I grew up in Mississippi," I drawled. "People might know you're gay, but they gloss right over the fact because it's not something one mentions in polite society. As long as you don't make an issue of it or embarrass anyone by bringing your boyfriend home for a visit, it simply is ignored."

Trevor nodded. "Discretion is the key, of course. Besides, there are enough goings-on, thanks to certain members of the community, to ensure that attention is usually directed elsewhere."

"I know just what you mean," I said, settling back in my chair for a good natter. "Let me tell you what I witnessed at the post office this morning!" I gave Trevor a quick but highly entertaining precis of the scene between Abigail Winterton and Samantha Stevens. He laughed, spewing smoke in his mirth.

"Abigail is rather a nasty old cat," he said. "You'd think she would have learned by now, with Prunella Blitherington slapping her down all the time. One of these days, the high-and-mighty Mrs. Stevens is going to show her what's what, and Abigail may never recover."

"So what's the story behind Mr. Stevens's accident?" I asked.

Trevor shrugged. "Who knows? He's got to be nearly thirty years older than his wife, and he's not in terribly good health. Yet he persists in trying to perform various macho feats, like hang gliding and bungee jumping, and he's going to kill himself one of these days. I daresay that Mrs. Stevens won't wear black too long afterwards, either. In fact, I wouldn't be surprised if she's the one who encourages him to do such foolhardy things in the first place."

"Sounds like a plot for a good English mystery," I observed.

"Be my guest," Trevor said. "After you've been in Snupperton Mumsley for a while, I've no doubt you'll have gathered enough material for *several* mystery novels."

"Not to mention romance," I said boldly.

Trevor laughed—a sound I was coming rather quickly to enjoy—but the phone rang. Any reply he might have made was lost as he picked up the phone after glancing apologetically at me.

"Good morning," he said smoothly. "The Book Chase."

A voice squawked at him. The light in Trevor's eyes went dark, and he turned slightly away from me. I stood as if to leave the room, and he motioned me back into my seat.

"I'm sorry," Trevor said into the phone, his voice betraying his irritation with the caller, "but I really cannot talk just now. I'll have to ring you back later." The voice protested in

Trevor's ear, loudly, but Trevor repeated himself before putting the phone back in its cradle.

"Sorry about that," Trevor apologized. "A book dealer who simply refuses to take 'no' for an answer on some of my stock he wants to buy."

I nodded. Trevor didn't know, of course, that I have exceptionally good hearing. Thanks to the magic little pills that make life in death so pleasant, I can no longer turn into a bat or into any other creature, but the sensitive hearing remains.

Even after having met the young man only once, I still could recognize the ill-tempered tones of Giles Blitherington on the other end of the phone line.

Was there some sort of relationship between Trevor Chase and the snotty young lord of the manor?

Chapter Five

After he ended his conversation with Giles Blitherington, Trevor Chase smiled at me, evidence of a slight strain in his face. I itched with curiosity. Why had he felt it necessary to lie to me about the phone call? He didn't realize I knew it was a lie, but it made me a bit wary of him, whereas before the phone call I was ready to invite him out to dinner.

I had gotten a bit too flirty too fast. That's not normally my style. I suppose it had been too long. After all, it had taken me some little while to get over Tris. Was I really ready for the dating game again?

Maybe not, I told myself. At some point I'd bring up the young lord of the manor and see how Trevor reacted. At the moment, though, I decided it was time to get back home.

I stood and offered Trevor my hand. "I've enjoyed meeting you, Trevor, but I'm afraid I must be getting home and back to work." The warmth of his hand in mine was almost sensual, at least on my part. I wondered what he thought about the dry coolness of my hand? Some men find it vaguely unsettling.

Apparently not Trevor. He smiled his beautiful smile as he escorted me to the front door of the shop. "I'm sorry you have to rush off," he said. "But I understand the demands of the writer's life, I assure you." He smiled again, broadly this time. "And, moreover, I believe I shall see you this evening." He unlocked the door.

Startled, I couldn't think what he meant. "I beg your pardon?"

Trevor laughed. "The village grapevine has you a new recruit to the Church Restoration Fund Committee. I'm a member of the board of the Snupperton Mumsley Amateur Dramatic Society. Don't disappoint me and say you're not coming to tonight's joint meeting!"

"I suppose I can't disappoint the village grapevine. Can I?"

I'd swear he winked at me, but his countenance was grave as he replied, "No, Simon, don't disappoint them."

I gave him one of my highest-wattage smiles, and he blinked. "See you tonight, Trevor." I left him standing in the doorway of his shop, slightly bemused.

Whistling a jaunty air, I reaccoutred myself with hat and sunglasses, gathered up my mail, and headed back down the High Street toward home. When I reached St. Ethelwold's, I paused for a moment to stare at its Perpendicular façade. The outside of the church was lovely, but I had been delighted to discover many Early English elements inside. The church was a charming blend of styles, and even such a supposedly godless creature as I could appreciate it. Like many Americans, I am secretly awed by the sheer antiquity of many of the buildings in England.

A stand of old trees shaded the large churchyard abundantly, so that even on this warm day, dark shadows here and there obscured some of the headstones. I was about to walk on toward home when a slight movement back in the shadows near the rear of the church caught my eye. I concentrated hard, and my vision sharpened. (There are some things I'm still attempting to master about this vampire business.)

For a few seconds, I could see into the shadows, and what

I saw astonished me. Letty Butler-Melville, clutching a basket of flowers in one hand and brandishing a pair of secateurs in the other, appeared to be engaged in a furious argument with a man whose identity I did not know. They weren't close enough for even my acute hearing to pick up what they were saying to each other. But to judge from the expressions on their faces, they weren't delighted with each other.

I let my concentration lapse, and the sharpness of sight faded. Walking on toward home, I pondered this small mystery of village life. Who could the man in the shadows be? He looked to be in his sixties, weather-beaten and rugged. Perhaps he was the sacristan and had failed to do something properly. Letty, the officious wife of the vicar, was upbraiding him for his dereliction of duty.

That made as much sense as anything. I'd keep an eye out for the man and try to figure out what the trouble might have been. I found it interesting that Letty Butler-Melville could rouse to such a pitch of anger. On the previous occasions when I had encountered her, she acted as if she didn't have the nerve to scare the proverbial goose. But in the heat of passion, she certainly looked different. The drab creature I knew had disappeared, to be replaced, at least momentarily, by a spitfire. Curious.

Reaching the door of Laurel Cottage, I decided that I'd had enough speculation for now. I put thoughts of the village firmly aside as, a few minutes later, I changed into my writing duds and got comfortable in front of the computer. It was time to start a new book, a time that normally energizes me as the ideas buzz in my head.

But for the moment I was a bit too unsettled by the events of the morning to focus as I should. Turning away from the computer screen, I picked up the mail I had received from Abigail Winterton. Glancing idly at the envelopes, at first I saw nothing that demanded my immediate attention. Mostly business correspondence, with perhaps a couple of fan letters. Nothing that couldn't wait.

One of the letters bore a Houston return address. I frowned, staring at the scrawl, trying to decipher the name of the sender.

Slowly, I slit the envelope with a letter opener and pulled out the folded sheet within. I spread out the letter and scanned the contents quickly. Then I went back and read it through again, carefully, taking in the full import.

Dully, I registered the date at the head of the letter, then checked the smudged Houston postmark. It had taken the letter three months to reach me, having been forwarded several times, from my old address in Houston to my hotel in London and now to Snupperton Mumsley.

Having had the news earlier would have made little difference. Jack would have died no matter whether I was there or here in England. The only thing I could have done for him, to have saved him, he wouldn't have accepted.

Jack Quinn and I had been best friends since I had moved to Houston from Mississippi nearly ten years before. I met him one night, my first week in Houston, at a bar in Montrose. He came home with me, but instead of going to bed together, we ended up talking all night and most of the next day. He became my dearest friend, the one who held my hand through every one of the ups and downs of graduate school, and I nursed him through one broken romance after another. He was an optimist, always thinking that the next one would be Mr. Right instead of Mr. Right Now.

Jack had a big heart, but love made him careless. Six years ago he came to me and confessed that he had tested positive for HIV. At first, I was furious with him. How dare he do this to me? How could my best friend be so careless with his life?

I didn't speak to him for a month, but I realized how stupidly selfish I was being. I called him one night to apologize, and he waved it away. He understood, he said, and he was sorry he'd made me so upset.

That was Jack. Nothing much seemed to faze him. Not even when I confessed that I was having a torrid affair with my major professor. Not even when I told him my new lover was a vampire who wanted to share his "gift" with me.

Jack did his best to talk me out of it. But by then we had both seen numerous friends and acquaintances die from AIDS complications. Late one night, after having attended yet another funeral, terrified by what was happening to those I cared so deeply about, I finally yielded to Tristan Lovelace's blandishments, and I let him turn me into a vampire.

It wasn't nearly as frightening as I had expected. Death, when it came, was almost a relief. I remember waking afterward, being filled with relief, knowing that now some things could no longer touch me. Tristan had explained everything carefully beforehand, and I knew much of what I should expect. I was happy with my new state of existence.

But for once, Jack couldn't share in my joy. I hinted for a while, then even came right out and told him that it wasn't too late. He could save himself, if he wanted to, by becoming a vampire like me. For whatever reason, he refused.

That began the rift between us. I tried keeping in touch with him, but as time passed, I became more and more caught up in my work, trying to finish the dissertation and put up with an increasingly difficult relationship with Tristan. So Jack and I drifted further and further apart.

I called him about a month before I was ready to leave for England, hoping at least to visit with him one last time. But he told me, the weariness evident in his voice, that he simply was too ill to see me. I said good-bye to him then, whispering softly, "I love you, Jack," into the receiver. I don't think he ever heard me.

And now I was staring, through crying eyes, at a letter

from an acquaintance informing me that Jack had died two weeks after I left Houston for England.

I folded the letter carefully and put it back inside the envelope. Pulling open the bottom drawer of the desk, I laid the envelope on top of the pile already nestled there. I shut the drawer, then turned my chair back to the computer screen.

Taking a deep breath, I focused once more on the task at hand. Time to start a new book.

Chapter Six

By the time I quit working to get ready for the meeting, I had written two chapters of my next minor masterpiece of mystery and mayhem. I am nothing if not modest about my achievements. The critics adore my mysteries, and I have enough awards from peers and fans to choke a Clydesdale. I shut down the computer, took my miracle pill, and dressed for my first encounter with the board of the Snupperton Mumsley Amateur Dramatic Society. *Had I but known,* as the saying goes.

I approached the parish hall on the dot of nine o'clock. In the light of a fading August evening, the hall looked to have been built in the 1950s, judging from its utter lack of character and charm. Utilitarian, I supposed. Functional but graceless. Like one or two of the residents of Snupperton Mumsley. Following the voices I could hear into the main hall, I found various persons onstage. A long table stood there, with most of the board and members of the Church Restoration Fund Committee seated around it. There was apparently very little difference in membership between the two groups.

Lady Prunella Blitherington was trying vainly to make her voice heard over the rest. I walked across the floor and sprang lightly up onto the low stage. As the din of conversation ceased upon my dashing entrance, I nodded to Trevor Chase. Lady Prunella rose from her position at the head of the table and deigned to introduce me. "My dear Dr. Kirby-Jones, mere words cannot express our *delight* in the fact that you have decided to join us tonight." She gestured imperiously. "Of course, you already know Abigail Winterton."

I inclined my head, and Lady Prunella continued. "May I present Trevor Chase, who owns the village bookshop?" There wasn't quite a sniff in her voice, but I could tell she didn't approve of Trevor. I smiled at him, and he winked at me. "We met earlier today."

At this, someone clumped out of the shadows at the back of the stage, where miscellaneous bits of scenery leaned and sagged. "Mother, I can't find it anywhere," Giles Blitherington complained, taking no notice for a moment that his mother was speaking.

Lady Prunella pursed her lips at this sign of ill-bred behavior on the part of her darling, but she allowed it to pass without comment. "Giles, darling, you remember Dr. Kirby-Jones?"

Giles smiled at me, tossing his head. Quite a change from yesterday's attitude, I noted. Was he flirting with me? I cast a quick glance at Trevor Chase, who was so obviously not watching Giles, it was almost funny.

Not waiting for a verbal response from her son, Lady Prunella continued. "May I present Mrs. Samantha Stevens, who is also a recent addition to our ranks." And an unwelcome one, to judge from Lady Prunella's ill-concealed distaste. Mrs. Stevens favored me with a glittering smile. "Dear Lady Blitherington," she cooed, "always so *delightfully* polite and proper. Dr. Kirby-Jones and I met in the village shop this morning."

I attempted to say something flowery and charming, but Lady Prunella cleared her throat loudly. "And may I also introduce Colonel Athelstan Clitheroe? Another member of our *select* little group." *Lady Prunella must approve of the colonel,* I thought, since she sounded almost cordial when she spoke his name. "Unfortunately, neither our dear vicar nor Jane Hardwick could be with us tonight. But we shall endeavor to uphold the charge given us, nevertheless." She smiled, rather like a hyena about to devour some disabled prey.

Her introduction performed, Lady Prunella plumped herself back down in her chair, which squeaked alarmingly beneath her bulk.

I turned my attention to the assorted persons around the table. Colonel Clitheroe interested me greatly, because he was the man I had seen earlier in the shadows of the churchyard with Letty Butler-Melville. Perhaps there was more to my little mystery than I had anitcipated. I made general noises of greeting to everyone and scouted about for a chair to pull up to the table. Giles, the gracious lout, had taken the only available one right in front of me. So much for flirting.

As the stage seemed recently to have been set for some sort of drawing-room comedy, replete with tea tray and two sofas, I rooted out an empty chair lurking behind one of the sofas. While I found a place to sit, between Trevor Chase and Samantha Stevens, Letty Butler-Melville came bustling in from somewhere backstage, wheeling a heavily laden tea cart before her. ·

Lady Prunella paid absolutely no attention as Letty began to serve tea except to remind her sharply, "Sugar, no milk!" *Robert's Rules of Order* evidently held no interest for our dear chairwoman as she launched into the business of that night's meeting.

"We have *all* agreed that we shall direct our energies to a production to benefit *dear* St. Ethelwold's and our *dear* vicar's efforts to keep the building in good repair. The *only* question remaining before us at this time is *what* play we should produce." She frowned at each of us in turn during an interval in which no one spoke but slurped tea instead.

"Obviously, in order to keep our production costs *down* so that we may give as much money as possible to *dear* St. Ethelwold's, we *must* save money wherever we can. I propose that in order to do so in a *most significant* way, we produce a play for which we will have to pay *no* royalties. Indeed, no author fees whatsoever, as the author has *kindly* consented to our using the play for these reasons."

Giles grumbled something into his teacup, but Lady Prunella affected not to notice. Samantha Stevens spoke up instead. "That is certainly *prudent* of you, Lady Blitherington. But, *do* tell us, who is the *generous* soul who has made such an offer?"

Abigail Winterton had been remarkably restrained to this point, I thought, but now she snorted loudly and clumped her teacup down in its saucer. She was about to launch into a tirade, but Lady Prunella fixed her with a basilisk stare, and the shopkeeper subsided.

"My own *dear* son has offered to let us produce his play *Who Murdered Mater?* I have no doubt that a clever whodunit will bring us a *huge* audience and thus help us raise a *goodly* sum for the church." In a rare moment of goodwill, Lady Prunella beamed at us all.

Samantha Stevens clapped her hands together and laughed, a silvery, musical sound. "What an absolutely *delicious* title, Giles! How *ever* did you think of it?"

Giles's face slowly suffused with redness, while Abigail Winterton and the colonel tried to be discreet with their amusement. Trevor Chase, in between casting venomous glances in Giles's direction, looked more and more as if he wished he were somewhere else.

Colonel Clitheroe cleared his throat. "My dear Lady Blitherington," he bleated. I was astonished at his voice; I had been expecting the stentorian tones of an Anglo-Indian officer, right out of Agatha Christie. But instead I heard the wimpy tones of a Caspar Milquetoast.

"Do you believe you're right about the whodunit," the colonel continued. "That *Mousehole* play still packs 'em in. Don't quite understand it myself, but still, there you are. Good show, and all that."

At least his dialogue was true to form, I thought. Yet another delicious stereotype in this charmingly stereotypical village. Where on earth did he come from?

"Thank you, Colonel," Lady Prunella beamed, not bothering to correct his mistake. If she even realized the title was wrong, that is. "One can always rely on your *sensible* approach to things." She paused to frown at the rest of us. "I take it, then, that we are *all* agreed?"

"Lady Blitherington," Samantha Stevens said, "one cannot disagree with you *in principle*. That is to say, I think a whodunit could be *just* the ticket. But I also think we should all have a chance to *read* the play first *before* we decide whether to produce it. After all, we don't know that it is quite, well, shall we say, *suitable,* for our purposes?"

In other words, it could stink to high heaven, I thought. You go, girl!

Stunned silence followed Mrs. Stevens's suggestion. I grinned, looking away from the tableau for a moment. Lady Prunella sat frozen, her mouth hanging open at the audacity of someone's challenging the abilities of her own dear Giles.

Lady Prunella found her voice. "Mrs. Stevens, you are only *lately* come to Snupperton Mumsley, so I will grant that you are *not* aware of the *manner* in which we do things here. My family and I have been *generous* patrons of the Snupperton Mumsley Amateur Dramatic Society since its inception, and as hereditary chairwoman of the group, I believe that I may speak *for* the board when I say that I would *not* have proposed the use of Giles's play were it not *eminently* suitable for production by our illustrious group."

Even with her hideous voice, it was an impressive speech. Once upon her dignity, Lady Prunella could have been Britannia bravely sailing forth to conquer the uncivilized nations of the world. But would it serve to put Samantha Stevens in her place?

Mrs. Stevens had an odd gleam in her eye, one that promised another battle, sometime in the future, with a different outcome. Lady Prunella had best not turn her back on her adversary.

"Dear Lady Blitherington," Mrs. Stevens said, her voice as smooth as cream, "of course you are right. I had not stopped to consider your *obvious* concern for the *group* in my own efforts to safeguard those same interests."

Lady Prunella, blindly considering this a victory, decided to be gracious. "Thank you, Mrs. Stevens. We all do so very much *appreciate* your interest in the group and your generous *support* of it." Perhaps Lady Prunella had belatedly remembered that Mrs. Stevens had as much, or more, money to offer the group than did the Blitherington family and it behooved her to kiss and make up. "As it so happens, Giles has brought copies of the play for everyone. I *knew* you would want to read it"—here she could not restrain a small, triumphant smile—"and here it is." With a flourish she reached beneath the table and pulled out a stack of scripts.

Abigail Winterton cleared her throat loudly, and Lady Prunella stared at her, arrested in mid-thwack. "A whodunit is all very well, Prunella," she said, "but perhaps those who will be coming to our play would prefer something a bit more *literary.*"

I found the sneer in her voice amusing. Evidently she was yet another of those tiresome persons who believed that simply because a work of fiction contained a murder or two, it was worthless as literature.

"And what would *you* suggest in its place, my *dear* Abigail?" The venom in Lady Prunella's voice could have felled a herd of elephants. Lady Prunella slapped her hand down on the pile of play scripts in a shockingly vulgar display of temper.

Proof against Lady Prunella's tone of voice, Abigail Winterton smiled, smugness smeered across her face like marmalade. "A drama which addresses the human condition as seen in the moral decay in a contemporary English village. Much like our own *dear* Snupperton Mumsley. And I'm sure the author would not ask for royalties, at least this once."

The room had grown absolutely still, and I watched with considerable interest as every gaze seemed riveted upon Abigail Winterton.

"Would you care to elaborate upon what you mean by *moral decay*, Miss Winterton?" Samantha Stevens's voice frosted the air.

Abigail Winterton preened before all the attention. "Well, if you *must* know, in this particular play—the author of which happens to be a *keen* observer of human nature— *moral decay* encompasses so many things. You all know what life is like in a village. For example, a village like our own dear, *dear* Snupperton Mumsley." She giggled. A most unfortunate sound, I assure you. "There are so many *secrets*, those shameful little things about one's past that one *never* wants the neighbors to know abour." She paused, smiling with delighted malice.

"It all sounds rather *tawdry* and unbearably *common* to me," Lady Prunella said, sniffing loudly.

"Perhaps," Abigail Winterton replied, "but the human condition so *often* is."

Trevor Chase said, sounding as if he were speaking with teeth clenched, "Why should the board approve putting on something like this? It sounds completely outrageous to me. We don't even know who the author is!"

Her eyes flat and hard, Abigail Winterton stared briefly at each member of the assembled group in turn, skipping only yours truly. "The author is someone *local* who for the moment prefers to remain anonymous. Having read it, I think it would be so *very* interesting to do this play. I'm sure the whole village would find it *vastly* amusing, don't you?"

"No, I don't!" Lady Prunella stood up. "Abigail, I do believe you've totally lost your mind. This is ridiculous. We have a *perfectly* good play to use. Why should we even *consider* the drivel you've suggested?"

Abigail Winterton gave that same malicious smile. "Oh, my dear Prunella, I could think of any *number* of good reasons why it would behoove the board to approve *my* choice of a play." Once again she stared around the table, leaving out only me. "I'm sure *most* of you would agree with me."

Lady Prunella sat down with a thump. Her face had paled. "Very well, then," she said in a weak voice. "Do you have copies of this play for us to read?"

Abigail Winterton's face turned shifty. "At the moment there is only one copy of the play, and the author hasn't wished to let it out of sight. Copies should be ready soon. You *all* will have copies as soon as they are available."

There were undercurrents here that I simply did not understand. At one point, I would have sworn that Abigail Winterton was threatening everyone in the room, with the exception of myself. I thought back over what Jane Hardwick had said about this woman, that she was sly and prying. Was she actually *blackmailing* them into performing this play? What *had* she discovered on her late-night rambles around the village? Copying Abigail Winterton, but doing it more subtly, I hoped, I surveyed the faces of everyone in the room. They had all had time to smooth over their shock, but I could feel all sorts of emotions rampant in the room. Vampires are very sensitive to strong emotion, and I felt it coming from everyone in the room, in varying degrees. The problem with so much emotion at once, however, was that it was difficult to isolate person by person. But someone in the room (and maybe more than one someone) was furious enough to kill.

"In the meantime," Lady Prunella continued, her former bluster gone, "perhaps we could look over Giles's play in the eventuality that the other play proves unsuitable." A last gasp of defiance, it seemed, but I thought that the conclusion was already foregone.

Nevertheless, we passed the scripts around and began peering cautiously inside them. Even if Giles's work stank, it would no doubt be preferable to whatever Abigail Winterton had devised. I settled back in my chair to read, while others around the table got up and wandered around the stage. Trevor Chase and Samantha Stevens were both walking and mumbling dialogue under their breaths, while Lady Prunella and Giles had a conference in one corner of the stage. Letty Butler-Melville pottered around the stage, fiddling with various props. Abigail Winterton thumbed disdainfully through Giles's play, and Colonel Clitheroe sat staring off into space.

I focused my attention on the script, and to my amazement, I discovered that it was actually quite good. The dialogue was snappy and sophisticated—not stolen straight out of Noël Coward or Oscar Wilde, as I had anticipated—and I looked at Giles Blitherington with renewed respect. He and Trevor Chase were now whispering furiously to each other, while Lady Prunella and Abigail Winterton faced off in another corner. The emotions coming from that corner were powerful indeed. Samantha Stevens resumed her seat next to me and said quietly, "It's actually quite good, isn't it?"

I nodded as the rest of the board resumed their seats around the table. I longed to ask her for an explanation of Abigail Winterton's behavior tonight, but now was not the time.

"Well, everyone," Lady Prunella said, "I suppose there is

nothing further to be said this evening. We have one play offered for our use, and I had thought that more than sufficient for our needs." Her temper flared for a moment, then went out. "Apparently, we shall have another one to consider, however, and Abigail will see to it that we all have copies to examine."

Abigail Winterton inclined her head graciously.

"Miss Winterton," Samantha Stevens said, "won't you tell us who wrote the play?"

Miss Winterton stood up. "You'll all know soon enough. Good night, everyone." She smiled one last time and walked to the stairs at one end of the stage. We watched in silence as she strode across the room and out the door.

An air of constraint had fallen upon the remaining group, several of whom eyed me with uncertainty. Ever sensitive to atmosphere, I stood, pushing back my chair. "This has been a most interesting meeting. I shall look forward to conferring with you all later, but now I *must* bid you good night. More work to do at home, you know."

Amidst faint wishes for a good evening, I followed the path of Abigail Winterton, meanwhile tuning my ears very carefully for what was going to be said as soon as they thought I was out of earshot.

Just as I reached the door, I heard Lady Prunella hiss to her offspring, "I hope someone offs the bloody bitch and saves us the trouble."

Tsk! Such language, I thought. But who knew that Lady Prunella could predict the future so accurately?

Chapter Seven

After a busy night of writing, I was pottering about the cottage the next morning, trying vainly to bring some sort of organization to my office, when someone knocked on the front door. In my favorite tattered writing togs, I wasn't best attired to receive visitors. I glanced at my watch. What would the neighbors think to see me dressed this way, scant minutes before noon?

Ah, well, I shrugged. They'd get used to me.

I opened the front door to the vision of a tall, handsome blond man in an off-the-rack suit. Despite the ready-made appearance of his clothes, my visitor filled them out well. He caught my glance as I made a rapid survey, but his face retained its look of polite inquiry. Behind him stood a chubby associate who was nearly a foot shorter. What have we here? I thought. They had rather an official air about them. I had a good notion just who they were.

"Good morning, sir," he said in a pleasant baritone. "You are Dr. Simon Kirby-Jones, are you not?'

"Yes, I am," I said, "and I don't believe I've had the pleasure."

"I'm Detective Inspector Chase, and this is Detective Sergeant Harper."

Ah, suspicions confirmed. I shook hands with the fair detective inspector, noting the strength of his grip and the warmth of his flesh. I gave him one of my best smiles, and he blinked several times. I can't put the "glamour" on anyone, the way more traditional vampires can (one of the side effects of my little pills). I have to rely simply on the force of my own personality. Which can be considerable, you understand.

"Won't you come in, Officers?" I stood back and gestured for them to enter the cottage.

"Thank you," Chase said, and he and Harper followed me into the sitting room.

"I must apologize for my dishabille," I said, "but I'm a writer, as you might have heard, and this is my writing kit."

"No need to apologize, Dr. Kirby-Jones," Chase said as he settled on the sofa. Detective Sergeant Harper chose a chair a discreet distance away and slightly behind where I was sitting, his notebook and pencil at the ready.

"To what do I owe the pleasure this morning, Detective Inspector? Are you part of the welcome wagon hereabouts?"

Chase shook his head. "Not today, I'm afraid. We're here on official business." He cleared his throat. "Dr. Kirby-Jones, I gather that you have only recently come to Snupperton Mumsley?"

I nodded. "That is correct."

"I believe you attended a joint meeting last evening of the board of the Snupperton Mumsley Amateur Dramatic Society and the St. Ethelwold's Church Restoration Fund Committee."

"Yes," I said.

"How well do you know any of the other persons who attended the meeting last night?" Chase asked.

"Not well at all," I said. "I met most of them only yesterday or the day before. Let's see. I had met Letty Butler-Melville and her husband, the vicar, on one or two of my flying visits here from London, but of course the vicar wasn't at the meeting last night. Lady Prunella Blitherington, her son, Giles, and Abigail Winterton I met two days ago at the vicarage. I met Trevor Chase, Samantha Stevens, and Colonel Clitheroe for the first time yesterday. I believe that accounts for everyone, with the exception of Jane Hardwick, whom I met at the vicarage two days ago. She was supposed to attend the meeting last night, but wasn't able to, for some reason."

"Thank you, Dr. Kirby-Jones," Detective Inspector Chase said. "That's admirably clear. So you had never met anyone in the village before coming here?"

"No," I said, intrigued by his insistence. "Could I ask, Detective Inspector, what all this is in aid of?"

"We are investigating a suspicious death," Chase said.

"Really? Whose?" I said, hoping not to appear ghoulish.

"Miss Abigail Winterton," Chase said.

No big surprise here, though I did register a heartfelt blend of surprise and dismay. Though death hadn't bothered me all that much, no doubt it had come as a nasty shock to Miss Winterton. "Oh, dear. What happened?"

"Miss Winterton's assistant at the post office found her dead this morning in her kitchen."

"And you suspect foul play?"

Chase inclined his head. "There are circumstances that lead us to believe that foul play is a possibility."

Good grief. This man should run for office.

"Then I will do everything within my power to assist you, Detective Inspector. We certainly can't have a murderer running loose in Snupperton Mumsley!"

Chase didn't appear overwhelmingly grateful for my fervently expressed offer to assist. "We don't know just yet, Dr. Kirby-Jones, how much help we're going to need from anyone." *Well, ouch!* That put me in my place. "Miss Winterton's death may simply be the result of natural causes, but we must make certain." He smiled again. "But I won't forget your offer of assistance." He fingered his mustache nervously.

I smiled back. "Whatever I can do, Detective Inspector."

"For a start," Chase replied, "you can tell us what you did last night after the meeting ended."

"In case I need an alibi, you mean?"

Chase nodded.

I described my evening and all its excitement, explaining that I needed little sleep (but not why, naturally) and that I had spent the night alone, writing. "Thus, Detective Inspector, I really have no alibi, unless you want to see the chapters I wrote last night."

"Not at the moment, Dr. Kirby-Jones," Chase said, faintly amused. "Now, could you tell me about what happened during the meeting last night?"

Hmm, I thought. How candid should I be? Should I tell him what I suspected was going on? Or would he think I was a gossipy busybody?

I launched into a description of last night's meeting, deciding that I might as well offer him the benefit of my impressions. Surely, as a newcomer and an outsider, I might have a fresher take on it all—and no doubt the others weren't as willing to be forthcoming if they were being blackmailed by Abigail Winterton, as I halfway suspected.

Chase's eyes narrowed when I repeated for him the gist of Abigail Winterton's speech about the "moral decay" in the village of the play.

"What did you think she was getting at, Dr. Kirby-Jones, with her description of this alleged play?"

I shrugged. "There were definitely some deep undercurrents in that room last night, and I'm not sure what she was after. I almost got the feeling that she was taunting the rest of the group, myself excluded, naturally, since I'm new here. And I never expected to see Lady Blitherington back down like that. In my brief experience of her, she doesn't seem the type to refuse a challenge, and Miss Winterton was most definitely offering some sort of challenge."

Chase nodded. "I see. Well, Dr. Kirby-Jones, we'll certainly keep all this in mind as we investigate. We might need to come back to you later and ask more questions, if you don't mind." He stood up, and his partner did, too.

"Oh, not at all, Detective Inspector," I said, rising from my chair. "I'll be delighted, as I said before, to assist you in any manner possible." I smiled graciously at him and received an enigmatic smile as my reward.

I showed the two policemen out the door, wincing slightly at the bright noonday sun. I stood watching the detective inspector as he and his sergeant walked back down the lane toward the center of the village. *What a lovely view.*

And the village isn't too shabby, either.

I stared across the lane at Jane Hardwick's cottage. I saw no obvious signs that Jane was at home, but I thought it might be worth my getting dressed and going over on the chance that she was home and ready to discuss the murder. I was convinced that Abigail Winterton had been murdered, you see. After all, the way she had been taunting the others last night, I wasn't in the least surprised something had happened to her.

On the way upstairs to change into something more respectable, I thought back to something Detective Inspector Chase had said. He had made reference to the "alleged" play. That was odd. Did that mean, maybe, that the police hadn't come across a copy of it? Maybe the murderer had stolen it!

Whoa, I told myself as I began changing clothes. *You're getting the cart well ahead of the horse. You don't even know for sure that the woman was murdered and you've already got half the book written.*

A few minutes later, I knocked on Jane Hardwick's front door and waited impatiently for some sign that Jane was at home. As I was about to turn away and stump back home in disappointment, Jane opened the door.

"Good afternoon, Simon," she said, standing back and motioning me inside. "I imagine you're all abuzz with the news. Isn't it terrible? Poor Abigail."

I apologized for calling on her unannounced, but she waved that aside. She ushered me into her sitting room, where I made myself comfortable on an overstuffed sofa. The room looked like something out of *Country Life* magazine. From the outside, Jane's cottage looked very much like mine, down to the brick and the pantiles on the roof. No doubt they had been renovated by the same person or firm a century ago. But the interior was much frillier here. I hadn't expected Jane to be the ruffles and bows type, but her sitting room looked like an English variation on that nauseating "country" style that is so popular with American yuppies. Yuppies who have never been within a hundred miles of a cow or a chicken or a functional churn, I might add. I'd have to overlook Jane's taste—or, rather, lack of it—in decorating.

"I've just had a visit from Detective Inspector Chase and his partner, and they told me that Abigail's death was being treated as suspicious. I'm sure she must have been murdered, Jane!"

"I don't doubt but that you're right, Simon." Jane frowned. "I can't say that I'm completely surprised that something like this has happened. Abigail was such a thoroughly unpleasant woman in some ways, and she's been behaving oddly, even for her, for quite some time now. Frankly, I suppose I'm more surprised that it has taken someone this long to do away with her."

"Then you don't believe I'm getting carried away?"

Jane shook her head. "The village grapevine is already at work, and I've heard three different stories so far. One, that

Abigail was poisoned. Two, that she was bludgeoned to death and the room was awash with blood. Three, that she was strangled." She shrugged. "I don't know how long it will be before the police release any official information."

"Detective Inspector Chase certainly wasn't very forthcoming with me, even though I gave him every opportunity," I complained.

"Yes, I'm sure you did! Now tell me, Simon, what did you make of the fair Robin?" Jane was patently amused.

I sighed. "Robin, eh? A lovely name. He's quite handsome, of course." I paused as a thought finally struck me. "His last name is Chase. Is he any relation to Trevor Chase?"

"They're distant cousins," Jane said. "Trevor once told me that they have a great-grandfather, or perhaps a great-great grandfather, in common."

"I don't know about you, Jane, but I'm terribly curious about our potential murder. You missed a most interesting meeting last night!"

"Tell me all about it," Jane urged, and I happily complied.

"I think you're right, Simon," Jane said when I had finished. "Abigail was daring them not to choose the play she was suggesting. I just wonder . . ." Jane trailed off.

"What?" I said when she failed to continue after a long few moments.

"I'm certain," Jane said, "that Abigail must have written the play herself."

I thought about it for a moment. "It definitely makes sense." Then I told Jane what Chase had said about the "alleged" play. "Perhaps it's gone missing, and I would think it was a prime motive for the murder, don't you?"

"Very possibly," Jane said. "From rumors I've heard over the years, Abigail was not above abusing her position as postmistress."

"You mean she tampered with people's mail?"

"From what I've been told," Jane replied. "She apparently

found out things about people in the village, and the only way she could have discovered some of it was to have opened their mail and read it."

"No," I said slowly. "That's not the only way."

"What do you mean?" Jane said, obviously startled.

I described what I had seen the night before last.

Jane's face shifted from annoyed to grim. "That explains a lot! I wondered how on earth . . ." Her voice trailed off, and she stared into my face. "She was even nastier than I realized."

"Do you think she was actually blackmailing anyone?"

Jane grimaced. "She must have been! People put up with her far longer than I would have thought possible, so she must have had some leverage. There must be some rather humiliating little secrets that folk here in the village don't want known."

"And maybe Abigail had written a play in which she exposed some of them?" I thought out loud. "If that were the case, then someone might be desperate to stop that play from being read by anyone else, much less performed in front of the whole village!"

"That sounds plausible," Jane agreed. "And if the police don't find a copy of this play, who's to know what Abigail was really planning?"

"One thing puzzles me, though," I said slowly. "If she'd been blackmailing people in the village all this time, why was she suddenly trying to humiliate them all publicly? If the play had been performed and all the little secrets had been put on public view, she wouldn't have been able to keep blackmailing them."

"That's a very good point, Simon. It doesn't make much sense, does it?" Jane frowned. "But, with Abigail, one never knows. She was more than a bit eccentric in all the time I've known her, and perhaps she was simply potty enough to think she could just keep twisting the knife."

"But someone decided to stop her once and for all," I said

grimly. "Do you have *any* clues as to what secrets she may have been planning to expose?"

"I'm still enough of an outsider here," Jane reflected after a moment, "that I've not been privy to *all* the stories of peccadilloes past. I've told you about the long-standing enmity between Abigail and Lady Prunella, which is very much old news hereabouts. I've observed some quite tantalizing interactions between our late, unlamented postmistress and Samantha Stevens, but I've not been able to decide whether it was sheer bloody-mindedness on Abigail's part or whether she actually knew something to Mrs. Stevens's detriment."

"Mrs. Stevens impressed me as a formidable opponent. I can imagine her quite easily doing away with someone who stood in her way and expecting to get away with it."

"Oh, yes," Jane nodded. "Quite so."

"What about Trevor Chase?" I asked. "What kind of dirt could Abigail have had on him?" I was more than normally curious about this, I realized.

"Other than the obvious, you mean?" Jane laughed, a sour note in her mirth. "Abigail was quite capable of all sorts of outmoded and highly prejudiced notions just because she suspected Trevor is gay. I know nothing against him myself, though who knows what scandals Abigail's fevered brain might have concocted or professed to have uncovered. We don't have any molested choirboys running about as far as I know!"

I laughed. "Surely choirboys would be more in the Reverend Butler-Melville's line?"

Jane waved a hand. "Don't be absurd. Despite the fact that Letty to all appearances has the charm of a damp tea towel, they are quite genuinely devoted to each other. Neville is that most boring of creatures, a uxorious husband. And Letty would do just about anything for Neville."

"I'll take your word for that, though I can still harbor a few fantasies."

Jane emitted a most unladylike snort. "There is more than enough fodder for your fantasies—if I've not mixed my metaphors unforgivably—hereabouts. Trevor, for one, and the appallingly spoiled scion of the Blitherington dynasty, for another."

I laughed in delight. "So Giles is gay? I am most definitely not his type, then, the way he glowers at me whenever I'm around."

Jane shook her head. "No, Simon, I'd say just the opposite. Giles is desperately unhappy. Wouldn't you be, considering his parentage?" She shuddered delicately. "You represent so much of what he'd like to be. Handsome, sophisticated, witty, intelligent."

"My, you do know how to turn a man's head," I observed, not without satisfaction. "Do go on!"

She ignored me. "Giles is an attractive young man, if he could only get over himself. I believe that's an American expression, isn't it?" She didn't wait for confirmation. "And quite apt, in this particular case. If he would only stop paying so much attention to himself and all the imagined 'slings and arrows of outrageous fortune,' he might accomplish something. Such self-absorption isn't attractive."

I thought of mentioning the bit of conversation I'd overheard in Trevor Chase's office yesterday, but for the moment I decided I'd keep that tidbit to myself. Trevor Chase certainly bore further investigation, for several reasons. And maybe Giles Blitherington did as well.

"Perhaps it's just a phase?" I grinned wickedly.

"With Giles it's almost an art form!" Jane said with asperity. "But at least he has some brains, unlike his sister."

"I've not yet had that pleasure," I told Jane.

"You're not missing much," Jane assured me waspishly.

"What about Colonel Clitheroe?" I asked. "He seems almost too Agatha Christie to be real."

Jane laughed. "I know exactly what you mean. But he

seems to be the real article, all right. He's a latecomer to the village, like you and me, although he's been here for nearly twenty years. I think he came here not long before the Butler-Melvilles, in fact."

This time I shared my tidbit of information with Jane about that curious scene I'd witnessed between the colonel and Letty Butler-Melville. Jane frowned.

"I've no idea what that could mean. In my observance, they've always been polite with each other. Friendly, but not friends, if you see the difference."

I nodded. "But there's obviously something going on there, and it bears investigation."

"And that brings us quite nicely to the point, doesn't it?" Jane observed, her eyes twinkling with mischief. "Speaking of Agatha Christie. So shall you begin twirling your mustaches and speaking of little gray cells?"

"Well, *Jane*," I said with particular emphasis on her name, "if you'll leave off your knitting and your gardening, I'll not twirl anything. But I can't help but be curious. This is the first time I've found myself right in the middle of a real-life mystery plot, and I see no reason I shouldn't poke my nose in."

"I doubt Detective Inspector Chase would agree with you."

I just grinned. "And there's reason number two. The handsome agent of truth and justice shouldn't be denied the help and brainpower of yours truly. Especially when I'm more than willing to give him every assistance possible."

"You're quite shameless, Simon," Jane said, "but you know it, and you don't need any further encouragement from me." Her mouth twisted in an ironic smile.

I stood up. "Quite. I'd better be toddling off home. There's not much else to be done until we know for sure that Abigail Winterton was murdered, and how. Work calls, and I'll just mull over the first step in my investigation. Are you in?"

Jane ushered me to the door. "Of course, you great ninny.

Do you think I'd miss a minute of the excitement? As unattractive and downright unpleasant as Abigail Winterton could be, I don't believe she deserved this. I'd like to see justice done, as I'm sure would you." Standing on her doorstep, I nodded, then said good-bye. She shut the door with a brisk snap behind me.

Whistling, I set off down the lane toward home. Snupperton Mumsley was proving to be far more interesting than I had ever dreamed possible.

Chapter Eight

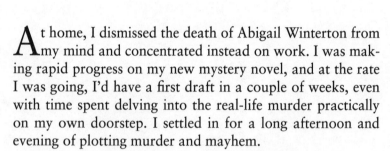

At home, I dismissed the death of Abigail Winterton from my mind and concentrated instead on work. I was making rapid progress on my new mystery novel, and at the rate I was going, I'd have a first draft in a couple of weeks, even with time spent delving into the real-life murder practically on my own doorstep. I settled in for a long afternoon and evening of plotting murder and mayhem.

By the time I was ready for a break from the computer—even vampires get stiff necks from too much time at the VDT—I was about ten chapters into a new Dorinda Darlington. More than enough to have earned myself some time off. I snuggled into my bed for a nap and woke up about two hours later, refreshed, ready to greet the dawn.

I spent a couple of hours catching up on fan mail, which normally I enjoy doing. But this morning I was impatient for the hands on the clock to reach a decent hour for calling on people. I was rarin' to go (as we say back in the Deep South, where I'm from) and start collecting information on possible suspects in Abigail Winterton's death. Now, mind you, no one had as yet officially confirmed the death as murder, but why let the little details dampen my enthusiasm?

Thinking about having to catch up on my backlog of correspondence and getting my office organized had given me an idea. I needed some subterfuge with which to approach some of the folk involved in the case in order to extract information from them. I didn't think that playing the brash, nosy American—which I can do all too well, thank you very much—would quite come off in this case. Vulgarity has its place, but this situation called for more subtlety.

I could chat with the various folk involved in this case and ask their opinions on finding someone suitable in the village to serve as a part-time secretary. And while we were discussing that safe topic, surely it wouldn't be a surprise if the conversation strayed to what was really on everyone's mind?

With whom should I start?

Lady Prunella Blitherington seemed as good a choice as any.

A quick call to Jane Hardwick gave me the information I needed. Lady Prunella, ever a creature of habit, usually walked her Precious (which Jane assured me was anything but) promptly at nine every morning. A chance encounter with the lady and her Peke was just the thing to start off my sleuthing.

I rummaged around in my closet and managed to find a track suit. I had bought it on a mad whim—one of those occasions, while I was still mortal, when I thought I might actually exercise enough to get myself into shape. But, alas, that kind of physical effort and I were not made to coexist happily. Fortunately, death brought me the figure I always aspired to in life. A cap and sunglasses completed my ensemble. The sun was bright this morning. Oh, for a cloudy day!

But Lady Prunella wasn't to know that I looked upon exercise with as much fondness as I regarded a stake through the heart. I could assume my camouflage, trot by her and her dog, express surprise at seeing her, and then launch into my oh, so subtle interrogation.

Track suit in hand, I rooted around for a pair of trainers. (Those are running shoes to you and me from across the Pond; learning to speak the language here is half the fun.)

Half an hour later, suitably attired, I was jogging down the lane toward the acreage that constituted the Blitherington estate. According to Jane, much of the family's lands had been sold off over the last generation or so, leaving the estate much diminished but still impressive enough. Lady Prunella liked to give Precious a chance to stroll down the lane from Blitherington Hall into the village, half a mile away, where she (Lady Prunella) was wont to stop and talk with folk while he (Precious) left his mark upon his favorite targets.

I met the lady and her dog moments after I had trotted into the lane near Blitherington House. I made a show of huffing and puffing a bit, hoping that Lady Prunella wouldn't notice the lack of perspiration upon my unlabored brow. This morning, however, Lady Prunella seemed much occupied with something else, so much so that she hadn't noticed me.

"Good morning, Lady Blitherington," I chirped. Anyone would think I absolutely *adored* exercise, I was so perky. "What a *pleasant* surprise!"

"Oh," Lady Prunella exclaimed, drawing back sharply on Precious's leash. The dog took one good, long look at me and retreated behind Lady Prunella, where he whimpered quietly. Dogs aren't terribly fond of vampires, and Precious had pegged me almost immediately. He wouldn't be happy until I was well away from him. Thankfully, Lady Prunella seemed as oblivious to the creature's distress as she was to most everything else.

"Dr. Kirby-Jones!" Lady Prunella invested my name with evidence of her displeasure at being so accosted. "You quite startled me."

"I do beg your pardon, Lady Blitherington! I was just out for my morning run. I do apologize for startling you."

Somewhat mollified, Lady Prunella warmed up a fraction. "That is quite all right, Dr. Kirby-Jones. After all, one is to be *commended* for exercising. A healthy *mind* in a healthy *body*, and all that." She unbent so much as to smile briefly at me. "*Others* could emulate your example instead of staying up to *all* hours and then *lolling* in bed most of the day."

The venom invested in that last sentence surprised me. To whom was she referring? I wondered. Her son and heir?

"You are quite right, Lady Blitherington," I assured her. I walked beside her and Precious as they began moving again toward the village. "There are so many things to accomplish in a day's time, one should make every effort to get up and get busy."

"Quite so!" Lady Prunella nodded vigorously in approval. "Your attitude is a *credit* to you."

"Thank you," I replied in my most modest tone. So this was the way to Lady Prunella's good graces. "I imagine that *you* have *tremendous* responsibilities here."

"Quite so!" Lady Prunella affirmed, much more cheerful now. "One *must* do one's best to uphold the social fabric and *all* the responsibilities of one's God-given *position* in life."

Or the position that one had married, I thought, remembering the tidbits I had gleaned from Jane Hardwick.

Lady Prunella sighed deeply. "Things are *much* different these days. One does not always receive the *respect* to which one is naturally *accustomed*."

Choking back a snort, I replied, "Our modern world simply no longer respects persons of good breeding the way it once did." I sighed heavily.

Lady Prunella cast a quick glance at me, not certain whether I was having her on, but my demurely innocent mien reassured her.

"Quite so!" she said forcefully.

"I must say, Lady Blitherington," I said, launching into my shtick, "that this was a fortunate meeting for me, because I

had hoped to ask your advice on a matter of some importance to myself. I asked myself last night, Now who, of all
the folk in Snupperton Mumsley, could give me the *best* suggestions toward finding someone suitable to assist me with
some occasional secretarial work? And I naturally thought at
once of *you*, my dear Lady Blitherington, because of your position of leadership in the village. I knew that *you* could advise me whether there is anyone at all *suitable* hereabouts.
After all"—I leaned closer and dropped my voice—"it would
simply *not do* to have someone unsuitable in one's home, and
with access to one's work."

Lady Prunella beamed at me, little knowing she was step-
ping right into a pile of manure up to her neck.

"My *dear* Dr. Kirby-Jones," she practically purred at me.
Even Precious was taken aback; he stumbled and fell flat on
his ugly little face. Then he started scrambling backward
again, for all the good it did him. Lady Prunella jerked him
up by his lead, far more interested in yielding to my blandishments than in comforting an unhappy dog. "If I didn't
know better, I'd swear you were a base flatterer." She simpered this time. Ye gads, what a sight!

"You are *quite* correct to be cautious in *this* day and age.
You simply would *not* believe some of the tales I could tell,
with regard to finding *suitable* servants for Blitherington
Hall. Such *attitudes* these young people have, and even the
older workers, who were reared to know and *appreciate* their
betters, why, you wouldn't believe how *rude* they can be, too!
When one is *only* trying to do one's *duty* toward those less
fortunate."

"I can imagine," I oozed in my most comforting tone.
"Such challenges you must face." She probably couldn't afford to pay many folks what they'd charge to put up with her
authoritarian ways. "But perhaps you might know of someone suitable, anyway?"

I could see the wheel turning in her mind. That little gerbil must get awfully tired sometimes. Lady Prunella was probably trying to come up with someone acceptable to me who also owed her something. That way she could collect information on yours truly without having to act directly herself.

"I *might* know of one or two persons," she finally admitted. "There *are* two women in the village, now somewhat retired, who have secretarial experience. One worked for my *dear* late husband, and another had considerable experience in the City before marrying and retiring here." She paused for a moment. "I do believe it *might* be best if I approached them on your behalf, since *you* are a newcomer here. Yes"—she nodded briskly—"that *would* be best. And if either of them is available, I will suggest that they call you to set up an appointment."

Quite the little stage manager, she was. I pursed my lips to keep from laughing. "My dear Lady Blitherington, you are *most* kind, most kind indeed! I shall await the outcome of your talking with these ladies."

By now we were within sight of the village. I'd better get to the main purpose of this conversation before Lady Prunella started her daily rounds (Jane said locals referred to it as "the Inquisition") among the shops.

"I must say," I said, dropping my voice to a confiding level, "that I was *most* distressed and shocked this morning to hear of the death of Miss Winterton. After all, one *doesn't* expect the police to show up on one's doorstep in the morning! I had met Miss Winterton only twice before. The poor woman! One is left wondering what kind of *accident* could have befallen her."

Lady Prunella threw me another surprised glance, this time not making much effort to mask her emotion. She stopped abruptly and seized my arm. "Dr. Kirby-Jones, I must tell you, Abigail's death was *not* from any kind of *accident!*"

I provided a suitable expression of dismay and horror.

"Surely," I sputtered, "you can't mean that her death was . . . was *deliberate?*"

Lady Prunella nodded grimly. "Yes, it *was* deliberate. Abigail Winterton was murdered!"

"How horrifying!"

Lady Prunella leaned closer and fixed me with her best basilisk gaze. "There is a *stalker* loose in our village, and Abigail was his *first* victim!"

"My dear heaven!" I gasped, playing along. "A stalker? Here? In this delightful little village?"

Lady Prunella glanced furtively around, checking to see that the information she was about to impart would not be overheard by less couth ears. "I know it *seems* impossible. Some *madman* has been stalking *me* for weeks. He's killed Abigail, and I'm probably *next* on his list!"

Chapter Nine

Ididn't have to work too hard to feign amazement after Lady Prunella's announcement. I should have figured she wouldn't miss an opportunity to dramatize herself. Could there really be a stalker loose in Snupperton Mumsley? Or had she simply witnessed the late unlamented on her midnight rambles?

"Dear Lady Blitherington," I burbled, "how absolutely *terrifying* for you! Someone has been *stalking* you? Have you notified the authorities?"

A decidedly shifty look crept onto Lady Prunella's face. "Why, no, I haven't. Not yet."

"But *surely* you must want the police to find out who is doing something so dastardly!"

"Perhaps *stalking* is not precisely the correct word." Lady Prunella backtracked with a noticeable lack of finesse. "There have been a number of unpleasant *letters* and an odd *shadow* or two at the windows of the drawing room at Blitherington Hall in recent weeks, rather late at night." She shivered. "There is most *definitely* a sense of *menace* in-volved, but not anything *substantial* enough to convince the police." More than likely, then, it was just Abigail Winterton, spying.

"Surely the *letters* you've received?" I insisted.

Lady Prunella sniffed. "I showed one to Police Constable Plodd here in the village, and he professed to find *nothing* actionable in it." She sniffed again. "The very notion! The letter made some *most* unpleasant—and *totally* unfounded—asseverations about my judging of the Women's Institute's annual flower show. The allegations were *monstrous,* I tell you." She shuddered delicately. "Such *calumnies* it contained."

Probably someone told her quite plainly that she couldn't tell a begonia from a beet and her *amour propre* couldn't withstand the shock.

"But why would someone want to do *you* grave harm?" I pretended an ignorance I didn't feel. Most likely just about everyone in Snupperton Mumsley had been annoyed to the point of aggression over something she had done once upon a time.

"I cannot *imagine!*" Lady Prunella drew upon her considerable dignity. "The person must be completely and irrevocably *unbalanced.* There is a *lunatic* loose in Snupperton Mumsley, and now poor Abigail has paid *dearly* for it." She sighed tragically, then said, "You must excuse me now, Dr. Kirby-Jones. I have errands I *must* finish." She turned to head into a nearby shop, Precious dancing with excitement on his lead, for it was the butcher's.

"But, my dear Lady Blitherington," I pulled her up short, "now that this dreadful thing has happened in the village, surely you *should* tell the police everything you know. After all, it's your *duty.*"

Lady Prunella marched back to where I was standing. Her eyes narrowed as she said, "I have already thought of that. You are right, of course. But in my experience, the officer in charge of this particular investigation has *scant* respect for his *betters*."

Oh, ho, I thought. *So Detective Inspector Chase refuses to kowtow to you, madam. Very interesting.*

"Oh, dear," I clucked in sympathy. "How very *trying* for you, Lady Blitherington."

"You can see, Dr. Kirby-Jones, why one doesn't have much *faith* in the police. A *savage* killer has struck my poor *dear* friend Abigail Winterton, and I could well be *next!*" Her voice rose on that last phrase, and Precious started whining.

I leaned closer and whispered, "But, Lady Blitherington, what if it weren't a mad stalker? What if it were someone here in the village that everyone knows and thinks is harmless?" I wasn't going to explain that I thought Abigail Winterton had been the "stalker." At the moment, at least, I thought the stalker and the murderer were different people.

Lady Blitherington drew back in horror. "Oh, surely not, Dr. Kirby-Jones. Surely *not!*" she protested.

"Let's just consider it for a moment, though. You had a far greater knowledge of poor Miss Winterton than I, and you are no doubt a very *shrewd* judge of character," I declaimed modestly. "Why on *earth* would someone want to harm Miss Winterton?"

Lady Prunella's brow darkened momentarily. She seemed caught in the grips of some internal battle. Finally, the urge to gossip won. "Poor Abigail was, as you no doubt noticed even in *your* brief acquaintance with her, rather a *bitter* person. She was *most* inclined to hold a grudge, no matter how *unfairly.* One sometimes had to overlook these *unfortunate* tendencies in order to make life bearable, though the dratted woman *did* go on so upon occasion."

"Against whom did she hold these grudges?" I asked, wondering what on earth, if anything, she would tell me.

"Any *number* of folk here in the village! Abigail was *al-*

ways imagining that someone had slighted her for some reason or another. She took offense over the *silliest* things. Though, mind you," here Lady Prunella leaned closer to me, "she did on occasion have *real* reason to bear a grudge."

"Really?"

Lady Prunella nodded vigorously. "Poor Abigail invested part of her nest egg in some *scheme* of that Stevens woman's husband, and she lost it when whatever it was *flopped.* I believe he had talked her into investing in some sort of joint venture. Can you imagine?"

"How distressing for her, though, to have lost money like that."

"Well, certainly," Lady Prunella acknowledged, "but she knew it was a *risk* when she did it. Letting herself be *swayed* by a City charlatan, mind you! You'll notice that Mr. High-and-Mighty Stevens and his wife haven't lost any noticeable amount of money lately." She sniffed. "There was *nothing* poor Abigail could do, though she talked about it to all and sundry, until Mr. Stevens threatened proceedings against her for libel."

"I can't imagine, though, that Mr. or Mrs. Stevens would have murdered her for that reason."

"Perhaps not." Lady Prunella frowned. "Abigail was also inclined to be somewhat *overzealous,* shall we say, in her inspection of the local mail."

I grimaced in distaste. "You don't mean she actually *read* other people's mail?"

Lady Prunella nodded. "I'm afraid so. There are things that she knew, things of a most *personal* nature, that she could have discovered *only* by violating the ethics of her position."

"Surely the offended parties could have had her brought up on charges of some sort?"

Shaking her head, Lady Prunella said, "I'm afraid that in a village this small it would *never* have done. The *offended parties* simply suffered the embarrassment as privately as possible. After all, Abigail never made her *news* public. She simply liked to *twit* one with her special knowledge from time to time."

"How unpleasant!" I said, sincerely for once. "Do you think this play she was talking about last night could have anything to do with her death?"

Lady Prunella turned pale. She seemed to fight for breath for a moment, then recovered herself with a great effort. "*If* there was a play to begin with! Which I sincerely doubt! I think it was just Abigail playing a *nasty* little joke on us all." She shook her head. "No, Dr. Kirby-Jones, I think that was just poor Abigail's *fevered* imagination!"

I'd certainly reserve judgment on that. No doubt folk in the village would hope that the play, if it had ever existed, never came to light.

"Well, this has been *most* enlightening, Lady Prunella, and I *must* beg your pardon for taking up so *much* of your time." I didn't want her to become unduly suspicious. "And you *will* let me know what you find out about a suitable secretary?"

Lady Prunella favored me with an uneasy smile. "Most certainly, Dr. Kirby-Jones. Most certainly." With that, she marched briskly into the butcher's shop, a much-relieved Precious leading the way.

I jogged toward home, wanting to get out of the ridiculous clothes before many of my new neighbors spotted me. I didn't want them to start expecting to see me do this every day. I shuddered at the thought.

At home I changed into more conventional togs while I speculated on what Lady Prunella had told me. Conspicuously absent from her recitation of grievances against Abigail Winterton had been any mention of her own ill will against the poor dear departed. In her own colossal self-absorption, Lady Prunella probably couldn't imagine that anyone would dare think *she* had a motive to do away with her nemesis. Not to mention the fact, I thought nastily, that she didn't have the brains to do it.

Appearances, however, could be deceiving. Yours truly being a perfect case in point. People meeting me rarely, if ever, suspected that I was dead. Lady Prunella could, after all, be hiding a formidable intellect behind a façade of effete aristocratic blather.

And maybe Jackie Collins would win the Nobel Prize for Literature, too.

Now comfortably dressed in country-weekend attire, I felt ready to call on the vicar and his wife in pursuit of my inquiries. I glanced at my watch. Nearly ten. Surely a decent hour at which to call upon the spiritual comfort of the parish and his helpmate?

A few minutes later, I opened the gate to let myself into the yard at the vicarage. Letty Butler-Melville was just coming out the front door, and we stood regarding each other in slightly surprised silence for a moment.

I found my voice first as I moved down the walk toward the front door. Letty Butler-Melville stood still, clutching a large hamper in her hands, watching me. "Good morning, Mrs. Butler-Melville. I trust you won't mind my calling upon you unannounced like this, but I wished to consult the vicar about a matter of some importance."

Letty Butler-Melville suppressed a sigh. "Not at all, Dr. Kirby-Jones. My husband is at home and is quite accustomed to consulting with parishioners. He will be delighted to see you." There was some undertone in her voice; whether simple annoyance at finding me unexpectedly on her doorstep, so to speak, or whether it lay somewhere deeper, I didn't know. But Letty Butler-Melville barely concealed her irritation, whatever its cause.

"You must excuse me," she continued briskly as she motioned me inside the vicarage. "I have many errands this morning. You'll find Neville in his study. I believe you will re-member the way." So saying, she pulled the door shut behind her, and I was left standing in the entrance hall of the vic-arage, staring blankly after her.

I shrugged. Maybe she simply didn't like me. After all, it had been known to happen. Or she just had more pressing matters on her mind. Like that scene in the churchyard yes-terday with Colonel Clitheroe. Such mysteries to ponder.

Wandering down the hall toward Neville's study, I noticed anew the shabby gentility of the furnishings. The Butler-Melvilles seemed to live comfortably in their fraying nest, but the place certainly could use a thorough cleaning, not to mention a bit of renovation here and there. Perhaps an anonymous donor could offer money for such purposes? One hated to think of dishy Neville living in surroundings that did him less than justice.

And here was dishy Neville himself, dozing in his chair. I coughed discreetly, and Neville's eyes fluttered open. Ah, I thought, those emerald eyes. The man was wasted here in Snupperton Mumsley. He really should be a movie star. Mel Gibson and Kevin Costner had nothing on him.

The vicar stood up hastily, dislodging a book from his lap. I caught a quick glimpse of its cover before it tumbled to the floor behind the desk, and I was amused—and gratified—to see that the book the vicar had been reading was none other than Daphne Deepwood's *Succulent Surrender*. Shouldn't the vicar be working on next Sunday's sermon? Or reading some edifying theological work? I wondered. What would the bishop think?

"Dr. Kirby-Jones!" Neville quickly overcame his embar-rassment at being caught napping and came forward with his hand outstretched. "What a pleasant surprise. What brings you here this morning?"

"Good morning, Vicar," I said. "I apologize for arriving unannounced like this. I do hope you will forgive me."

"Not at all, not at all!" Neville motioned me toward a seat in front of his desk. "You should feel free to call here whenever you like. I'm never too busy to talk with one of my parishioners."

"Thank you, Vicar; that's most reassuring," I told him, settling comfortably into the battered-looking leather armchair. "I met Mrs. Butler-Melville at the front door. She seemed in quite a hurry, but she told me to come on in."

The vicar beamed with pride. "Dear Letty is the most amazingly industrious woman. Such a perfect helpmate for a vicar! She is on her way to check in on several of our elderly parishioners. Letty visits the shut-ins and the ill among our little flock without fail. I don't know what I—or they—would do without her ministrations. She has abundant energy and takes such good care of us all."

A part of me wondered why the vicar himself wasn't out and about visiting some of these poor folk, who would no doubt be the cheerier for one of his dashing smiles rather than the dour—and dubious—pleasures of his wife's sour visage and her oddly raspy voice. But perhaps I was doing Letty Butler-Melville a grave disservice. Maybe she lit up like a Christmas tree in the presence of those who sorely needed kind words and chicken soup. Neville certainly seemed a fit testament to his wife's skills at caretaking.

"I'm sure the people of Snupperton Mumsley frequently have cause to be very grateful to Mrs. Butler-Melville for her many good works," I said, all in hopes of seeing Neville smile again.

He did not disappoint me. "Quite so, Dr. Kirby-Jones, quite so." He continued beaming. "Now, what can I do for you this morning?"

Quickly, I explained my need for a secretary and asked for his recommendations of someone suitable. Dear Neville gave the matter his utmost attention, as if I had brought him the most thorny moral dilemma to unravel.

After several moments' thought, Neville reached for pen and paper and jotted down several names and phone numbers. He handed the paper across the desk to me. "I'm sure, Dr. Kirby-Jones, that you'll find any of these women most suitable."

"Vicar, please, I must insist that you call me Simon. You've made me feel quite welcome here in Snupperton Mumsley, so much so that I'm beginning to feel quite at home here."

"Of course, Simon. We're delighted to have someone of your accomplishments here in the village."

I inclined my head in modest thanks. "And thank you for these recommendations." I waved the piece of paper at him. Perhaps at some point I'd actually get around to contacting one of the women listed there. "One has to be careful these days. And after what happened during the night to poor Miss Winterton, one has to wonder just what the world is coming to!"

Neville had been fondling a pipe he had retrieved from a rack behind his desk, but at my words he dropped the pipe with a clatter onto the desk. His face clouded, and he stood abruptly, surprising me. "Simon, I'm afraid I'm forgetting my manners. Would you like some tea?"

"That would be most kind of you, Vicar," I assured him, and he moved briskly off to the kitchen to fetch the tea. I sat waiting patiently, wondering why an allusion to the death of Abigail Winterton had unnerved him.

Chapter Ten

Neville returned shortly with the tea things—no doubt left in readiness for his elevenses by his doting spouse—by which time he seemed to have regained his equanimity. He served us both efficiently, and I took a grimacing sip of the tea. Ye gads, but they must have cast-iron stomachs to endure this abomination.

Masking my distaste with a cough, I alluded to my earlier statement. "Vicar, I regret having distressed you by my mention of Miss Winterton's mysterious death. But I'm afraid she has been much on my mind ever since the police called upon me yesterday." *Not to mention the identity of her murderer,* I added silently.

Neville looked away for a moment. "You have no need to apologize, Simon. I have a most unfortunate failing in one of my calling, I fear. Such news as that of poor Miss Winterton's death quite oversets me, and it is only with great effort that I can face such unpleasantness." He turned to me again with a boyishly sheepish grin. Anyone would forgive so handsome and charming a minister of the Lord this little-bitty failing of his. Excepting, perhaps, the bishop, and he very well might be as susceptible to Neville as the rest.

"It does credit to your finer feelings, I'm sure, Vicar," I re-assured him. He did bring out that urge to comfort *him* rather than the other way around.

"Thank you, Simon," he said. "You are most understanding. I have known poor dear Abigail for so long, naturally, and her death is such a shock. One simply doesn't expect such tragic accidents to occur."

Surely he couldn't be that dim. "But, Vicar," I pointed out gently, "do you really think it was an accident?" I put an ever-so-slight emphasis on that last word.

For a long moment, Neville seemed likely to swoon. I was ready to rush to his aid should he succumb, but manfully he recovered himself from the shock. "I, hmm, well, I hadn't thought about that, Simon." His voice wavered a bit. "Do you mean that Abigail didn't have a heart attack during the night? That's what Letty told me had probably happened."

He had to be putting on some sort of act for my benefit. He couldn't be *that* unworldly. Unless, perhaps, his wife was trying to shield him from something, and that bore further thought. At the risk of sending *him* into cardiac arrest, I decided to try harsher tactics. "No, Vicar, it doesn't seem to me that she did. Surely the police wouldn't be treating her death as suspicious if there weren't some odd circumstances about it. Don't you think she might have been murdered?"

At that last, most hideous word, Neville turned ashen. I cast about for some water to throw in his face, just in case, but with a magnificent effort, eyes blinking rapidly and chest heaving deeply, he calmed himself.

"But, but," he sputtered, "why on earth? Why would anyone want to *murder* Abigail?"

"My dear Vicar, I have no idea. I've just come to the village, remember, and I know very little about its inhabitants. Surely *you,* as spiritual guide and counselor, must know who among us might have reason to do something so cold-hearted?" I sat back and awaited further swooning.

Neville obviously possessed more mettle than I realized. He faced me directly and spoke with great determination. "Simon, that is an absolutely appalling notion. No one of my acquaintance here in the village could be so utterly ruthless as deliberately to take someone else's life! The whole notion is preposterous! There has to be some other explanation."

He made a good show of innocence outraged, but I thought fear lurked there somewhere. Fear that he was mistaken in his rosy view of his parishioners? Or fear that someone near and dear to him was a cold-blooded killer? What did he know, if anything, that could be pertinent to the case?

"What about that play she was talking about the other night at the meeting? The play all about the *moral decay* in a village like this one?" I affected an air of innocent inquiry.

"That is the most absolute rot," Neville thundered, and I was taken aback. I had no idea his voice was that powerful. He continued in a milder tone. "Snupperton Mumsley is a quiet village, full of hardworking and God-fearing souls. You are a newcomer here, and I must make allowance for that. You simply haven't had the chance to become acquainted with the people here. There is no *moral decay.* The idea is complete and utter nonsense! Poor Abigail had a tendency sometimes to try to dramatize herself, and I'm afraid this was simply one more instance."

"Don't you think it makes the timing of her mysterious death even more strange?" What color *was* the sky in his little world?

"No, it's preposterous. I'm sure her death will turn out to be some rather unfortunate accident." The more he talked, the more agitated he seemed to become. He was afraid of something, but I had no idea what.

"Vicar, are you going to be okay?" I was becoming rather alarmed. He really did look quite done in. Was it the fear? Or just his "unfortunate failing" at its most extreme?

Neville waved a hand weakly in my direction. "I'll be fine,

Simon, but perhaps you wouldn't mind leaving me for now. This is all most distressing, and I must have some time to contemplate it all." His voice grew stronger. "Yes, time for prayer and reflection. That's what I must have." He gazed at me, those beautiful eyes pleading with me.

How could I resist? I should be hard-hearted and grill him further, while his resistance was low. I'm no longer human, but despite what you might think, I'm not completely lost to the finer feelings. At least not where a handsome man is involved.

"Of course, Vicar. I quite understand," I said as I stood. "Please forgive me for distressing you so."

He stood with me. "Don't think about it any further, Simon, really. I'll be fine . . ." His voice trailed off forlornly.

My sense of humor, inconvenient at the best of times, almost got the better of me then. A picture of his face at that moment would have moved even the most hard-hearted to give thousands to famine relief or whatever charity you might name. Pain for the human condition was nobly etched in his face, distress radiating from those remarkable eyes, sorrow aching upon his lips. He was most definitely wasted in Snupperton Mumsley.

Assuring the vicar that I could see myself out, I left before I disgraced myself completely and giggled right in his poor face.

I wandered back home, wondering what my next move ought to be. I could call and see if Jane was at home and share the fruits of my morning labors with her. I was sure she'd be quite amused at my efforts at interrogation. Thinking back over the meager amounts of information that I had gleaned, however, I decided that perhaps I didn't want to share everything with Jane just yet.

However, I reminded myself as I unlocked the door to my cottage, I had only just begun. Whistling the old Carpenters song softly, I advanced into my office. The light on my answering machine was blinking, and I stopped to play back my messages.

The cool voice of Samantha Stevens flowed out into the silence. "Dr. Kirby-Jones, I apologize for ringing you on such short notice, but I wondered whether you might be available to join us for dinner this evening? My husband is most eager to meet you, and I trust you will not mind indulging him while he recovers from his accident." She went on to give me her phone number, asking that I call back and leave word with her husband's secretary about tonight and get directions as well.

Most interesting, I thought, jotting down the phone number. I had nothing else planned for this evening, and I might as well meet the mysteriously injured Mr. Stevens and further my acquaintance with his wife. Would there be a way in which I could—discreetly, of course—bring up that little matter of Abigail Winterton and her lost nest egg?

I'd have to ponder that one awhile. "I say, old chap, rumor hath it that you swindled the dear departed out of her life savings, what?" Not quite the done thing. No, something more subtle would be required.

After all, that alleged business deal gave Abigail Winterton motive to murder Mr. Stevens, and not the other way round, as far as I could see. But perhaps old Abigail had been carrying on a torrid affair with Mr. Stevens and the icy Samantha had caught wind of it and decided to rid herself of her rival once and for all.

I laughed aloud. That would take more imagination than even I possessed. Daphne Deepwood most emphatically would not go for it.

Perhaps, though, the dear departed had stumbled upon some deep, dark secret that one of the Stevenses would rather not have anyone know. If the late, unlamented postmistress really did snoop through the mail, goodness only knew what she might have winkled out. And that certainly didn't limit the field to the Stevenses. Anyone in the village was fair game for blackmail, provided the existence of guilty secrets.

The whole village hadn't been present at the meeting, of course, so the group of potential murderers was probably limited to those in attendance that night. Unless everyone else at the meeting immediately went home and started spreading the word throughout the village about Abigail Winterton's play (I was going to consider it hers, for the ease of discussion), then the murderer was most likely someone at the meeting.

Until the police officially confirmed that Abigail Winterton had been murdered and released some details as to just how it was accomplished, I could carry my speculations only so far. I could imagine several rather lurid scenarios in which one of my fellow committee members had snuck into Abigail's home during the night and batted her over the head or strangled her. But until we knew a bit more, all this speculation didn't serve much purpose.

I stared at the piece of paper in my hands. Might as well call Mrs. Stevens and accept her invitation to dinner. I punched in the numbers and listened to the burring of the phone. A prim, cultured voice answered, and I stated my purpose in calling. The voice, strangely androgynous, calmly took the news of my arrival for dinner and just as calmly gave me directions to the Stevens estate. I thanked it (for it had never introduced itself) and rang off.

Wandering into the kitchen, I got myself a glass of water. Because of those little pills I keep mentioning, I do get a bit dehydrated from time to time. I don't understand the way the darned little things work; I'm just grateful for most of what they allow, minus the occasional supernatural side effect. I've yet to experience the odd desire to bay at the moon that some have reported or the excessive growth of hair on various parts of the body. I'm hairy enough as it is.

The doorbell rang, and I set my empty glass down in the

sink. By the time the bell rang the second time, I was opening the door. There, standing ever so handsomely on my doorstep, was none other than Detective Inspector Robin Chase, stroking his mustache.

I smiled. The game was afoot.

Chapter Eleven

I invited the policeman in. He was alone, I was delighted to see. Perhaps I had misinterpreted his reason for this visit. Maybe it wasn't because they were finally ready to admit Abigail Winterton had been murdered. Maybe he simply wanted to see me again.

And maybe Wile E. Coyote would finally catch that elusive Road Runner. I stifled a sigh as I led the way into my sitting room. At least I was better dressed this time.

"May I offer you something to drink, Detective Inspector?" I asked as I gestured for him to find a seat. He chose the most comfortable chair in the room.

"No, thank you, Dr. Kirby-Jones. I won't take much of your time," he assured me.

"What can I do for you, Detective Inspector?"

"We're continuing our inquiries, Dr. Kirby-Jones, and I wanted to go over your statement with you again." He paused to pull a notebook from his pocket.

"So Miss Winterton's death was not an accident?"

"We are now officially treating this as a case of murder," Chase responded.

"How did it happen? You must know by now that all sorts of rumors are spreading rapidly around the village."

Chase regarded me with a speculative smile. "Such as?"

"Oh, that she was bludgeoned to death, that she was strangled, that she was poisoned. Just about any variation you could name."

Chase shook his head. "I shouldn't be surprised."

"So, how did it happen?" I repeated.

"Miss Winterton was strangled to death."

From the look on his face, it must have been a grim sight. "The poor woman!" I said. "How hideous." And I meant it. She might have been irritating and sly, but she had not deserved such a violent death.

"Do you have any leads yet, Detective Inspector?" I asked after a brief silence.

"We are pursuing several lines of inquiry at the moment, Dr. Kirby-Jones," he replied smoothly. "I did want to ask you a few more questions, if you wouldn't mind."

"Certainly not," I said. "Fire away."

"Tell me again about this play that Miss Winterton talked about that night of the meeting."

Aha! I thought. *So the play* does *have something to do with the murder.* Quickly I repeated what I had told him before, and he nodded occasionally during my recital of the facts.

"Did you not find a copy of this play somewhere in her house?" I asked.

For a long moment, I thought he wasn't going to answer, but finally he said, "No, as a matter of fact, we haven't yet found it. If it indeed ever existed."

"Do you think she could have been making the whole thing up?"

"It's possible, I suppose, but it's more likely that whoever killed her took it away to keep us from discovering it."

I whistled softly. "Whatever was in that play must have been dynamite."

"Unless we find a copy or talk to someone else who had read it, we'll never know," Chase said.

"Do you think that Miss Winterton had written it herself? If she didn't, then whoever wrote it might come forth now."

Chase shrugged. "If someone else did write the play, this murder might convince him or her to remain anonymous. For the moment, we have to concentrate on other angles to the case."

"Like who had some more concrete motive to do away with her, you mean?" I said mischievously.

He nodded, trying not to smile. He was relaxing nicely. I was a bit surprised that he had been so forthcoming with me. Perhaps this meant that I was not a suspect in the case.

"I'm afraid I must ask you again, How well did you know Miss Winterton?" He consulted his notebook. "You told me previously that you've not been in the village very long, Dr. Kirby-Jones. Any chance that you knew the victim before coming here?"

He wasn't all that relaxed, after all.

I shook my head. "I had never met the woman until three days ago, at the vicarage. The vicar invited me to attend a meeting of his committee to raise money for St. Ethelwold's restoration project, and Miss Winterton was one of the committee members. That was the first time I had met her."

"You hadn't been into her shop, you hadn't had a letter or package to mail?"

"Until this weekend," I told him for the second time, "I had actually spent very little time in the village since coming to England three months ago. There is so much red tape to get through in order for an American to live here. I stayed in London most of the time, making only quick trips down here occasionally to check on things. I hadn't gone into the shop or the post office until two days ago, when I sent a manuscript to my agent in London. The third, and final, time I saw her was that same night at the meeting of the dramatic society."

"So she was essentially a stranger to you?" Chase asked.

"Yes," I agreed.

"Did you observe anything else that night at the meeting, or in your previous intereactions with her, that might shed some light on our investigation?"

How candid should I be with him at this point? I wondered. The worst he could do, I supposed, was dismiss me as a nosy American. I demurred. "Well, I have already picked up the odd piece or two of gossip."

Chase smiled encouragingly. Naughty man! I believe he knew the effect it had on me.

"A little bird—or two—has told me," I continued, matching him smile for smile, "that Miss Winterton was not above peeking through the mail, looking for interesting tidbits."

Chase smiled. "Could you tell me, then, Dr. Kirby-Jones, who these informants were?"

This was a bit of a sticky wicket. Should I rat on Lady Prunella and Jane? I frowned, considering.

Chase observed my hesitation. "I assure you, Dr. Kirby-Jones, that I won't reveal my source unless it's absolutely necessary."

I made a further show of my reluctance, but really, I could see no good reason to demur. "Both Jane Hardwick and Lady Prunella Blitherington mentioned to me in conversation that Miss Winterton was prone to a bit of snooping through the mail."

"In other words, she was potentially a blackmailer," Chase said.

"My, how direct you are! Yes, that's what I do mean. At least that's what I inferred from what I was told. It's dreadfully sordid, of course, but there you are. A time-honored, but excellent, motive for murder."

"And the body's in the library, and Miss Marple is peering over the hedge in the rose garden." Detective Inspector Chase positively twinkled at me.

"If you want to look at it that way," I acknowledged.

Chase frowned, and the sun went most definitely behind a cloud. "Please do remember, Dr. Kirby-Jones, that murder is not a parlor game. Someone deliberately and brutally strangled Miss Winterton, and it's my job to discover who did it." He rose and stood looking down at me.

"My dear Detective Inspector Chase"—I stood, my face the tiniest bit flushed with irritation—"I quite understand that. I will endeavor to give you every assistance possible in doing your job, without the least interfering in that process, I do assure you." I smiled disarmingly at him. "I do want to stay on your good side, after all."

"I'll rely on that, Dr. Kirby-Jones. I appreciate your helping us with our inquiries."

"Anytime at all, anytime at all," I promised as I escorted him to the front door. "Please feel free to call me whenever you need me . . . for anything."

He turned at the door, rubbing his mustache quickly with one finger. "I'll be in touch."

And with that I had to be content.

I had no doubt that before this thing was resolved, I'd see plenty more of the delicious detective inspector. Which was fine by me.

For the moment, I decided that I might as well call upon his cousin, that other delectable Chase, and see what I could ferret out in the case of the strangled postmistress. I waited until the policeman was out of sight, put on my hat and dark glasses, then let myself out the front door of Laurel Cottage.

A pleasant ramble down the lane took me to the Book

Chase. When time allowed, I really must explore more of the village and its environs. From what I had observed thus far, the setting was delightful. I reassured myself, yet again, that I had done the right thing in choosing to settle here. America no longer held much charm for me. I refused to let myself brood about Jack, or about Tristan Lovelace, and relationships gone by the wayside.

Trevor greeted me warmly when I stepped inside the bookstore.

"Simon!" He came forward with hand outstretched. "How nice to see you again. Can you believe what has happened? It's monstrous!"

"Yes, wasn't it the most awful shock? Your cousin came to see me just now, by the way. Has he been by here yet?"

Trevor sniffed and shook his head. "Not yet. Robin will, as always, leave me until the last moment possible." *Obviously not a lot of love lost there. Hmm . . . jealousy, perhaps?*

"That's a shame. He's quite handsome," I said mischievously.

Trevor's eyes narrowed. "Don't waste your time there, Simon," he said, his teech clenching. "Robin won't be interested, I assure you." He turned away. "What can I do for you this morning?"

The friendly mood between us had vanished abruptly. I barely knew the man. Surely he wasn't jealous? There must be something in the history of his relationship with his cousin that caused this.

"I said he was handsome, I didn't say he was available," I observed innocently, and Trevor turned back inquiringly. "I thought I'd like to poke around among your collectibles upstairs, if that's all right. When I was here the other day, I didn't take time. As you might expect, I'm quite the bookaholic, and one of the treasures I've been desperately seeking for years could just be lurking on the premises."

Trevor smiled, his good humor suddenly restored. "Please

go right ahead, Simon. I'm sure there must be something you want on the premises. Help yourself." He waved me upstairs.

It was a good thing there was no one else in the shop at that moment, I thought as I climbed the stairs to the second floor. (Or should I call it the first? This translation bit was sometimes a bit confusing.) The conversation hadn't gone quite the way I had planned. So much for an interrogation of Trevor Chase. I'd have to think of some other gambit. And what had he meant by "something you want?" Was that an invitation, or was I simply reading more into it than was warranted?

I spent a lovely half hour browsing through the shelves, and I did manage to locate one treasure I had long wanted. In a locked case, Trevor had what looked to be a mint copy of Dorothy L. Sayers's *The Nine Tailors*, my favorite of her books. I had to have it. And, thanks to Daphne Deepwood and Dorinda Darlington, I could afford it. There were several other, minor items that I wanted as well. This sale would very likely make Trevor's day. If not his month.

Heading back down the stairs, I paused halfway as I picked up part of a conversation.

"There's not a thing you can do about it!" Giles Blitherington was saying heatedly.

"Don't threaten me, boyo!" Trevor responded with quiet fury. "Abigail Winterton tried it, and look where it got her!"

Chapter Twelve

I paused on the stairs, hoping I might hear more of the argument, but at the most inopportune moment, the front door of the shop opened, its bell tinkling. Drat and blast!

I continued down the stairs to find Trevor assisting the newcomer, a perky young blonde with a toddler in tow, and Giles browsing through the history section. He just happened to have my book on Eleanor of Aquitaine in his hands.

Giles seemed a bit startled to see me. He glanced down at the book in his hands, then back up at me. For once the sulky look wasn't spoiling his handsome face.

"I say, Dr. Kirby-Jones, this is a pleasant coincidence," Giles said, tucking my book under his left arm and then extending his right hand for me to shake. The warmth of his voice surprised me.

"Good afternoon, Mr. Blitherington," I responded, taking his hand in mine. Strong, firm, and very warm, I found. Did I imagine it, or did he give me just the tiniest extra squeeze before releasing it? His eyes betrayed nothing but innocent interest.

"Are you a reader of history?" I asked when he pulled my book out from under his arm.

He nodded. "Actually, yes, and the medieval period has always fascinated me. I wonder . . . Would you mind signing this for me? I've not read it yet, and I am much looking forward to it."

"My dear fellow," I assured him, "I'd be delighted." Well, if he really wanted to buy and read my book, he'd go up a few notches in my estimation. Maybe there truly was a brain lurking behind that cover-model exterior.

We moved to the counter, and I drew a pen out of my pocket and signed the book with a flourish. Trevor glowered at both of us while trying to seem not to do so, and Giles paid for the book. I told Trevor about the books I wanted from the upstairs case, and muttering something under his breath, he went upstairs to retrieve them for me.

"I say, Dr. Kirby-Jones," Giles said as soon as Trevor had vanished up the stairs, "I wonder if I might talk with you privately about something?"

Curiouser and curiouser. I had had him on my list to interrogate, naturally, and there was no time like the present. Whatever it was he wanted, perhaps it might work to my advantage in questioning him about Abigail Winterton and her murder.

"Certainly, Mr. Blitherington. Would you like to accompany me to my cottage as soon as Trevor has my books ready? I can offer you something to drink, perhaps, while we talk."

"Thank you," he said, looking more relieved than the situation warranted, I thought. "That would be most excellent."

Trevor watched us both suspiciously when he came back downstairs a few moments later, arms laden with books. I took my time inspecting them, ensuring that I was getting good value for my money. Really, his prices were most reasonable. I nodded, he rang them up and wrapped them for me, and I wrote him a check that made his eyes glow with pleasure, at least momentarily. My leaving with Giles Blither-

ington in tow seemed to spoil the mood a bit. Further interrogation of Trevor Chase would have to wait.

Giles remained silent on the short walk to my cottage, and
I didn't attempt to engage him in conversation for the moment. I unlocked the door and ushered Giles in, leaving my
parcel of books on the table near the door.

"Welcome to Laurel Cottage," I said, escorting Giles into
the sitting room. "But perhaps you've been here before?"

Giles shook his head as he surveyed the room. "Actually,
no. When Professor Lovelace lived here, I was never allowed
near the place. I was too young." He turned to face me with
a wicked grin. "And he was too dangerous, of course. He
might have corrupted me." Something about Giles's voice informed me that he wished Tristan had.

"Could he have?" I asked, raising one eyebrow rakishly.

"Oh, most assuredly," Giles said. "But it was not to be." If
his tone was anything by which to judge, he had obviously
made up for lost time.

"How about some tea?" I asked.

Giles pouted slightly, as if disappointed by the suddenly
mundane turn of the conversation. "How about something a
bit more exciting? Like Diet Coke, perhaps?"

I laughed. "Can do. Be back in a tick."

I left him in the sitting room, wandering around and looking at the paintings and furnishings. Humming softly as I prepared our drinks, I mused on just what Giles could be after,
seeking me out like this. A date? Or, to be blunt, a quick roll
in the hay? The sexual energy emanating from that young
man could make even my cold blood stir.

Back in the sitting room, I served Giles his drink. He had
made himself comfortable on the sofa, adopting a pose similar to mine when I had entertained Detective Inspector Chase
earlier in the day. Really, the boy (I shouldn't call him that,
for he was at least twenty-five) was quite shameless. I could

get to be quite fond of him. He reminded me of myself at that age. Only a few years ago, mind you.

I took the chair more recently filled by said detective inspector. Assuming that worthy's inquisitive air, I asked Giles something that had been puzzling me for two days. "Do you mind my asking, Do you have an elder brother?"

Puzzled, Giles shook his head. "No, I'm the only son, and my sister is the only daughter in the family."

"Then why aren't you called Sir Giles? Isn't it a hereditary title?"

Giles rolled his eyes. "Because no one ever remembers that I am Sir-bloody-Giles, that's why! With my dear mummy running around, playing lord of the manor enough for both of us, no one pays much attention to me." I thought for a moment he was going to lapse into a sulk. But, amazingly, he laughed, a rich, deep sound that was completely infectious.

I laughed, too, and he looked back at me, eyes twinkling. "It doesn't seem to bother you that much."

Giles shook his head. "Honestly, no. I don't much care whether people call me that. My mother is the one hung up on titles, but even she forgets it most of the time. Though my father has been dead for nearly ten years, he lives on in her memory so strongly that she forgets that I inherited the title and the estate and not she."

An interesting sidelight on the rather trying Lady Prunella, to be sure. This conversation was revealing aspects to Giles's character that I never would have thought existed. Why, the boy seemed to have bottom to him, if I could use that so-very-English phrase.

"Then I shall call you Giles," I said, and he grinned before taking a sip of his Diet Coke.

"I believe you said you wanted to talk to me about something?" I prompted him after several moments' silence.

"Oh, yes," he said, leaning forward, his pose forgotten for

the moment. He set his glass down on a coaster on the table in front of him. "I want to apply for the job as your secretary."

This was the one thing I hadn't expected. Sir Giles Blitherington, wanting to be *my* secretary! My, my.

"Did your mother tell you I was looking for someone?" I asked, to stall for a moment.

Giles nodded. "Yes, and she has no idea that I'm asking you for a job. She'll make quite a scene, of course, if you should actually take me on, because it's not proper to one of my station." Here he grinned impishly, and I was ready to hire him on the spot. Not to mention for the sheer joy of annoying his mother.

"I can perhaps understand her point of view," I said mildly. His face fell. "But I wouldn't let that keep me from giving you serious consideration." He cheered up at that. "Provided, of course, you are actually qualified to do the job."

He nodded enthusiastically. "I'm quite adept at computers, really. I know several word-processing programs, and if I don't know yours already, I can learn it very quickly. I type very fast as well, and I even know shorthand, believe it or not. Mummy would be horrified if she knew." He grinned. "Actually, she has seen some of my shorthand scribblings, but I told her it was Greek. Which I was supposed to have learned at school, of course."

"Then I presume you understand the alphabet and the rudiments of filing as well?" I said dryly. "Are you any good at research?"

He sobered for a moment. "I know you heard what that harpy said about my being sent down from university, which is true, unfortunately. But I'm quite capable of assisting you in research despite my lack of a degree." He tried to hide his embarrassment, but he wasn't yet sophisticated enough to pull it off.

"Why do you want this job?" I asked him bluntly. Perhaps his money was tied up in the estate and he needed the job for the most basic of reasons.

His answer surprised me. "I want to be a writer," he said simply. "I know of your reputation in your field, and I've read some of your work. I could learn a lot by working with you, not to mention the potential contacts."

That last was certainly shrewd. Knowing the right people in publishing meant as much, if not more, than actually having the talent to write these days.

"But you already are a writer," I responded.

"What do you mean?" he asked, visibly startled.

"Your play," I reminded him. "I finished it, actually, after all the brouhaha the other night when Miss Winterton died, and I think you have talent."

He glowed briefly, but then the light went out. He looked darned uncomfortable, and I couldn't imagine why. "Thank you, but that's not the kind of work that I want to put my name on. That was my substitute for therapy." He smiled, trying to make a joke of it, but I wasn't quite convinced.

"That's as may be," I said, "but you can obviously put words together, and you have a sense of dramatic structure."

"But it's not a novel, nor is it a biography," he said, a trifle impatiently. "I'm more interested in other types of writing. Will you consider me for the job?"

I sighed. He didn't realize it, but he'd been hired five minutes ago. I might be making a terrible mistake, but something told me this was the right thing to do.

"It's yours," I told him, and his eyes sparkled with elation.

Giles flopped back against the sofa, grinning broadly. "You mean you're really going to let me work for you?"

I nodded. Hadn't I been clear enough?

"When do I start?" he asked eagerly. "I've nothing planned for this afternoon if you're ready for me to start right away."

"Giles, don't you even want to know what I'm going to pay you?" I asked, highly amused and—to be honest—quite flattered.

He waved that away. "I'm sure you'll be more than fair, Simon. May I call you Simon?" I nodded. "I've more than enough money, I assure you. In fact, you don't even have to pay me if you don't want."

That was a bit too much noblesse oblige for me. "No, Giles, I insist we keep this on a business footing. You'll be paid the going rate. As soon as I find out what it is."

"Fine, fine," he said, glowing with happiness. "When do I start?"

I sighed. Was I really ready for this? "Very well," I said, standing up. "Come with me into my office. If you're that eager, you might as well start getting my files sorted out this afternoon. It's got to be done, and I didn't relish doing it myself, frankly."

Giles was every bit as quick a study as he promised, and after fifteen minutes, I left him restoring my files to some semblance of order. I had to swear him to secrecy about the existence of Daphne and Dorinda, and he promised he'd not breathe a word, though his eyes grew big with excitement.

I stood in the doorway for a moment, watching him root happily through my papers. If this was what he wanted, he was quite welcome to it, I thought, shaking my head.

I had picked up our glasses and was ready to take them back to the kitchen when the doorbell rang. Now, who could that be? I wondered, most originally.

I set the glasses down on the hall table and opened the door.

Letty Butler-Melville stood there, her finger poised on the bell, ready to ring again.

"You!" She looked up at me, fire in her eyes. "I cannot believe how completely insensitive you are! You, you *American*!"

Chapter Thirteen

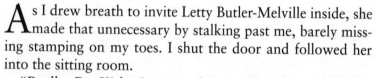

As I drew breath to invite Letty Butler-Melville inside, she made that unnecessary by stalking past me, barely missing stamping on my toes. I shut the door and followed her into the sitting room.

"Really, Dr. Kirby-Jones"—she continued her harangue, arms akimbo, hands on hips, her voice husky with emotion—"I had thought you a much more sensible individual." Despite the fact that I was a lowly American? "How *could* you upset poor Neville with such tales?"

"My dear Mrs. Butler-Melville," I protested, "I do assure you that I had no wish whatsoever to discompose the vicar to such an extent. I had no idea that he was so sensitive to, er, bad news."

The vicar's wife didn't seem much mollified by my conciliatory tone. One hand now twitched at the ever-present scarf around her throat while she kept glaring at me.

"I realize that you are only lately come to Snupperton Mumsley, Dr. Kirby-Jones, but surely even in your benighted homeland you don't descend upon unsuspecting souls and burden them with such horrendous and preposterous stories."

Good grief! I thought. *Someone needs desperately to tell this woman how the cow ate the cabbage.* Normally I am the politest of souls (and please don't be persnickety about vampires not having souls at this very moment), but when faced with such out-and-out hostility, I feel my own hackles rising.

"Perhaps you have been too busy scurrying about doing your good deeds for the parish," I said, my tone indicating that her good deeds probably included humping every available man over the age of consent, "but *while* you were on your errands of mercy, I was informed by no less a personage than Detective Inspector Chase himself that poor Miss Winterton was most foully murdered." I glared hard, and she took a step backward.

This cow suddenly got more of the cabbage than she ever bargained for, I noted with satisfaction. Letty Butler-Melville went white, and her right hand twisted her scarf so hard, I thought she'd choke herself right in front of me.

"Mur-murdered?" she finally managed to croak through her constricted throat. "But I thought it was an . . . an accident! I had no idea it was murder!"

Making a show of my concern, I approached her and, taking hold of her right arm, steered her gently to a chair. "Can I get you something? Some brandy, perhaps? Or maybe some hot tea?"

She shook her head. "No, thank you," she whispered. She stared up at me, her eyes wide with fear. "How . . . how did it happen?"

I took a seat in a nearby chair and watched her carefully. "She was strangled."

"Oh, dear God," she said, her voice tight and low. "God have mercy upon her soul." She crossed herself nervously.

I wasn't completely convinced that Letty Butler-Melville's obvious distress had all that much to do with the state of Abigail Winterton's immortal soul. There seemed to be something rather calculating about the vicar's wife, even *in ex-*

tremis. Deciding to take advantage of the situation, I observed casually, "You know, the thing that puzzles me is, why would someone want to murder her? I had met her only briefly on three occasions, and I can't see what someone would have had against her." And I didn't bat an eyelash at the lie.

Letty Butler-Melville's face hardened almost imperceptibly. If I hadn't been watching her intently, I would have missed it. "Abigail could on occasion be difficult about some things," she finally said, "but like you, I can't imagine what would move someone to do something so vicious as this."

She stood up abruptly. "I must get back to my husband, Dr. Kirby-Jones. I will ask you in the future to remember my husband's sensitive nature and to do your best not to upset him. Neville must guard his strength in order to shepherd his flock, and I am certain you can understand why I must be so protective of him."

I was beginning to have a few ideas about that, but I refrained from sharing them with her at this very moment. I had no doubt that Mrs. Vicar and I would tangle again at some point in the not-so-distant future. She was afraid of something, and I wasn't sure just yet what that was. But I would find out, I promised myself. She was a tougher nut than her husband, but I'd get something out of her eventually.

"Let me show you out, Mrs. Butler-Melville," I responded, not giving her an inch. She stared hard at me, then stalked ahead of me to the front door of the cottage. With a barely audible sniff, she stomped out the door and down the lane toward the vicarage.

"What was all *that* about?" Giles asked from behind me.

He stood in the doorway of my office, a stack of files in his hands. His handsome face quivered with curiosity.

"I'm sorry," he went on, "but I couldn't help but overhear a little of it. She was upset about something."

I nodded. "I discovered today that the vicar has a rather delicate constitution when it comes to emotional distress, and apparently I upset him. She came to tell me not to do it again."

Giles snorted in derision. "Oh, is that all! I should have known. Nothing gets Mrs. Butler-Melville so excited as a threat to the vicar's peace of mind."

"No kidding!" I said. "After that little scene I'm almost convinced that dragons are not extinct, after all."

Giles laughed. "She has only one little chick to defend, and she does it with a vengeance. We've all learned not to bother the vicar with anything. *She* won't stand for it."

"Does the man not have a backbone?" I asked.

"Not noticeably, no," Giles said, laughing. "Otherwise, do you think any man that attractive, with a reasonable amount of ambition, would stay in Snupperton Mumsley for twenty years?"

I shook my head. "No, I suppose not."

"My mother says that when he first came here, he was quite different. Much more energetic, much more involved in his actual clerical and pastoral duties. But over the years, he's turned into what you see now." Giles grinned. "Of course, I was very young when he first came here, so I don't remember much about him."

"Interesting," I commented, wondering whether I should broach the subject of Abigail Winterton's murder at this point.

Giles gestured at the folders in his hands. "I have questions about some of these, if you have a moment."

"Certainly," I said, and followed him into my office.

Giles dropped the folders onto the top of my now-bare desktop and spread them out. I stood next to him as he went through his questions. At one point, he leaned closer to reach a folder that had slipped slightly out of reach, and when he had grasped it, he didn't move back. His arm rubbed against mine, and when he turned his head to look at me, his face was disconcertingly close.

I stepped casually back and answered his question. His eyes flashed briefly with disappointment. A moment later, I left him, after giving quick instructions on several boxes that I wanted unpacked and sorted.

I retrieved those abandoned glasses from the hall and took them to the kitchen, where I rinsed them out in the sink. As the water ran, I thought about what had just happened in my office. I wasn't naive enough to think that Giles's brushing against me like that had been accidental. Giles was certainly not naive, at least not in matters of that nature, and I could spot a come-on when I saw one. I sighed. What was he really after? The job? Or me?

Frankly, I was as much irritated as I was flattered. He was undeniably attractive, and he was only about ten years younger than I (that is, if I were still alive and aging at the normal rate). What was it about this village? I laughed aloud. How many other gay men were there wandering about? No wonder Tristan had enjoyed it so.

I had to admit that Giles was a good bit more attractive, as far as personality went, than I had first suspected. Away from his mother, he was quite different. But was I ready for Lady Prunella as a mother-in-law? I shuddered at the thought.

A loud crash from the direction of my office caught my attention. I reached the door of the office quickly and stopped in the doorway. Giles was sitting on the floor in front of one of the overly laden bookshelves, a box of my assorted office knickknacks and junk spilled on the floor beside him. He looked surprised but otherwise unhurt. I walked in and reached down to offer him a hand. He took it and hoisted himself up. As he did, we both heard a loud rip. The back of his shirt had caught on something on the bookshelf behind him, and the shirt tore as he stood up.

Giles stood facing me, a rueful grin giving him a most boyish look. "Sorry about your things," he said. "I was checking the boxes on the shelves for more files, and I got a bit overbalanced. If anything is broken, I'll replace it."

"Don't worry about that," I said, surveying the damage on the floor. "There was nothing particularly valuable in that box. But what about your shirt?"

Giles shook his head. "Nothing terribly expensive, I assure you. And more than a bit aged, else it wouldn't have torn so easily." He twisted around, and I could see that the shirt was indeed ruined. It had ripped up the back to almost the neckline.

Staring at Giles's back. I got quite a surprise. He pulled the shirt off over his head, his back toward me. Spread across his back, extending around over his left shoulder, down his left arm to the elbow, and onto his chest, as I could see when he turned to face me again, was a large and beautifully executed dragon tattoo. The dragon breathed fire across his chest, which was lightly furred with dark hair. Giles grinned when he saw the expression on my face.

"Yet another little secret from Mummy," he said.

"I can imagine," I responded dryly. "One doesn't expect a flower of the English aristocracy to have such colorful taste in body decoration."

Giles stepped closer. "You can pet him if you like. He doesn't bite."

I flashed him one of my better smiles. "No, but I imagine you do."

"Only if you ask nicely," Giles assured, his eyes doing their best to tempt me.

I stepped back, and Giles's face fell. "It's not that I'm not tempted," I told him honestly, "because you are just about as attractive as you think you are." I flashed him another smile, even higher wattage this time, and he smiled back, charmed despite himself into forgiving me. "But I don't mix business with pleasure." For now, I added silently.

"Fair enough," Giles said, but something about his tone told me he wouldn't stop trying.

And, at that opportune moment, the doorbell rang.

Chapter Fourteen

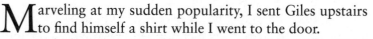

Marveling at my sudden popularity, I sent Giles upstairs to find himself a shirt while I went to the door.

"Good afternoon, Simon," said Jane Hardwick after I had opened the door. "May I come in?"

I gestured with my left hand, realizing belatedly that I was still holding in it Giles's abandoned shirt.

"Have I interrupted your cleaning?" Jane asked, slightly puzzled.

Giles chose that moment to come bounding back downstairs. "How's this one, Simon?" he asked. "It looked as if it might fit."

Giles paused at the foot of the stairs, and I could see that, indeed, the shirt did fit. Very snugly, that is, showing off his well-muscled arms and chest. "Oh, hello, Miss Hardwick. How are you?" he inquired politely.

"Quite well, Giles," she responded. "And you?" She looked at me with an amused glint in her eyes.

Giles smiled and said, "I'm doing very well, thank you. But if you'll both excuse me, I had better get back to work." So saying, he disappeared into my office and closed the door, but not before I had thrust his torn shirt into his hands.

I accompanied Jane into the sitting room, where she chose everyone's favorite chair and sat down. I dropped onto the sofa and stared at her. "Well, go ahead," I told her after waiting in silence for nearly a minute.

"Go ahead?" she asked innocently. "Why, whatever do you mean, Simon?"

"Go ahead and ask me how Giles got his shirt torn and why he was upstairs in my bedroom," I answered, starting to see the humor in the situation.

"Why, Simon," Jane purred, "I never expected you to have such a dirty mind. I'm sure poor Giles somehow tore his shirt—most innocently, of course—and you simply offered him the use of another."

I pretended to glower at her. "Very funny."

"But that doesn't quite answer what Giles meant about getting back to work," Jane continued, ignoring my attempt at humor.

"I got the bright idea that I needed a secretary. Really, it started out as a dodge with which to approach some of the suspects and grill them without their realizing it," I explained. "The trouble is, Lady Blitherington told Giles, and he came to me to apply for the job." I paused for a moment. "And I hired him."

I fully expected Jane to chide me for getting myself into such a situation, but she surprised me.

She looked quite thoughtful. "This may be just what Giles needs, Simon. How clever of you to have thought of it."

Jane puzzled me. "From our earlier conversation, I had rather got the idea that you didn't think much of Giles."

She shook her head. "No, I've always thought he had potential, but I knew it was going to take the right person—a man, naturally—to bring it out in him." She smiled wickedly. "And something tells me that you may be just the man to do it."

Groaning, I leaned back into the sofa. "'Enry 'Iggins I'm not," I protested in my best imitation cockney.

"The best part of it all," Jane went on gleefully, "is Prunella's reaction once she finds out. I hope I'm somewhere nearby. This is going to be tremendous fun."

"I'm delighted to be able to provide you with so much amusement," I told her dryly. "What*ever* did you do before I came to Snupperton Mumsley?"

Jane held up a hand, silencing me. Moments later, Giles's head popped into the sitting room. "I've done all I can for now, Simon," he informed me. "I have something I have to do this afternoon or I'd stay longer." His tone expressed his regret at having to leave. "So I'll just push off now if you don't mind. What time would you like me to be here in the morning?"

I avoided looking at Jane. "How about ten o'clock?"

Giles beamed at me. "That's fine. See you then. Your servant, Miss Hardwick." He nodded at Jane and then was gone. The front door closed behind him seconds later.

"What on earth have I gotten myself into?" I asked the air around me.

The air steadfastly ignored me, as did Jane.

"Now tell me, Simon, what have you discovered about Abigail's murder?" she asked.

I sighed. "Pitifully little thus far. Detective Inspector Chase told me that the police are indeed treating it as murder, but I'm sure you knew that already."

Jane nodded impatiently.

"I've talked to Lady Prunella, the result of which is getting myself saddled with her son. I talked to the vicar and earned the undying enmity of his dearly beloved, and I spent a lot of money at Trevor Chase's bookstore." That reminded me. "I also overheard a bit of an argument between Trevor and Giles." I repeated the little that I had heard. "So what's the deal between those two?"

"I've never been entirely certain," Jane admitted after a moment's silence, "just who is chasing whom with those two. They seemed to go out of their way to avoid each other when Trevor first moved to the village. That was about a year after Giles got sent down from Cambridge. Or was it Oxford?" She shook her head. "Not that it matters greatly. But within a year or so they seemed to have overcome whatever initial antipathy there had been between them. They seem to blow hot and cold with each other. It's rather a strange relationship, and I've not figured it out yet."

That was quite an admission from her, I thought. "Very interesting," I said. "Trevor seemed a bit jealous this morning when Giles talked to me, but I couldn't figure out which way the feelings were directed. Did he want Giles to himself? Or did he fear that Giles might make a play for *me?*" I shook my head. "Rather odd vibes from him."

"There is some mystery attached to Trevor Chase," Jane said. "He's never talked that much about his background before he came to Snupperton Mumsley. From what I know, he was an English master at some minor public school before he came here. He inherited money from some aged relative, which enabled him to give up teaching and purchase the bookstore. He seems to do well enough at it."

"So you never tried to find out more about his past," I said.

"No," Jane said. "There never seemed to be enough reason to warrant *that* much nosiness on my part." She smiled wickedly. "But perhaps I was wrong. At this stage, the more we know about everyone's past, the better."

"And that includes the vicar and his overprotective wife," I commented, then went on to relate to Jane the story of my encounters with the Butler-Melvilles.

"Perhaps I should have warned you about Letty," Jane said. "But I had no idea you'd go right to Neville and burden him with such distressing news." She laughed. "The poor man is so easily overset. Or at least he pretends to be."

"Do you think it's his way of avoiding the less pleasant aspects of his calling?"

"Wouldn't surprise me in the least, Simon. Our vicar is not the world's most energetic caretaker of souls."

I reprised my brief conversation with Letty Butler-Melville, and Jane looked very thoughtful. "Letty can be so prickly that it's difficult to get much out of her. But we'll have to try again. The question is, what would be the best approach?"

"I think I might leave that one to you," I said. "The woman gives me a headache." (No, before you ask, vampires don't get headaches that easily, but old patterns of speech are hard to lose sometimes.)

"We've been thinking about motive," Jane said, "but what about the method of murder?"

I nodded. "Yes, whoever did it had to be fairly strong. I imagine strangling someone takes a bit of strength."

"Abigail was not a large woman, but she was quite active. She would not have been easy to overcome unless someone sneaked up on her from behind."

Jane paused, and I knew we were both imagining the same scene in our minds. A rather unpleasant one it was. I shuddered. The poor woman! She had suffered a very nasty death, whatever her sins.

"If we get in the murderer's way," I said lightly, to break the sudden tension, "we could be targets as well." I grinned. "Though we are impervious to most of the usual methods."

Jane laughed. "You have to admit, Simon, that as amateur sleuths go, you and I are going to be disgustingly difficult to get rid of unless the murderer just happens to stumble upon our little secret."

I shuddered at the thought of a stake through the heart. That's the one thing that will still do away with us, irrevocably. Unless, of course, you take away our magic little pills for a few days and then expose us to the sun. Or maybe pump us full of garlic. Ye gads, I was giving myself the willies with such gruesome thoughts.

Turning my mind from such unpleasantness, I focused on the case at hand. "What we need," I said to Jane, "is to find out more about the secrets that would have been worth killing for, things Abigail Winterton knew that were dangerous for someone."

"That's obvious, Simon," Jane commented as I paused.

"Yes, quite," I said a bit testily. "I was thinking out loud. If I may continue"—Jane nodded, smiling sweetly—"the question *is*, how do we go about digging up the dirt?"

"I fancy," Jane said, watching my face closely, "that a little expedition to the post office is in order."

"How on earth are you going to snoop around at the post office at this time of the day? I'm sure it's sealed off as a crime scene, don't you think?"

Jane shook her head. "I didn't mean this very *moment*, Simon! In the dead of night, naturally, when the rest of Snupperton Mumsley is fast asleep. When creatures of the night are abroad." Her voice dropped to a sepulchral whisper. "When vampires can break and enter and not get caught."

"Oh, goody," I said, delighted. "What time shall I meet you?"

"A bit after the witching hour should suffice, don't you think? About one?" Jane said. "By that time we should be done with dinner at the Stevenses and the rest of the village is sound asleep."

"So you've been invited to dinner as well," I said, a bit surprised. I had thought I was the guest of honor.

"Yes, Mrs. Stevens likes to have a balanced table, and you and I will join her and her husband and their little ménage."

She refused to answer my questions in response to her

choice of words. "You'll see what I mean tonight." She stood up. "I must get back to my work. We are expected at seven-thirty for cocktails and dinner at eight. Shall I drive, or will you?"

Fascinated to find out what kind of car Jane drove, I said I'd ride with her and that I'd be at her door promptly at seven-fifteen. I showed her out and closed the door behind her with a sense of relief. After all the busyness of the morning and afternoon, I was more than ready for a bit of time to myself. As always, there was writing to be done, not to mention the fact that I had to figure out what I was going to have Giles do when he reported for work the next morning.

I had just changed into my comfortable and shabby working clothes when the doorbell rang yet again. "Drat!" I muttered over and over as I moved swiftly downstairs to the door. This was getting to be ridiculous.

I swung the door open, not quite having wiped the scowl off my face. There stood Trevor Chase, a book clasped in one hand and a bouquet of flowers in the other. Maybe this wasn't so ridiculous, after all.

Chapter Fifteen

"**D**o come in, Trevor." I stood back to allow him in. After all, the man had brought me flowers.

"What lovely flowers," I commented as Trevor stepped into the hallway.

"Oh, dear," Trevor said, turning to me with a small frown nestling in his beard. "I had forgotten these. They're for my neighbor. She's housebound at the moment, and fresh flowers do so cheer her." His eyes expressed his apologies for unintentionally misleading me.

So much for my presumption! I smiled ruefully as Trevor thrust the book he had been carrying into my hands.

"This, however, *is* for you."

I examined the book carefully. "Why, thank you, Trevor. How did you guess?" It was a lovely, bright copy of Cyril Hare's *An English Murder*.

"Do you have it already?" he asked anxiously.

"Actually, no, I don't." And now I was stuck in one of those awkward moments. Was this intended as a gift? Or was Trevor simply bringing some of his wares on a house call?

"When I saw what you liked earlier today, I told myself, Simon must have this one, too." Trevor smiled brightly. "A little gift from me to you. Consider it my personal welcome to the village."

"Well, thank you very, very much, Trevor." I gave him a warm smile, and his eyes dazzled a bit. "You'll have to pardon my dishabille," I said as I led him into the sitting room, "but these are my 'working' clothes. I can't write unless I'm wearing something worn-out and comfortable."

Trevor eyed me from his vantage point on the sofa. "Not at all, Simon, not at all. It suits you." From the expression on his face, he was enjoying the view. Not that I was exposing anything *private*, mind you.

"I must apologize for interrupting your work," Trevor continued.

I waved that away. "Not at all. I was just coming back downstairs from changing clothes. I haven't started work, so you've not actually interrupted anything."

Trevor relaxed into the comfort of my sofa. "That's good, then. I can imagine that you sometimes must be quite taxed by interruptions from those who don't understand the necessities of the writer's life."

I inclined my head slightly. "That's true, but I can assure you, few ever make the mistake of interrupting me a second time." For a brief moment, I let him see my fiercest expression, and he shrank back a bit into the sofa.

"Yes, I quite see what you mean," Trevor said faintly.

"Not to worry, though," I continued. "I always make allowances for my friends." I smiled again, and Trevor relaxed.

"What are you working on these days?" Trevor asked. "A new biography?"

I wasn't ready to confide to Trevor the full extent of my literary endeavors, so I employed the truth selectively. "At the moment, I'm still deciding. Once I've settled in here, I'll make up my mind. But one possibility is a biography of the Empress Maud."

Trevor nodded enthusiastically. "I've always found her intriguing. One wonders what Henry the First was thinking, trying to force his barons into supporting her. I shall look forward to that book with great interest."

I dipped my head modestly. "Why, thank you, Trevor. I can only hope that the book will live up to your expectations."

Trevor laughed. "I seriously doubt that you fail at anything you undertake, Simon." He paused for a moment. "I trust that you *are* settling in well here in the village despite the rather strange goings-on of last night."

"You mean the murder?" I asked him coolly.

He started. "Murder!"

"Yes," I said. "Detective Inspector Chase came by to see me earlier today to ask more questions and to inform me that the police are now treating Miss Winterton's death officially as a murder inquiry." I watched his face closely. "Hasn't he been by to see you?"

Trevor's mouth twisted bitterly. "Not yet. My dear cousin always assumes that I am of the least importance in any group. I'll hear from him at some point, however."

Good grief, the man could sound quite nasty when he chose. I'd do well to remember that.

"Murder!" Trevor repeated. "How sordidly nasty! The woman could be quite annoying for no apparent reason, but that doesn't explain why someone would murder her."

"For someone unbalanced," I observed mildly, "mere annoyance might be enough."

"Snupperton Mumsley has perhaps more than its share of eccentrics," Trevor said with a touch of frost in his voice, "but none of them seems quite the murdering type."

I shrugged. "I've not been here long enough to know anyone that well. But I've already picked up hints from more than one quarter that the late, and largely unlamented, postmistress was decidedly inclined to poke her nose into other people's business. Where it most assuredly was not wanted."

Trevor laughed. "That's an understatement if ever I heard one. The woman wasn't satisfied until she knew where you came from, what your parents did, and so on. Like some self-appointed bloody social register."

And those with something to hide, I thought, would be greatly disconcerted by the woman's nosiness. What was it that Trevor was hiding? His tone was too harsh to be merely a snide comment; there was something personal here. He gave every appearance of coming from a solidly middle class background, but was he hiding some shameful secret? That he grew up in the slums somewhere? That his mother dressed him in polyester when he was a child? That his father secretly did embroidery when he wasn't driving a lorry?

I recalled the brief scene between Trevor and Giles Blitherington that I had overheard earlier today. Trevor must have something to hide or he wouldn't have used such strong language with Giles. And had Giles threatened him with exposure? Could what Trevor had said to Giles be construed as an admission of guilt in the death of Abigail Winterton?

"Sometimes the secrets we find most painful," I said with nonchalance, "are terribly innocuous and downright uninteresting to other people. Having them broadcast around the village would be irritating, but sometimes it's better to get things into the open, where they have no power to harm you any further."

And if that wasn't an invitation to unburden himself, I don't know how much clearer I could make it. I watched Trevor closely to see how he would react.

"Perhaps so," Trevor said. At the moment, he gave little appearance of having taken my point to apply to his own case. "Tell me, if you will," he went on, attempting to change the subject with little subtlety, "what it was that Giles was so intent on burdening you with earlier."

I frowned slightly. He was definitely fishing for something or surely he wouldn't have been so blatant.

"Giles can be quite a pest," Trevor went on hurriedly when I didn't respond immediately. "I know well from personal experience that he is very importunate when he wants something and one doesn't yield right away."

Curiouser and curiouser. "I'll admit that my first impression of him wasn't very good," I said. "But upon further acquaintance, I can see that he has some most interesting possibilities." Should I tell Trevor the news that I had hired Giles as my secretary? What if Trevor were correct and Giles *was* a pest? I shrugged. I had no doubts about my ability to rid myself of any kind of pest; thus, I wasn't unduly worried about Giles. But I *was* curious about Trevor and his motives in trying to discredit Giles with me.

"I grant you," Trevor said in a studiedly casual tone, "that Giles can be very appealing whenever things are going his way, but the moment you tell him no, the situation changes dramatically."

Despite his attempts to appear otherwise, Trevor was sounding more and more like someone with the proverbial ax to grind. I had expected better of him. What on earth had Giles done to him to warrant this kind of backbiting?

"I assure you, Trevor," I said, frost in my voice, "that you need not worry about my welfare. I am more than capable of handling any situation which Giles—or anyone else, for that matter—might contrive." I fixed him with a direct glare, and he wilted visibly. "What has Giles done to you that you're so bitter about him? He may be a bit spoiled, from what I've seen, but that doesn't mean he's harmful."

Trevor sighed and ran a hand through his hair. "I might as well tell you the truth, Simon."

At last we were getting somewhere, I thought with satisfaction.

"I knew Giles before I came to the village," Trevor said. "In fact, I was his tutor at university."

"Before he was sent down?" I asked. Hadn't Abigail Winterton said Giles had been expelled?

Trevor nodded. "And, unfortunately, I was the reason he was sent down from Cambridge." He took a deep breath. "He became obsessed with me and wouldn't leave me alone. It became most painfully embarrassing, I can assure you. No matter where I went, or with whom, there he was. I was hesitant about doing anything official, but he had become so obsessed that his work was suffering, and I was able to use a certain amount of influence to get him sent down."

"And then you ended up living here in the same village?" That sounded like too much of a whopping coincidence, even for me.

Trevor nodded wearily. "I had inherited some money from a relative, and I was tired of tutoring wretches like Giles. I wanted to own my own bookshop, and I found the one here in this village for sale. I had no idea, at the time, that this was where Giles lived. By the time I found out, it was too late."

"And has he continued to pester you with unwanted attentions?"

"No, thank goodness," Trevor said, his eyes shifting away from mine for a moment. "He seems to have matured enough that he doesn't indulge his adolescent passions to the same extent. He does come into the shop to talk to me occasionally, but most of the time he leaves me alone."

"And this is what you were afraid of?" I asked him. "You were afraid that Abigail Winterton had found out and that she would broadcast it to the whole village?"

Trevor nodded unhappily. "Can't you see, Simon, how difficult it would be if that were to become known? I'd be a laughingstock."

"Perhaps," I said. "But if you were the victim, it really wasn't your fault."

"I know that," Trevor said impatiently, "but it doesn't

matter. Giles is Sir Giles Blitherington, for God's sake! Even as unconventional as he can be, he still commands respect around here because of his name and his family. Do you think I want to match my good name against his in a contest of rumors?"

"I can see why you'd rather not," I conceded. "But if Giles no longer makes any attempts to bother you, I can't see what relevance the past has. Who's going to tell the story, and for what purpose?" *Now that Abigail Winterton is dead,* I added silently.

If Trevor were truly this worried about his so-called shameful secret, he might conceivably have a motive to murder Abigail Winterton. But did he really feel that shame deeply enough to kill? And with Giles a living, everyday reminder, how could he expect to keep the secret hidden forever?

But how would Abigail Winterton have found all this out? I couldn't imagine Lady Prunella confiding something like this in her favorite adversary, and I didn't think Giles would be indiscreet enough to tell her himself. If she truly had been reading everyone's mail, she might have discovered the information that way. If someone had been indiscreet enough to write something down.

Despite what Trevor said, though, this could give Giles as much motive to kill Abigail Winterton. His good name locally wouldn't be much proof against scandal in a situation like this. Giles—and his mother—would have as much, or more, to lose as Trevor did.

"You may be right," Trevor said. "As long as Giles keeps quiet, everything will be all right." He shrugged. "I've settled in here, and I like the village and my life as a bookseller. I just don't want anything to unsettle it."

Like murder, I thought.

But murder changes everything; Trevor might soon find his

secret exposed, one way or another. What would his cousin, the detective inspector, do in this case? But perhaps he already knew. I didn't voice that thought aloud, however.

"Please promise me, Simon," Trevor said earnestly, "that you won't say anything to Giles about this? As long as he thinks I haven't told anyone, he won't get angry and do something to get back at me."

Had I misread Giles completely? I wondered. I'd have plenty of opportunity to evaluate him for myself if he continued to work as my secretary. I didn't relish working with a murderer, but at least I'd have the opportunity to get a better sense of his character.

"I don't think I'll be bringing the subject up with Giles anytime soon," I assured Trevor dryly. "I must tell you, however, that I have engaged Giles as my secretary. I need help with some of my research and correspondence, and Giles seemed most eager to work with a published writer."

Trevor went completely still at my news. "I hope you won't regret this," he said finally. "Perhaps Giles has matured enough that he won't try to take advantage of you in some way. But you can't say I didn't warn you."

"No, Trevor, I'll remember what you've said and weigh it very carefully." I grinned. "And I'll assure you, yet again, that I'm more than capable of looking out for myself."

Trevor stood abruptly. "I had better be going." He picked up his flowers from where he'd laid them earlier. "If I don't get these to my poor neighbor soon, they'll wilt completely."

"Quite so," I said, standing, then leading him to the front door.

"Good afternoon, Simon," Trevor said, standing on the doorstep.

"Thank you again for the book, Trevor," I replied. "It's a lovely addition to my collection."

Trevor smiled, but his eyes remained distant. "You're most

welcome. I hope it brings you pleasure." He turned and walked away. I had the sense of a door closing, and not the one whose latch was in my hand.

Well! I thought. *That was certainly strange.* I shut the door and leaned back against it. *Giles a stalker? Trevor the object of an obsession? Whoever would have guessed? Maybe I had better call up Ruth Rendell and invite her over for tea and advice.*

Shaking my head in amusement, I headed to my office to work.

Chapter Sixteen

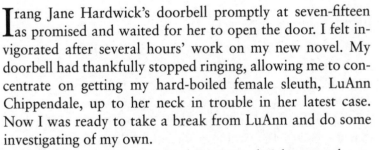

I rang Jane Hardwick's doorbell promptly at seven-fifteen as promised and waited for her to open the door. I felt invigorated after several hours' work on my new novel. My doorbell had thankfully stopped ringing, allowing me to concentrate on getting my hard-boiled female sleuth, LuAnn Chippendale, up to her neck in trouble in her latest case. Now I was ready to take a break from LuAnn and do some investigating of my own.

The door swung open, and Jane Hardwick stepped out, locking the door behind her. She looked the very picture of the ultra-respectable English spinster in a sensible black dress accented with jet-and-silver earrings, broach, and necklace. The denizens of Snupperton Mumsley would never have guessed she'd been dead for over four hundred years.

After a calm "Good evening, Simon," Jane led me behind her cottage to her detached garage. I wasn't in the least surprised to find that her car matched her image perfectly: a black Volvo, every inch of it gleaming in the soft evening sun. I made myself comfortable in the passenger seat, though I felt a bit odd sitting on this side of the car without a steering wheel in front of me. Yet another of the adjustments necessary for life in England.

During the brief drive to the Stevenses' estate, just a few miles outside the village and up a long, winding drive, Jane and I discussed plans to raid the post office later that night. Jane was hopeful that we could find something among Abigail Winterton's effects that could point the way toward a solution in the case. I thought the police might well have beaten us to the punch, but Jane demurred.

"Abigail had such a quirky way of doing things," Jane explained, "that whatever records she might have kept very likely defied any attempts by the police to uncover them. I think it's worth our doing a little snooping. I have an idea where Abigail might have kept evidence of her activities."

More than that she refused to say, telling me, with that infuriatingly enigmatic smile, to be patient.

By then we had crested a slight rise that hid the Stevens domicile from view and I couldn't restrain a gasp of amazement as the house came into view down below us.

"House" was a completely inadequate word to describe what I could see. "Is it a real castle?" I asked. I hadn't heard that there was a surviving medieval castle in the immediate area of Snupperton Mumsley.

Jane laughed as we got out of the car. "No, Everard Stevens had it built. He'd always fancied living in a castle, so he had one built for himself."

"Looks to me like his architect must have been drunk and cross-eyed, at the very least!" I said, leaning back against Jane's car, staring in wide-eyed amazement.

Castles can be majestic, awe-inspiring, defiant. This one seemed to be begging for sympathy. Maybe because whoever designed it had been three sheets to the wind while drafting the plans or maybe because the contractor who built it thought he was the Salvador Dali of the building trade. It looked suitably Gothic, at least—the kind of place where you'd expect to find guys like me hanging from the rafters. Disguised as bats, of course. But if I knew any bats (and I don't, I assure you), I believe they'd be embarrassed to call this travesty home.

The proportions were off, for one thing. The towers were too thin, like strands of pasta pasted on a squat and bulging meatball. Then there were the various colors of stone employed in construction. The result was a crazy-quilt type of effect that made the whole edifice seem like a postmodernist interpretation of "medieval." I shuddered.

Jane laughed again. "I thought you'd enjoy seeing this place, Simon. I'm pleased that I was the one to bring you here for the first time. The expression on your face is priceless."

"Something tells me this won't be the last surprise of the evening," I muttered as I followed Jane over the bridge spanning the moat. Too bad we couldn't drive right inside the walls of the castle, but whatever idiot had designed the place had made the main gate barely big enough for two normal-sized beings to squeeze through.

Jane preceded me across the yard and up the steps to the front door. She lifted the huge brass knocker, which seemed to be some strange heraldic device, and let it clang three times against the door.

A few moments later, Lurch opened the door. I blinked in surprise. Had we suddenly stepped into an *Addams Family* rerun? The butler was a dead ringer (and I use the term advisedly) for the actor who played the Addams's family retainer.

Except for her voice. At least I thought it was "her" voice. It was pitched just high enough that I concluded its owner was likely female. I peered more closely as Jane introduced me. Yes, "Dobson" was a woman, no doubt a refugee from the Soviet women's basketball team of a decade or so ago.

She'd had more than her share of steroids and male hormones, to judge by the hair on her upper lip and the shaggy eyebrows, but Dobson was most definitely female. I think.

Dobson gestured for us to follow, leading us toward what was likely the drawing room. I glanced around at the entranceway of the castle. There was lots of marble, with exquisite statuary cheek by jowl with stuffed trophy animals of various kinds. There were expensive tapestries hanging on the walls and equally dear carpets on the floor, but the effect was more "I've got lots of money, get it" than "welcome to my comfortable home." Surely the elegant Mrs. Stevens hadn't furnished this place to her taste?

Lurch—I mean Dobson—opened a door, and Jane swept regally through, with me trailing dutifully in her wake, wondering all the while what further horrors awaited us. The drawing room continued the same mishmash of elegance and kitsch that I had observed already. There seemed to be no unifying theme at work in the decor here except poor taste. I shook my head at seeing a Georgia O'Keeffe stuck on the wall next to what surely was a Constable. Both artists I admired. But right next to each other?

Then my attention was caught by the person awaiting us. Dobson had quietly departed after announcing us to the room's sole occupant. I wondered suddenly whether this was the British headquarters of the Society for the Propagation of Androgyny because I was yet again faced with an individual of indeterminate gender. It wore beautifully tailored clothes that were gender neutral, had a sleek cap of lustrous black hair, worn short and curling around the face, and features that were attractive but asexual.

"Good evening, Jane? How are you?" It spoke in a pleasantly modulated voice that gave me no clues. Turning to me, it said, "How do you do? I'm Hilary Thomas, Everard Stevens's executive assistant."

"Good evening, Hilary," Jane said, casting a smiling

glance at me, enjoying my puzzlement. "I'm delighted to present Dr. Simon Kirby-Jones, our latest addition to the village."

"Welcome to Morland's Folly, Dr. Kirby-Jones," said Hilary Thomas. I smiled involuntarily at the name of the castle. Someone, at least, had an educated sense of humor. No matter that it probably had poor Jane Austen spinning in her grave.

"Thank you," I said, extending my hand. "Er, um . . ."

"Please, call me Hilary," it said, grasping my hand and shaking it firmly. "Everyone does. I see no need to stand on ceremony."

"Very well," I said. "Hilary it is. And I'm Simon." I tried not to be too obvious as I scanned Hilary, looking for some of the more obvious indications of gender. No prominent breasts, no suggestive swelling in the crotch of those beautifully tailored pants, and the carefully placed ascot at the neck kept me from finding an Adam's apple—or the lack thereof.

Hilary indicated a nearby sofa. "Please, won't you be seated? Everard and Samantha will be down any moment. May I offer you something to drink?" Jane and I both accepted small gin and tonics and made ourselves comfortable.

Moments later, the doors of the drawing room opened, and Samantha Stevens swept in, followed by a man hobbling on crutches. Trailing in his wake was a devilishly ugly hulk of a man, dressed in a dark suit, who watched the man on crutches very carefully, as if he were ready to step forward at any moment to pick him up and carry him, if need be.

The man on crutches was, as I expected, Everard Stevens. His wife, coolly elegant in ice blue silk and diamonds, introduced us. "Everard, may I present Dr. Simon Kirby-Jones? He wrote that biography of Eleanor of Aquitaine which you admired so much."

"Yes, I know," Everard Stevens told his wife testily. "It was my leg I broke, not my brains, my dear."

Samantha Stevens appeared not to hear the tone in her husband's voice as she quietly greeted Jane, and the two of them chatted while our host claimed my complete attention. Everard Stevens shook my hand firmly, then hobbled backward and dropped onto a nearby chair. "Apologies for my hopping around, but I broke my leg skiing in Switzerland recently. Just now beginning to get around again."

"No apologies necessary on my account," I assured him as I settled back into my seat and observed him.

Everard Stevens was in his late sixties, definitely older than his wife, but by how much only her plastic surgeon knew for sure. Stevens had the craggy kind of face that makes some men even more attractive the older they get, and his eyes burned with a fierceness that bespoke the ruthless man of business. Even with the crutches, he was physically imposing, though he was dwarfed by his attendant. The attendant, introduced briefly as Parker, remained quietly in the background, but I could feel the pent-up energy in him. He was ready to spring, I fancied, should anyone pose a threat to his employer. If I should ever have need of a bodyguard, I'd want a Parker on my side. He was big enough, and no doubt strong enough, to get rid of most obstacles in one's way. Even if that meant murder; he certainly looked sinister enough to me.

Like nosy postmistresses, perhaps? My mind turned irresistibly to the murdered Abigail Winterton. If she had got crossways of Everard Stevens, he'd only have had to sic Parker on her. With a quick jerk of his huge hands, he could have snapped her neck in two.

But I had put the cart well ahead of the horse once again. I hadn't the least notion that Stevens had any reason to want Abigail Winterton dead. From what I had heard, it was the other way around.

Stevens and I chatted for a few minutes longer about my work, then we talked about my impressions of Snupperton

Mumsley. That was still the topic when we went in to dinner. The dining room was a large chamber, echoing with our footsteps. At one end stood a fireplace big enough for roasting an ox or two. The huge table could easily accommodate thirty people. It seemed rather a waste to have it set for only the six of us, but we formed a cozy crew at one end of the table. Dobson, assisted by a most feminine looking maid, served our dinner and poured wine. The food, as I expected, was quite good, with no hint of garlic that I could detect. The china on which the food was served was so stunningly hideous that it was no doubt incredibly expensive. Bad taste so often is. I kept my eyes averted from the so-called art on nearby walls. Hunting pictures, with graphic illustrations of gore, are not to my taste. I detest the sight of blood, real or imaginary, especially when I'm trying to eat, though I consume only small amounts, of course.

At the table, I discovered that there was no real conversation to speak of; rather, there were orations from the head of the household. Everard Stevens held forth on any number of topics, pausing only occasionally for encouraging noises from his wife or his secretary or his bodyguard. I'm not quite sure what purpose Jane Hardwick and I were supposed to serve, because after his initial mentioning of my work, Stevens never again broached the subject, as I had expected he might. Eventually, eyes glazing in boredom, I seized the opportunity, when an uncharacteristic lull occurred, to dare a conversational gambit of my own.

"Rather shocking, isn't it, that there has been a murder in the village?" I said brightly, watching the faces of the lord and lady of the manor with great interest.

Samantha Stevens smiled slightly, while Everard Stevens was so nonplussed that he let his mouth hang open for a moment.

"I didn't know poor Miss Winterton all that well," I went on while Stevens struggled with the shock of actually hearing another voice besides his own, "so I can't imagine why on earth someone would murder the poor creature. What do you think, Mrs. Stevens?"

Thus called upon, Samantha Stevens cast a quick glance at her husband, then answered. "I, of course, knew poor Abigail much better than you, Dr. Kirby-Jones, but I confess that I, too, am in a quandary over her unfortunate death. I sometimes found her difficult, albeit usually well meaning, but that doesn't explain why someone would murder her."

"Quite so," Jane Hardwick said. "Abigail could be a sore trial at times. And to think how the village will suffer without her." Jane leaned across the table a bit and fixed me with a telling look. I wondered what she was about. "Simon isn't aware, naturally, of the significant role which Abigail played in village affairs. She was the mainstay of much of the charitable activity in the village."

Samantha Stevens nearly spluttered her wine all over the table. "Mainstay! She was a busybody, if you ask me! She thought she had to be in charge of everything that went on, especially anything to do with St. Ethelwold's. I'm surprised the vicar managed to get dressed in the morning without her express permission!" She gulped at her wine. "Between her and Lady Blitherington, they made it nearly impossible for someone truly experienced in fund-raising and committee work on a national level to accomplish anything of significance."

The heat of jealousy in Samantha Stevens's voice gave me a startlingly bizarre idea. Could Mrs. Stevens have possibly murdered Abigail Winterton for blocking her attempts to take control of charitable affairs in the village?

Chapter Seventeen

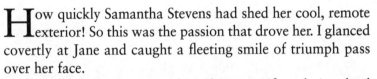

How quickly Samantha Stevens had shed her cool, remote exterior! So this was the passion that drove her. I glanced covertly at Jane and caught a fleeting smile of triumph pass over her face.

"I imagine that you must have been significantly involved in various fund-raising projects in London, Mrs. Stevens," I commented, sincerity and admiration oozing from my voice.

In response, Mrs. Stevens reeled off a list of charities that made my head spin. The woman wasn't kidding when she said she had experience. I speculated whether being "retired" to Snupperton Mumsley didn't make her even edgier. With that thought in mind, I said, "But since we're so close to London here, you probably still are actively involved with that work."

A pained look crossed Mrs. Stevens's face and was quickly gone. Everard Stevens spoke up, "No, Dr. Kirby-Jones, my wife and I decided that, once I retired from affairs in the City, we would both retire. After so many years of devoting ourselves to my business interests and to her charitable work, we thought we would rather have more time for ourselves and our leisure."

I wondered just how much input Samantha Stevens had really had in that decision. From the tautly controlled look on her face, I thought probably very little at all. If she no longer had her activities in London to keep her busy and Abigail Winterton (and probably Lady Blitherington as well) had kept her from positions of power in the village, the woman could be so frustrated, she might resort to violence of some sort. Suddenly, Abigail Winterton's taunting about Everard Stevens's accident didn't seem that ludicrous. Frankly, I couldn't blame Mrs. Stevens for wanting to get rid of her husband if he were stifling her needs and ambitions to this extent. Not to mention the fact that he was a crashing great bore. I observed her with a new respect. She could be a formidable foe if she chose, I was sure.

"Retirement has allowed us to travel more," Everard Stevens went on. "At least when I don't have stupid accidents that make travel difficult."

Samantha Stevens smiled enigmatically as she took another sip of her wine. "We traveled extensively before Everard's retirement," Mrs. Stevens said, "but of course we were always at the mercy of the needs of business, not pleasure. Now we may go where we like, when we like."

Her voice sounded dutiful, but her eyes told another story. Jane and I exchanged glances with amusement. No matter how tough a businessman Stevens may have been, I had little doubt that his wife (or should I say "widow?") would one day have her way.

"I can't imagine wanting to waste time on committees here in this little village," Everard Stevens went on, oblivious to Jane's broad smile. "All they want is a check, and we can contribute that without my wife having to dirty her hands with the actual fund-raising."

Mrs. Stevens paled at that beautifully brutal display of tactlessness. Her hand tightened on her wineglass, and for a moment I thought she might smash it in her husband's face.

"Money is naturally of great significance," Jane said, her voice calm but authoritative, "but without someone of great organizational skills and persuasive personality to guide the efforts, any committee will find it difficult to succeed in its goals, no matter how worthy the cause."

Everard Stevens blinked in surprise at being put so neatly in his place, while Samantha almost purred with joy. She tossed off the rest of her wine and stood. "Ladies, shall we adjourn to the drawing room and leave the men to their amusements?"

Since she had used the plural of the word, I was curious to see how Hilary Thomas, who had remained mostly silent during the meal, would react. Was Hilary a lady? Apparently she was, for she rose along with Jane and Samantha Stevens and departed the dining room. That was one little mystery solved.

Dobson didn't follow, but I suppose one can't be a butler and a lady at the same time. At least not socially.

Dobson did, however, fetch some expensive Cuban cigars, which she then offered each of us in turn. I accepted one happily. One of the benefits of death, you see. Smoking can't hurt me. Though I don't smoke that often, I do so enjoy a good cigar.

Stevens, Parker, and I sat and smoked for about an hour, with Parker and me listening to Stevens explain, in gruesome detail, the problems with the British economy and why Margaret Thatcher was the greatest prime minister in the history of Great Britain. I made a couple of attempts to turn the conversation back to Abigail Winterton, with some hopes of finding out more about her grudge against my host. But the River Bore was in full spate, and I sat back and enjoyed my cigar. Finally, Dobson stood behind Stevens's chair and coughed loudly. That was apparently the signal for us to rejoin the ladies in the drawing room.

As we came into the drawing room, Jane was entertaining

Mrs. Stevens and Hilary Thomas with a pithy review of some play she had seen in London the week before.

Everard Stevens took over the conversation immediately, changing the subject to some topic of interest to himself while the rest of us watched the hands on the clock move slowly around. After twenty minutes of Stevens's perorations on Basque separatism, Dobson came into the drawing room with a horse on a leash.

At least it looked like a horse, but it was actually a dog. I haven't the slightest notion of what breed it was. Huge and ugly, it looked as if it could eat several small children for breakfast. Upon sight of this canine behemoth, Stevens immediately lost the thread of his remarks, and a goofy look spread across his face.

"Dere is Daddy's big boy! Come to Daddy, sweet boy." Remarks in that vein kept flowing, becoming more nauseating by the moment. The creature, whose name was Junior, stood in front of Everard Stevens and licked his master's face happily. Stevens was soon dripping all over the place, and the whole scenario was completely disgusting. I watched with fascination as Mrs. Stevens averted her gaze entirely. The poor woman had my entire sympathy now. I wondered whom she would enjoy getting rid of more, her husband or his dog?

Eventually, Stevens remembered his guests long enough to adjure us to admire Junior. (The mind simply reeled at the implications of that name.) We did so dutifully, though if the damned beast had tried to lick me, he would have been awfully surprised. But he took one look at me and, even as stupid as he appeared, knew enough to keep his distance.

Stevens continued crooning at his horrid pet as the rest of us watched in horrified fascination. My ears pricked when Stevens said something about that "nasty lady who won't ever bother my sweet boy again!"

"Did someone take exception to your handsome pet, Mr. Stevens?" I said brightly.

"What?" Stevens jerked his head up, out of range of Junior's slimy tongue. "Oh, that. That damned interfering busybody of a postmistress was always on about poor little Junior here whenever we went into her pathetic excuse for a village shop. She screeched at him and upset him terribly. My poor boy!"

"Obviously she had no sense of appreciation for what a fine animal Junior is," I said, and Stevens bought every syllable of it.

"His pedigree is certainly more august than hers ever was," Stevens snorted. "Bloody woman tried to make trouble for Junior, saying that he hadn't spent the proper time in quarantine when I brought him over from the United States. But that was sheer nonsense. She was trying to get back at me."

"She was a spiteful shrew," Samantha Stevens agreed. "But Everard was able to prove that Junior had spent his duly allotted time in quarantine, and that was the end of that." She gave her husband a speaking glance, and, wonder of wonders, he said no more.

After that exchange, the conversation dwindled enough to bring the dinner party to a close, and Jane and I left shortly after that. We thanked our host and hostess for a most diverting evening. That was the most tactful word I could devise. I couldn't help but think that some version of tonight's amusements would make its way into one of my books someday.

Once we were safely ensconced in Jane's car and heading homeward, I said, "You were right, Jane! There's no way I could have imagined anything like that."

Jane laughed. "Something you have to experience to believe, as I know only too well. That poor woman has a lot to put up with in that place. But she married him, for whatever reasons. I can only hope the money makes up for most of what she endures."

I laughed along with her. "That's the bad part about making a bargain with the Devil. You're stuck with him, and his dog, one way or another."

"They've only been retired here in the village for a little over two years," Jane said. "I'm willing to lay odds that Everard Stevens doesn't survive five years of retirement."

"I wouldn't bet against you, Jane," I said. "Something tells me he is not long for this world. Because I don't imagine divorce, at this point, would have the same satisfactions as widowhood."

"No, mere divorce would be no compensation," Jane agreed.

"Very interesting," I said, changing the subject, "what you managed to bring out about charitable works. It sounds to me as if Mrs. Stevens had a motive, twisted though it might be, to get rid of Abigail Winterton."

"I thought it worth a gamble," Jane said. "I knew that Abigail had done her best, along with Prunella, to keep Samantha on the fringes of any kind of organized charitable activities here. The only instance in which they failed was the board of SMADS. The vicar, of course, is useless against such determined busybodies as Abigail and Prunella."

"How were you able to get yourself involved in such works?" I asked. "Surely they wouldn't be keen on having someone with your abilities to outshine them?"

"Thank you, Simon," Jane said as she drew her car into her garage. "But when I first came to the village, things were a bit different. Lady Prunella's mother-in-law was still living, and it was she who had control of such things in those days. She and I hit it off immediately, so I became involved in things before Prunella or Abigail could do much about it. They grew rather used to me, but once the Dowager Lady

Blitherington passed on, Prunella and Abigail took over. They fought with each other all the time, but they did stand united over one thing. One or the other of them controlled every committee of any significance in the village."

I followed Jane to her front door. "Politics, even on this level, can be dirty. I think we've found a possible motive for the murder."

Jane unlocked her door and opened it. "Yes, we have. But just how probable is it? Though I must admit I'm vastly amused by the notion of Samantha Stevens as a murderess, it doesn't seem strong enough a motive. There are probably others yet to be uncovered."

"What about Everard Stevens and his beloved dog? Could he have had his keeper, Parker, go after Abigail because of the fuss she kicked up over Junior?"

Jane shook her head. "I don't think so, Simon. There were definitely bitter feelings on Abigail's part, but as you heard, Stevens was able to prove that the dog had been through the proper quarantine. Abigail was just trying to annoy him, and she succeeded, but it was only momentary. That happened a year ago, and though both parties harbored a grudge, I don't think it's the motive for murder in this case."

"I knew it was a long shot," I said, "but worth a try. What a hideous beast." Which applied equally well to dog and master, I reflected.

Jane laughed as she stepped inside her cottage. "Meet me here at one and we'll proceed with our raid on the post office. And perhaps we'll uncover something even more interesting."

"And incriminating," I said, smiling. I glanced at my watch. It was almost eleven. "Only a couple of hours. Well, I'll have time to get some work done. Until then." Jane nodded and shut the door.

I loped off down the lane to my cottage, my mind mulling over the possibilities. We had established a tenuous motive for Samantha Stevens. Her husband seemed to be out of the running—for the moment at least. A pity, for he was rather a nasty specimen, and it would be most rewarding to see him in the dock, on trial for murder.

I unlocked the front door of my cottage, my mind still on the possibilities of Samantha Stevens as a murderer. How could I work it into something more substantial if I were to use it in a book, for example? I went upstairs to change clothes. I might as well dress in what I'd wear for our commando raid at one A.M. Then I could work right up until the time to meet Jane.

Other than the couple of small lamps that I had left burning downstairs in my absence, I hadn't turned on any lights. I paused on the threshhold of my bedroom, suddenly aware of another presence. I focused, and I could make out a lump of something—or someone—in my bed.

"It's about time you got here," a voice complained.

Chapter Eighteen

"Giles!" I said, flicking on the lights. "What the bloody hell are you doing here?"

Giles Blitherington regarded me sleepily from the bed. "Not much," he yawned. He patted the bed beside him. "I could be doing a lot more, though, if you'd care to join me." He winked lasciviously at me.

Need I say that he was beneath the covers of the bed, with his naked torso exposed? His dragon tattoo and hairy chest very much in evidence, Giles presented a tempting picture. His hair was a bit tousled from his nap in my bed, and his eyes made promises he seemed only too willing to keep.

I thought about yanking the covers off him and throwing him out of the cottage. Instead, I sat down on the bed near him and regarded him with my sternest gaze. He matched me glare for glare, unrepentantly.

"What am I going to do with you?" I said softly.

Giles grinned. "I should have thought that was pretty obvious for a clever man like you, Simon." He reclined against the pillow and regarded me seductively.

"Giles, this is no time to be funny," I said severely.

"I agree with you completely, Simon," he responded. He reached out with his right hand and clasped mine in his. He brought my hand to his mouth and kissed it, slowly and lingeringly.

"Oh, hell!" I said. I thrust his hand down against the bed, out of the way, then leaned over and kissed him.

After an enjoyable few minutes of that, I sat back and watched Giles. He almost purred with contentment. "Very nice, Simon," he said, his breath a bit short. "In fact, much more than very nice."

"Well, you'll have to be content with that," I told him, getting up from the bed. "I want you out of my bed, dressed, and downstairs in my study in five minutes." I smiled at him to take some of the sting out of my words, but I meant what I said. He recognized that, thankfully. His mouth twisted in a pout, but his eyes evinced resignation. I turned my back and headed out the door before he could throw off the bedcovers.

In my office, restless, I wandered about, shifting stacks of papers here and there. What was I going to say to him? I went over to the window, pulled back the curtains, and pressed my forehead to the glass. The moon shed a tranquil glow over the lane. There was no sign of a car, so Giles must have walked here. As I watched, I caught a glimpse of movement in Jane Hardwick's yard. A dark figure slipped out from the side of Jane's house and made off down the lane. I couldn't see enough to tell who it was, but from the size and the way the person moved, it looked an awful lot like Jane.

Frowning, I turned away from the window. What was Jane doing? Some investigating of her own before I joined her later, I supposed. I looked up from my reverie, and there was Giles, dressed but still seductively tousled looking. I forgot all about Jane for the moment.

If Giles only knew what self-control I'd had to exert to resist him, he'd be very flattered. I sighed inwardly. What had I got myself into by agreeing to hire him? Should I fire him now and be done with the whole situation? I wavered. I didn't want to dismiss him entirely, I told myself, at least not while Abigail Winterton's murder remained unsolved. He was a suspect, and I should take this opportunity to interrogate him.

I sat down behind my desk and motioned for Giles to take the chair across from me. He did so, frowning slightly.

Giles started to speak, but I stopped him. "No apologies necessary, Giles," I said. "I am very flattered, believe me. But I'd prefer to keep our relationship on a professional basis. If you can't abide by that, then I'll have no choice but to dismiss you."

Giles breathed deeply. "I shall abide by your rules, Simon," he said. "But I'll warn you, sooner or later, I always get what I want." His eyes sparkled wickedly, and his mouth curved in yet another seductive grin.

I found myself smiling in return. "That's as may be. If it happens to coincide with what I want, then there's no problem. But we'll just have to see, won't we?"

"I'm willing to wait," Giles assured me. "Some things are worth waiting for, after all."

"Yes, they are," I agreed softly, watching him. He was so very appealing, but I wanted to know him better before I made any kind of personal commitment. Working together should provide enough opportunity for getting to know each other. We'd either quickly tire of the situation and each other or it would become even more difficult to maintain a professional distance. Either way, it was worth the gamble.

As long as he wasn't a murderer.

Spurred by that thought, I plunged in. "As long as you're here, Giles, I've something I'd like to talk to you about."

Giles sighed tragically. "Since I seemingly have nothing better to do, go right ahead, Simon."

"Tell me about you and Trevor Chase," I said, not mincing words.

"Trevor and me?" Giles sat up straight in his chair. "What do you mean, Simon? There is nothing going on!"

I didn't believe him, not only because of what Trevor Chase had told me earlier in the day but because Giles had a rather shifty look at that moment.

"Perhaps there's nothing going on at the moment," I said, stressing those last three words, "but surely something went on in the past. Level with me, Giles. I promise I'm not going to hold past indiscretions against you."

Giles rolled his eyes. "It's just so embarrassing, Simon. God, if you only knew."

"Just tell me."

Giles stared down at his hands for a moment. "I first met Trevor when I went to university eight years ago. He was my tutor, and I found him madly attractive. I've always liked older men." He grinned at me. Then he turned somber again. "And Trevor was attracted to me, that much was obvious. Things got rather out of hand after that, and I was as much to blame as he was at the beginning. But I quickly realized that he was obsessively jealous. He followed me around, keeping an eye on me, because he feared I was having an affair with someone else. The whole situation was too Grand Guignol for words."

"So Trevor was stalking you?" I said, intrigued by this different interpretation of the story.

Giles nodded. "More or less. I couldn't handle his obsessiveness, and I told him I didn't want to see him again. But he wouldn't leave me alone. I threatened to report him to the appropriate university authorities and so on, and he must have believed me, because he went to them before I could. He made me out to be the villain, and I ended up being sent down as a consequence. My work had been suffering because he was making my life miserable. I couldn't concentrate on my studies, I couldn't do anything very well. He made my life an utter living hell for months."

"How did he come to live in this village, then?" I asked.

"That's where it gets even nuttier," Giles muttered. "He had been down to Blitherington Hall once, and at some point after I was sent down, he came into some money. He bought the bookshop in the village and moved here about six years ago. I was walking down the street one day and looked up and there he was, smiling at me from the doorway of his shop."

"So he followed you here?" I asked.

Giles nodded unhappily. "I thought at first that he was going to follow me around all the time and make my life hell again, but he hasn't. He has more than once made it plain that he'd just as soon take up where we left off, before I realized he was starkers, that is! But I told him in no uncertain terms that I wasn't interested."

"Did Abigail Winterton know about any of this?"

Giles looked startled. "Her? How could she unless someone told her? I certainly wouldn't, and I doubt Trevor would have."

"From what I hear," I said, "she wasn't above opening the mail and looking for interesting tidbits."

"Blackmail, you mean?" Giles almost laughed. "I suppose I wouldn't have put it past her, but she wouldn't have had much luck with me. All I would have had to do was sic my mother on her and that would have been that."

"But *could* she have known about it?" I persisted.

Giles considered that. "If she did go through and read one's mail, then yes, she could. Trevor wrote me a couple of rather indiscreet letters. I burned them immediately after reading them. But old Winterton never said anything to *me* about them. After all, I was the innocent one. That is, mostly"— at least he had the grace to appear slightly abashed—"but the old cow probably tweaked Trevor about them plenty."

Upon quick reflection, I was inclined to believe Giles's version of the story. No doubt he was spoiled and could be temperamental when he didn't get his way, but I didn't think he was obsessive. Impulsive, yes. As well as self-centered. But not (I hoped) obsessional.

His explanation of Trevor's turning up in Snupperton Mumsley seemed more convincing than Trevor's version. It would have been a whopping great coincidence for Trevor to have bought a bookshop in the one village in England where Giles lived without Trevor's having known about it in advance. Naturally, such coincidences do occur in real life, but this one seemed a bit much. That tipped the scales in Giles's favor. For the moment at least.

"Then you think Trevor might have more to lose if the story were broadcast around the village?" I asked.

Giles shrugged. "I suppose. He might find it more than a bit humiliating. And my mother would make his life miserable if she knew."

"Such being the case, how did you explain your being sent down? You must not have told her the truth."

"No," Giles said, "of course I didn't tell her the truth! Her hold on reality couldn't take it. Some version of it, mind you, but not the complete truth. My mother thinks I was simply too gifted for the jealously pedestrian minds of my tutors and that everything was their fault." His wicked grin flashed again.

"It wouldn't embarrass you if the truth came out?" I asked.

"Of course it would, Simon," Giles said in exasperation, "but I could live with it. I'm more embarrassed over the opportunities I wasted than for anything else. I could have had a first-class degree, but I screwed that up." His tone was bitter with self-reproach. "I know full well that I handled the whole situation poorly, and I've paid for it. But that little secret isn't worth killing for, if that's what you're after. At least I wouldn't have killed anyone to keep it quiet!" He glared at me with something approaching distaste.

"I believe you, Giles," I said, and I meant it. Was it simply my own hormones taking over? Or did Giles seem truly sincere, more so than Trevor had been? Perhaps I wanted to believe him more than I wanted to believe Trevor. Giles had managed to get past my defenses much faster than I had been willing to admit.

Giles stood up. "Thank you, Simon. I appreciate that." He looked across the desk at me, his eyes now warm again. "I'm more than a bit spoiled and selfish, I know, but I promise you I'll abide by your rules. When you're ready for something more than a professional relationship, I'll be waiting."

I stood up and walked around the desk. "I'm glad you understand, Giles." I pushed him toward the door. "Now, go home. I expect you here in the morning, ready to work. No slacking, mind you!"

"I'll be here"—Giles laughed—"and you'll have trouble keeping up with me."

"That I don't doubt," I answered wryly.

Giles left smiling, and I stood in the doorway of my study, staring at the closed front door of the cottage. I suddenly realized I had never asked Giles how he had gotten in. I had likely forgotten to lock one of the two doors to the cottage. But I wouldn't put it past the very enterprising Giles to have picked a lock. He was a young man of many parts, as I was quickly discovering. Nothing at all like what my first impression had indicated—but perhaps his mother simply had that effect upon him. I could easily understand *that*.

I glanced at my watch; it was now a few minutes past midnight. I had better get back to my original plan. I trudged upstairs again to get myself dressed for tonight's undercover activities and couldn't help laughing at my unintentional pun.

What further adventures would the night bring?

Chapter Nineteen

At the stroke of one I knocked softly at Jane Hardwick's front door. The door swung quietly open, and Jane motioned me inside. From the dim light down the hall, I could see that Jane was dressed completely in black: slacks, sweater, trainers, gloves, and a black scarf tied around her hair. I was similarly attired except for the scarf. I had no need to wrap my dark head or my face, since it was covered with a dark beard. The days when vampires could shape-change or make themselves invisible are gone. That's one of the tradeoffs we made for those dandy little pills I keep mentioning.

"Where were you going earlier?" I asked her. "About an hour ago?"

Jane's hand stilled as she reached for the doorknob. "You saw me, then?" She sighed. "And I thought I was being so careful. I did a quick reconnoiter at the post office, if you must know." She looked up at me as she pulled the door shut behind us. "Since you don't seem to have much experience at dead-of-night skulking, I thought I'd better have a look beforehand in case there were any nasty little surprises waiting for us, like a policeman on duty, watching the post office."

"Not a bad idea," I admitted, ignoring that little jibe about my lack of experience. "Lead on, Macduff."

I had been looking upon our expedition as something of a lark, but Jane was serious as ever, frowning at my attempt at levity. "Now, Simon, stay close by me," she whispered as we walked down the lane toward the post office. Thanks to all the trees lining the lane, we were able to stick to the shadows. The moon cast a faint glow, and the street lamps were few and far between. Just past the church Jane turned down a small lane I had not noticed before. It took us behind the buildings on High Street, and after a few moments, Jane stopped behind the cluster of buildings and opened a gate. This, I presumed, led us into the yard at the back of Abigail Winterton's shop.

In the faint shine of the moon, combined with fitful light from the street lamp in the front of the shop, I glimpsed Abigail Winterton's garden and the rubbish tip at one end. To judge from the dejected appearance of the few pitiful flowers leaning out of the ground in various haphazardly placed pots, she hadn't been much of a gardener. Jane gave me little time to observe much more, however, for she grabbed my arm and pulled me toward the back door. She fumbled for a moment with the lock, and then the door opened. Obviously, Giles Blitherington wasn't the only inhabitant of the village adept at picking locks. (I *had* locked my doors; Giles was proving to have some unusual habits for a minor peer of the realm.)

Once we were inside, Jane closed the door and pulled a small flashlight out of her pocket. The thin beam of the light played over the room. Abigail Winterton hadn't been much of a housekeeper, either. Apparently, she had been too busy with running the store and the post office, not to mention her various committees, to pay much attention to the washing up. The dishes in the sink looked—and smelled—as if they had been there for several days. My nose wrinkled in disgust.

As Jane's beam of light slid across the sink, I swear I saw something scurry out of sight.

"Surely we don't need to look for anything in here," I said to Jane, my voice low but well above a whisper.

Momentarily startled, Jane whirled around, flashing the light across my chest. "Sorry, Simon, I lost track for a moment." Jane wrinkled her nose, too. "No, I don't think what we're looking for will be in here. I hadn't realized Abigail was such a poor housekeeper. Rather sad, isn't it?"

Jane focused her light on the floor on the other side of the table, away from the door. Bearing mute witness to Abigail Winterton's last resting place was an outline on the floor. I shuddered in distaste. Somehow it seemed worse that the woman had died, struggling horribly, no doubt, in the squalor of this ill-kept kitchen. Jane muttered something under her breath and, without waiting for my response, headed out of the kitchen and down the hall to a set of stairs. I glanced curiously into the two rooms we passed on the way, but without the light I couldn't see much of anything. Whatever Jane's goal, it was upstairs.

I followed Jane up the creaking stairs to a narrow room across from the landing. Abigail Winterton's bedroom, as it turned out. There were obvious signs of disarray here as well, but nothing like the kitchen below. Here, it seemed to me, the disorder had more to do with a search of the premises than the deceased's disinclination to clean.

"Looks like the police have already gone through everything," I said to Jane.

"Yes, I expect you're right," Jane replied. "But one would like to think that they'd make more of an attempt to tidy things up afterward."

"Who's going to complain?" I said. "Did Miss Winterton have some relative who's going to kick up a fuss?"

"No," Jane said. "You're right. There's no one to bother."

Jane flashed the light around the room, avoiding the windows and the large mirror over Abigail's dressing table. The furnishings here were in sharp contrast to those I'd glimpsed in the kitchen. Miss Winterton had spent what money she had making her boudoir (and I was convinced that was the word she would have used) ultrafeminine and very comfortable. Silks and satins abounded, with lots of ruffles and lace on everything, the color scheme old rose, pink, green, and cream. No doubt a lovely, cozy room when viewed at its best. The flashlight roamed across the bed, revealing a flimsy negligee draped across the foot. I couldn't quite (and didn't want to) imagine the late Abigail Winterton wearing it.

I felt a real wave of pity for the woman who had died. She had been unpleasant, by most accounts, and I had certainly found her so, even on my brief acquaintance. But this room revealed a more vulnerable side of her, and I liked her the better for it, even while I pitied her. Remembering the sad state of her hair on the three occasions when I had seen her, not to mention her odd notions of dress, I thought that perhaps all she had needed was someone to take her in hand. The way it happens sometimes in the romance novels I write.

Speaking of which, I espied a set of bookshelves on the other side of the bed. Jane focused her flashlight on them, and I could make out the spines of several of my own books (those by Daphne Deepwood, that is) on the shelves. I crossed the room to pull a copy of *Silken Shadows* from the shelf. From the state of the book, this must have been one of Abigail Winterton's favorites. Either that or she had bought it fourteenth-hand, because it was ready to fall apart.

Jane had come to stand beside me, and I took the flashlight from her and played it over the shelves. She had every one of my books, even my mysteries. She had obviously been a fan of mine, and I never knew. (I spared a brief thought, wondering what *she* would have thought had *she* known.) Curious, I glanced at the other books: Mary Jo Putney, Laura Kinsale,

Kate Charles, Susan Moody, Georgette Heyer, to name a few. I was obviously in good company.

"If she had known that you wrote those books," Jane said softly, "she would have been beside herself. I can't tell you how many times she rhapsodized over the latest Daphne Deepwood. She practically *forced* me to read them."

"And?" I couldn't help asking. Any writer with a pulse— or without—would have done the same.

Jane laughed. "They were quite good, actually. And I thought you handled the details of life at Bess's court very well indeed in *Silken Splendors*, wasn't it?"

"Thank you, Jane," I said, stunned. "Coming from you, that means a lot. I've never known anyone who was actually there, of course."

Jane laughed again. "Oh, I can tell you some tales, believe me. And I might actually let you write them into one of your books."

I was rapidly getting distracted from the matter at hand. I started to question Jane right then and there about things that had been making me curious for years, but Jane shushed me. "This is not the time or the place, Simon. Need I remind you?"

I laughed. "You're right, of course, Jane, but I'm not going to forget what you said. You can bank on that!"

"No need, Simon. I'll tell you all sorts of deliciously scandalous things later, I promise." She sat down on the bed for a moment. "We have to concentrate right now, however, on ferreting out Abigail's secrets."

"Are you certain that she would have kept records of some kind of her blackmail?" I sat on the bed beside Jane, the copy of my book still in my hands. "I mean, we're not absolutely certain that she was blackmailing anyone. We just know that she was incredibly nosy, and that's it."

"It's enough for a start," Jane said tartly. "In my more

than four centuries on this earth, I've known my share of blackmailers, Simon, from every walk of life. They're all very much of a pattern—nasty, repulsive creatures who generally got what they deserved in the end. In my experience, at least. I doubt Abigail was any different. She was sly and self-serving, and she would have kept some sort of records, if for nothing else than to gloat over her knowledge."

"I yield, then, to your greater knowledge and experience of the breed," I said, gesturing extravagantly with the book in my hands.

Said book slipped out of my hands and went flying against the wall. As the book flew, something slipped out of its pages and fluttered to the floor. Jane and I nearly bumped our heads together in our haste to retrieve it.

Jane got to it first. She held a thin square of paper, folded several times. She opened it gingerly, since the paper was yellowed with age and well creased from having been folded inside the book.

Jane held the paper in her lap and flashed the light onto it. It was a newspaper clipping from nearly thirty years ago. "Student dies in ski accident" the headline read. I skimmed the article quickly, then looked blankly at Jane.

"Did Colonel Clitheroe have a son?"

Chapter Twenty

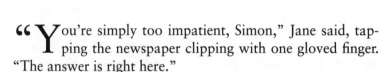

"You're simply too impatient, Simon," Jane said, tapping the newspaper clipping with one gloved finger. "The answer is right here."

"Oh," I said. I had stopped reading the moment I saw the name. Lester Clitheroe had been an honors graduate of Oxford University, a former divinity student on holiday in Switzerland, I read further, when he died in a tragic accident. He had apparently skied off the side of a mountain into a crevasse, and the body was never recovered. His companion on the holiday, his fellow student Neville Butler-Melville, had tried to save him, but to no avail. The crevasse into which Lester Clitheroe had disappeared was simply too deep and too difficult for anyone to attempt a rescue. Survivors included the victim's parents, Athelstan and Georgina Clitheroe.

"So he was the colonel's son," I commented needlessly.

"Apparently so," Jane said dryly. "I can't imagine that there is more than one Athelstan Clitheroe in the world."

"Why on earth would Abigail Winterton have such a clipping?" I asked Jane.

"Part of the pattern of a blackmailer is collecting all sorts of information about one's targets. Goodness knows what else Abigail might have uncovered about the colonel's past. This doesn't seem to be of much use, but you never know."

"Hmm..." I looked at the clipping again. "Maybe our dear vicar murdered this Lester Clitheroe. Maybe it wasn't an accident at all and Miss Winterton somehow found out about it. Maybe it's the vicar who killed her to cover up this heinous deed in his youth."

"Really, Simon, you do have the imagination of a novelist," Jane said lightly.

I wasn't certain that Jane had intended that as a compliment, but I refused to take offense. "We'll see," I muttered. I leaned forward and picked up another of Miss Winterton's romance novels from the shelf. Riffling through the pages, I found more bits of paper. Jane followed my example and started searching along with me. After going through every book on the shelves, probably at least two hundred, we had quite a collection of papers. Many of them were news clippings, but some of them were simply bits of notepaper on which someone had jotted down cryptic scribblings.

I sat back and surveyed our treasure trove. "So, what do we do with all this? Surely we can't keep it all. The police should have it, don't you think?"

"You're quite correct, Simon," Jane concurred. "We can't keep this evidence. It must be turned over to the police. But after we make copies of everything, don't you think? There's no reason we can't do that first, surely." In the glow from the flashlight I could see her vulpine smile.

I laughed. "A woman after my own heart. Yes, let's make copies first. I even have a small copying machine in my office in the cottage. But how do we arrange for the police to have this evidence without exposing our little venture in housebreaking?"

Jane thought for a moment. "I'll call Detective Inspector

Chase and tell him I need to get some books of mine that Abigail had borrowed. I've no doubt I can be persuasive enough. And no comments from you, Simon!" She paused to shine the flashlight in my face. "Once we're up here, I'll pick up one of the books and manage to discover the paper inside. The good detective inspector will catch on very quickly, I'm certain."

"And how are the papers going to get back into the books?" I asked. "After we copy everything, we bring all the bits and bobs back and stuff them into the books again, I take it?"

Jane laughed. "You do have a talent for stating the obvious, Simon."

I helped Jane stack the papers into as neat a pile as we could manage; then we wrapped them all in an extra black scarf Jane had brought along. We sat on the bed for a moment, surveying the room.

"Do you suppose there's any use in our trying to find a copy of that play?" I said.

"The police don't seem to have been as thorough as they should have," Jane said, indicating the papers rolled up in her scarf. "They might have overlooked it, though I should think it would be more difficult to hide."

I borrowed the flashlight from Jane and shone it discreetly around the room. "And if Abigail herself was the author, she doesn't seem to have written it on a computer."

"Abigail was rather distrustful of modern electronics," Jane said. "If she wrote the play, she did it the old-fashioned way, either by hand or on a typewriter. There's an old manual typewriter downstairs in the shop."

We made a cursory examination of the room, trying the most unlikely places, hoping to chance upon a copy of the mysterious play, but our efforts yielded us nothing except a few nosefuls of dust.

We eased back downstairs and into the night. I checked my watch, and it was only a few minutes past the three-quarter hour. Our stealthy activities hadn't taken very long.

We walked silently through the night back to my cottage. Inside my office, I quickly set up the copy machine, turned it on to let it warm up, then asked Jane if she'd like some tea while we worked. She said she would, and I departed to the kitchen to prepare the tea.

When I came back, Jane was busily copying Abigail Winterton's collection of papers. I took over while Jane sipped at her tea. The job was tedious, for it took time to line the scraps of paper up properly on the copier, then remove them and set up another batch. But after half an hour, we had copied everything. I made a copy of the copies for Jane to take home and study on her own. Then I took a last gulp of my tea, helped Jane wrap the originals into her scarf, and we hustled back down the lane to put the evidence back where it belonged.

By the time we were finished, it was nearly four A.M. Jane and I decided that we'd both like a chance to rest a bit before tackling the next job: making sense of Abigail Winterton's collection of papers. We agreed to meet a bit past ten in Jane's cottage. That would give me time to set Giles to work on something, then get out of his way for a while. And out of temptation's reach, I thought with a flash of humor.

Back at home, I napped for an hour, then was up again, watching the glow of dawn spreading and working away at my next best-seller. What a comforting phrase! That's all the stimulus I need to start writing.

By the time Giles knocked on my door at nine, a whole hour early, I was suitably dressed for my visit to Jane, plus I had a long list of tasks for Giles. That should keep him busy for a couple of days at least.

I responded to his cheeky "Good morning, handsome!"

with a rueful smile and a shake of the head. When I handed him the list of tasks, he merely grinned and said, "No problem, Simon. Your wish is my command."

"And you're incorrigible, Giles! But I suspect that you revel in that fact."

He offered me another cheeky grin, then set to work. I sat at my desk, doing a bit of research for the masterpiece-in-progress until time to go to Jane's. Giles worked quietly, occasionally humming to himself. I pretended not to recognize the tune to "Going Outta My Head Over You." He was even more shameless than I can be—when the occasion warrants.

A few minutes before ten, I put aside my work, adjured Giles to behave, and then walked slowly to Jane's cottage.

Jane opened her front door before I had the chance to knock, and she hurried me inside to a spot on her sofa. I plumped down and made myself comfortable, and I laid beside me the folder containing my copies of Abigail Winterton's papers.

"Why the all-fired hurry, Jane? Whatever has got into you?" I asked in amusement. In the brief time I had known her, I had never seen Jane in a hurry over anything. She was always so calm and detached.

"I'm burning with curiosity, Simon. Aren't you?" Jane almost snapped at me.

"If you were that curious, why didn't you start reading through these papers on your own?" Goodness me, it really was amusing to see this side of Jane.

Jane fixed me with a glare that could have frosted even Gloriana herself. "Because I've had other matters to attend to this morning, Simon. Such as calling Detective Inspector Chase and arranging to meet him at Abigail's to find those books I lent her. Two o'clock this afternoon. Not to mention calling at the chemist's to pick up a refill of my pills! With all that out of the way, we can concentrate for a while on this."

She waved a hand to indicate the papers. "I think the first thing we ought to do is number the pages of our respective copies so that we can refer to them more easily."

"Yes, good idea, Jane," I said. She came to sit beside me on the sofa. I drew out my favorite Mont Blanc from my jacket pocket, and we commenced to organize and number the pages of our copies.

Once that was done, we started with page one. At some point, we might have to cut the pages apart and reassemble them in a different fashion, depending on their subjects. In another life, I think I would have made a good cataloger in a library. I like having things organized myself (though you'd never tell it by my messy desk), and Jane seemed to share that tendency.

Jane and I read the various bits on page one together. The first one puzzled me because it seemed to be an accounting of some sort. There was a name at the top of the scrap that said "Harriet Jenkins"; beneath it were figures representing years, and across from the years were various amounts, like three pounds or five pounds. There were gaps between years, and sometimes the amounts were large, sometimes small. But over the course of some twenty-five years, Harriet Jenkins had apparently paid out over three hundred pounds to Abigail Winterton.

"What's the story behind this, do you think?" I asked Jane.

She laughed. "Harriet Jenkins is known throughout the parish for her prize-winning roses. I'd guess that if we checked the years indicated here, they would correspond with the years in which Abigail was judge for the parish flower show."

"Little thank-you gifts, do you think?" I said cynically.

"But of course, Simon. Nothing so crude as a bribe, natu-rally." Jane laughed again. "Harriet does produce some lovely roses, but that collection of blue ribbons means more to her than I would have suspected."

A similar record on page one caught my eye. "What's the story, then, with this Diana Daye?"

Jane thought for a moment. "Ah, yes, she raises Pekingese. Blue ribbons at the parish dog show, I would imagine."

Evidently prize Pekes were worth more than roses, or else Diana Daye was wealthier. The sums she had paid out amounted to well over fifteen hundred pounds.

"What do I do to get myself chosen as a judge for some of these things, Jane? Sure sounds like a good way to make money!"

Jane offered me a very pained look. "For the sake of our friendship, Simon, I choose to believe that was a joke. In poor taste but nevertheless a joke."

"But of course, Jane," I said, a tiny bit nettled. "I assure you I haven't the least need of taking money from these poor folk." The woman certainly had a fastidious sense of humor. Maybe if she were around me long enough, she'd lighten up a bit.

We found numerous other records of payments like these. It seemed that Abigail Winterton had done a thriving business in handing out prizes at various parish contests. There were some names that Jane didn't recognize, so she suspected that Abigail might have extended her operations to the county level.

In addition to the accounts of monies paid, we found numerous news clippings, most of which detailed some sort of indiscretion or incident involving locals. Jane observed that a number of those involved had since moved from the village. Evidently they found it easier to move away than to put up with Abigail Winterton's intrusion into their privacy.

There were several clippings involving Everard and Samantha Stevens. At one point, about five years ago, Mrs.

Stevens had caught her husband in flagrante delicto with a chorus girl in an apartment they owned in Paris. The resulting injuries to the chorus girl and to Mr. Stevens had been worthy of several inches of type. I approved Mrs. Stevens's gumption; she wasn't as passively accepting of her boorish husband as I had thought. She was also capable of violence, as I pointed out to Jane.

"Most interesting," Jane agreed. "She certainly bears watching."

We came again to the clipping about the death of Lester Clitheroe. "I wonder what significance this has?" I said aloud.

"We'll have to call upon Colonel Clitheroe and try to find out something more about his family. There may be a story there, or it may be nothing more than a terrible tragedy." Jane tapped her fingers restlessly on the paper. "I've never been inside the colonel's cottage. He's a bit reclusive, though he does involve himself in some things. But he is an avid gardener." She turned to look at me. "Your garden is in desperate need of help, Simon, don't you think?"

Catching her idea, I nodded enthusiastically. "Of course. And since I've heard the colonel is such an expert, surely he can advise me on what to do. Capital idea, Jane!"

"Perhaps we can call upon him around tea time. I'll call him later and sound him out," Jane said.

"But you seem to be quite the expert as well," I pointed out. "To judge from what I've seen of your garden. Won't the colonel think it rather odd that I'm consulting him rather than you?"

Jane's eyes narrowed as she stared at me. "No, I think not." She sighed heavily. "First, I have others do the work on my garden, Simon. I'm no expert. Second, the colonel is a man who would think it only natural that another man, namely you, would wish to consult him rather than me, a mere woman."

Well, I wasn't going to argue with *that,* so I turned a page and focused on the next bit of scandal-in-the-making. There had been a few full-page items among Abigail Winterton's collection, and this was one of them. A letter, which seemed to be a copy, it was dated nearly eight years ago and was signed by one Alistair Hinrichs, who appeared to be a Cambridge don. The letter was addressed to Giles Blitherington, and in it Professor Hinrichs bewailed the shabby treatment Giles had received at the hand of Trevor Chase. Furthermore, Professor Hinrichs assured the "darling boy" that he would be happy to assist in any attempts to clear his name so that he could resume his place at Cambridge. For whatever reasons, Giles had apparently chosen not to accept the offer, for he had never gone back to Cambridge. Or perhaps Hinrichs had promised more than he could deliver.

If nothing else, however, it corroborated to some extent Giles's version of what had happened between him and Trevor. I mulled it over for a moment, then told Jane what I was thinking. I briefly sketched for her the two different versions of the story that I had heard and then asked her what she thought.

"I can corroborate Giles on at least one point," Jane said immediately. "I do know that Trevor was fully aware of where Giles lived because he came to Snupperton Mumsley to spend a few days with the Blitheringtons that Christmas after Giles's first term at Cambridge. So Trevor most assuredly lied about not knowing where Giles lived. And if he lied about that, I'm inclined to think that he may have lied about everything else." She fell silent for a moment. "Giles is definitely spoiled and used to getting his own way, but most of the time, he's not really spiteful or malicious. I think that I would have to believe Giles's version of the story."

I felt more relieved to hear that than I would have cared to admit to Jane. Or even to myself.

"That being the case," I said, "do you think any of this gives Trevor a motive for murdering Abigail Winterton?"

"If the full story were ever to come out, Trevor would be completely humiliated," Jane said. "The Blitheringtons have been here since the year dot, and that still counts, believe me. Lady Prunella is tolerated, even affectionately in some quarters, because she does manage to do quite a lot of good, sometimes despite herself. Trevor would most definitely be seen in a bad light, and the villagers would ostracize him. He'd have to leave. But would he kill to stop that from happening? Or because he got tired of the blackmail? I'm not sure."

I agreed with Jane. She knew him better than I, certainly. It could be a very powerful motive for murder. But perhaps someone else had had a more compelling one.

We went back to our reading. There was a clipping of the wedding announcement of Neville Butler-Melville and Letty Clivering cut from an Oxford paper twenty-five years ago. The couple had honeymooned for a month in Denmark, where they had originally met the year before, according to the article.

Neither Jane nor I could figure out what significance this one had other than an interest in the vicar's life. But one question did occur to me.

"She didn't even know the man at that point, did she? I mean, Abigail Winterton didn't. So how could she have known to cut out and keep this clipping? And from an Oxford paper, nevertheless?"

"To answer your last question first, Simon, Abigail subscribed to newspapers from all over. That I knew already. As for her interest in Neville, well, he's almost a local boy. He grew up in a nearby village, and Abigail probably has known him for a long time." She indicated the wedding announcement. "And by the time he and Letty married, Neville had al-

POSTED TO DEATH   167

ready been assigned to our parish. He assumed his duties immediately after his honeymoon. He and Letty have been here ever since."

My eyes had drifted back to the page while Jane talked, and I was idly skimming. Then my eyes riveted upon something.

"Good grief, Jane!" I said excitedly. "Just look at this!"

Chapter Twenty-one

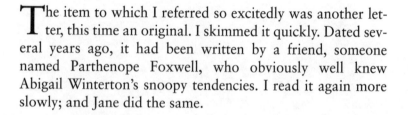

The item to which I referred so excitedly was another letter, this time an original. I skimmed it quickly. Dated several years ago, it had been written by a friend, someone named Parthenope Foxwell, who obviously well knew Abigail Winterton's snoopy tendencies. I read it again more slowly; and Jane did the same.

> Dear Abigail,
>
> As always, the arrival of your latest missive filled me with anticipation, for you never fail to entertain me—one who lives where the most excitement to be obtained comes from discussing marrows with my nearest neighbor. How I do long for the excitement you seem to find in your Snupperton Mumsley!
>
> Your latest letter, replete with the antics of your dearest old friend *Lady Prunella Blitherington* was a jewel even for you. How that woman can live with herself after the way she constantly undermines your efforts to achieve something of positive

good in her little feudal enclave is beyond me!!! [I nudged Jane and pointed to this sentence. Jane read it in a glance, then gave a most unladylike snort of derision.] *But we have discussed her megalomania before, haven't we, my dearest Abigail?*

It sounds as if the recent parish flower show was another roaring success, thanks in large part, I have not the slightest doubt, to your judging this year! You seemed to be simply purring *with satisfaction when you penned your description of it. My congratulations, as ever, my dear!*

I was struck also by your description of the handsome young man who has just assumed the proprietorship of your village bookshop. 'Tis truly amazing to me how coincidence sometimes operates in our lives, for surely this is the same Trevor Chase with whom I once taught at the school in the next village. (Ah, those lovely, heady days before retirement!) All the female staff were quite taken with young Trevor. So handsome and fresh, right out of university in his first posting, and we did all sigh after him a bit. But, alas, it was to no avail, for we soon discovered that his preferences lay elsewhere, shall we say? (I still cannot bring myself to say the word, dear Abigail, but I have no doubt that you know exactly what I mean.) All became apparent when Trevor was caught in a most compromising position with the mayor's son. The mayor being the mayor, of course, managed to keep things quiet, and young Trevor found himself looking for another post right away, down south. One cannot but hope that he learned something from that debacle!

The letter meandered on for several more paragraphs, but the rest of it mattered nothing to Abigail Winterton's murder. I looked at Jane, who had finished reading when I did. "A few more nails in the coffin, do you think?" I asked.

Jane winced. "I do wish you wouldn't use that expression, Simon. It brings back terrible memories of Paris during the Terror. Sometime when I feel like it, I'll tell you the story."

"Sorry," I said, intrigued. I had little doubt that I could get several novels' worth of material out of Jane's life. I hadn't written a novel set during the French Revolution. What an exciting possibility!

"Back to earth, Simon," Jane said sharply. "You'll have more than enough time to fictionalize my exploits later!"

Jane had got to know me rather well, in all too short a time, I considered. I resisted rolling my eyes at her.

"To go back to your inelegantly expressed point," Jane said, gesturing toward Parthenope Foxwell's letter, "yes, this does add further motive for Trevor Chase. This is even more humiliating, I'd say, than his obsessive pursuit of Giles Blitherington."

"And even more dangerous," I observed, "since it's hearsay."

Though it pained me to think of him that way because of the favorable first impression he had created, Trevor Chase was now looming large as our chief suspect in the murder of Abigail Winterton. How quickly the view can shift once details are added.

There were several more pages of items from Abigail Winterton's collection, and Jane and I turned the page to go on. There were two items on this page, both notices clipped from the local newspaper and dated a little over twenty-five years ago, though several months apart. According to one of the clippings, Sir Bosworth Blitherington had returned from a two-month visit to Kenya, on some mission on behalf of the government. The date on the piece was March 3. The second item was an announcement of the birth of a son, Giles Anthony Adrian, to Sir Bosworth and Lady Prunella Blitherington, on October 31 of that same year.

For a moment I couldn't figure out what was significant about these two items. Idly, I realized that they must have been clumped together in one of Abigail Winterton's books or they never would have gotten copied together on the same page. Then it hit me. I did a rapid calculation, and I was a bit stunned by the result.

I looked at Jane, and Jane looked back at me, her eyes wide with surprise. "Maybe Giles isn't a Blitherington, after all?" I said.

Jane nodded. "It looks to be a distinct possibility, Simon. Either Giles was rather a late baby, which is entirely possible, or Lady Prunella foolishly got herself pregnant by another man while her husband was on the other side of the world."

Oh, dear, I thought. This was a complication I hadn't counted on. Could this give Giles a reason to have murdered Abigail Winterton? Of course it did! He wouldn't be entitled to the estate if he were proven a bastard. This distressed me more than it should.

Then I brightened. Perhaps his mother, who would be even more humiliated were the truth known, had murdered Abigail Winterton. Lady Prunella made a much more attractive suspect.

Jane was staring thoughtfully into space. "This one is going to be rather difficult to suss out, Simon."

"What do you mean?" I asked stupidly.

For once Jane didn't react impatiently at my denseness. "One can't simply walk up to Lady Prunella and ask, 'My dear Lady Blitherington, who is Giles's father? Your husband or some lover?'"

"No, I see what you mean," I said, light breaking through

the sudden fog in my mind. "There must be some other way. What about family resemblances? Does Giles look like Sir Bosworth at all?"

Jane shook her head. "From the family portraits I've seen, Giles is the image of his maternal grandfather. Who was, if I may say so, a very handsome man."

"Maybe some notion will present itself later," I said, sighing heavily. "This is getting more and more tangled."

"Just like the plot in one of your mysteries, I suppose," Jane said.

"Ha ha," I said sourly.

I turned the page and found another set of accounts. At least I thought they were accounts, but they were certainly odd ones, if so. This time there were only initials at the head of the list, but I thought that "LBM" must indicate Letty Butler-Melville. What reason could Abigail Winterton have had to blackmail the vicar's wife? What dirt could there possibly be clinging to such a figure of rectitude?

Jane was also absorbed in scanning the list. There didn't seem to be any notation of figures. Instead, there was a rather curious shorthand, which I could not interpret no matter how I tried.

"What does it mean, Jane?" I finally gave up.

Jane grimaced. "I think it's a list of committee assignments. For example, 'FR' could indicate the flower rota for St. Ethelwold's. For the longest time, Letty Butler-Melville has handled the flower rota, and she did an excellent job of it, too. You can't imagine the petty jealousies and bickering that can be caused, all by who does the flowers and when for the church." She laughed briefly. "About four years ago, Letty suddenly announced that Abigail had kindly consented to take over that duty for her, to free her to do other things."

I looked down at the paper. There was a date beside the "FR" that corresponded with that year. Other entries, for that and succeeding years, showed that Abigail Winterton was getting increasingly greedy for power, spreading her control over various small activities, like running the church's annual Jumble Sale and Bazaar. Jane interpreted the various notations for me.

"This explains something that had been puzzling me for some time," Jane said. "I had thought that Letty simply had tired of Lady Prunella's high-handedness in assuming that she was naturally the one to run everything and was simply trying to shift her out of various committees by favoring her rival. But evidently Abigail was blackmailing her into it."

"How?" I asked, and Jane simply shook her head.

We hadn't found anything in Abigail Winterton's collection of material that gave us a lead except Neville Butler-Melville's connection with the death of Colonel Clitheroe's son.

"Perhaps your idea about Neville's having murdered Lester Clitheroe and staging an accident wasn't so far-fetched, after all," Jane admitted. "Letty would certainly go to great lengths to protect her husband. Perhaps even murder."

"And he'd never even know what she had done," I added, and Jane nodded.

"Letty shields him from as much unpleasantness as possible. Including blackmail, I'd be willing to bet," Jane said darkly.

The remaining few pages contained evidence of Abigail Winterton's profiting from her various positions of influence in the village. She had raked in various sums from numerous villagers who wanted badly, it seemed, to win prizes for flowers, jams, pets, and so on.

Jane and I set the papers aside and consulted. "Since our chief suspects were already those who were present when Abigail Winterton died, I suppose we can dismiss from the list those poor people who were paying Abigail money to win the 'best in show' prizes," I said.

Jane agreed. "Lady Blitherington, Giles, Trevor Chase, Mrs. Stevens, and Letty Butler-Melville are stronger suspects, certainly. The colonel may figure into this somehow, perhaps something to do with the death of his son. We'll have to dig something out of him when we visit him at teatime."

I stood up, and Jane accompanied me to the front door. "Do you suppose," I said, struck by a sudden thought, "that Detective Inspector Chase already knows about Trevor's past?"

"Most likely," Jane replied.

"That would explain the antipathy that Trevor seems to have for his cousin."

"No doubt," Jane said dryly. "I would imagine that Trevor is more than a bit uneasy at the moment."

I nodded. "I certainly would be."

Jane reminded me of the date for tea she planned to make with Colonel Clitheroe, and then I walked back to my cottage.

The day was sunny and warm, full of the heady scents that I had always associated, at least mentally, with a summer in England. The village was quiet and peaceful in its late-morning langour. Not for the first time, I couldn't really believe I was here. And would be for as long as I wanted. Sighing happily, I opened my gate and proceeded up the path to the front door of Laurel Cottage. Inside, I called a quick "hello" to Giles, who answered briefly, evidently absorbed in what he was doing. I went into the kitchen and to the back door in order to have a look at the back garden. I had to have something to say to the colonel this afternoon when Jane and I were going to visit him, ostensibly to talk about improvements to my garden.

I hadn't the least notion what most of the plants were. Horticulture has never been my thing. But the flowers grew in colorful profusion all around the garden, which covered perhaps half an acre. To my untrained eye, the effect was lovely, if a bit undisciplined. Not the orderly perfection I had glimpsed in many English gardens. The garden could remain as it was as far as I was concerned. But if I had to follow through with having something done because of our need to question Colonel Clitheroe on his own turf, then I would. Who knows? I asked myself. I might actually *enjoy* gardening. Or watching someone else do it.

I was just closing the back door when I heard the bell at the front door. Calling, "I'll get it," to Giles, I strode quickly to the front of the cottage.

I barely had my hand on the knob when the door was thrust open by Lady Prunella Blitherington. I stumbled backward, and the door crashed against the wall. Lady Prunella had in tow Detective Inspector Robin Chase, who, I noted quickly, seemed more than a bit embarrassed by Lady Prunella's behavior.

"This is the man, Detective Inspector!" Lady Prunella screeched and pointed a finger at me. "Arrest this man for corrupting my son!"

Chapter Twenty-two

For once in my existence, I was totally speechless, stunned by Lady Blitherington's accusation.

Then all hell broke loose around me. Giles had come out of my office at the sound of his mother's voice. Upon seeing Giles, Lady Prunella began screeching even louder, waving her arms around madly, like a helicopter out of control. Giles, obviously furious, was trying to drown out his mother. Detective Inspector Chase was doing his best to quiet them both but was having not one whit of success.

Suddenly, I found my voice. "Quiet!" I thundered. I have a very powerful voice when I exert myself, and the windows in the cottage rattled. Startled, Lady Prunella and Giles fell silent, while poor Detective Inspector Chase took a step backward.

"Lady Blitherington, what is this ridiculous charge you're making against me?" I fixed her with the proverbial basilisk gaze, and she wilted a bit, even as overwrought as she still was.

"You've corrupted my son!" she said. "You wicked, *wicked* man! Arrest him, I tell you!" She motioned once again at Detective Inspector Chase, trying vainly to stir him to action.

"My dear Lady Blitherington," Detective Inspector Chase said with weary patience, "I have been trying to explain to you that offering your son a job as a secretary does *not* constitute corruption." Then he lost his temper at the absurdity of it all. "And for heaven's sake, ma'am, your son is an adult, after all!"

I couldn't help myself. I burst out laughing. Partly in relief, I must admit. Upon hearing Lady Prunella's accusation, I had had visions of Giles confessing some sort of torrid seduction scene to his mother in which I figured largely as the evil, dissipated roué and Giles as the innocent dupe. It sounded suspiciously like the plot of one of my novels, now that I thought about it.

Giles laughed along with me. If anything, Lady Prunella looked more affronted than before.

"I'm *delighted,*" she said icily, "that you find the situation *fraught* with amusement. It is obvious to *me* that my misguided son has fallen *completely* under the spell of this, this *American!*" She invested that last word with so much loathing that I knew I'd not be invited to tea at Blitherington Hall anytime soon.

"Mummy, I told you before," Giles began with admirable patience, "that I wanted to get a job. I want to be a writer, and working with Simon will be valuable experience for me. He's very successful, and he knows many influential people in the publishing world. Surely you can understand that?" Giles cast an apologetic glance in my direction, and I shrugged.

"But, Giles, a *secretary?*" Lady Blitherington wailed. "What will people say when they hear that Sir Giles Blitherington is a *secretary*, of all things?"

"Perhaps, Lady Blitherington," said Detective Inspector Chase mildly, "they might admire him for working to find his own way into his chosen profession."

Lady Blitherington greeted this attempt at helpfulness with

a skeptical sniff. "Why couldn't you have told me about this yourself, Giles? I had to hear it from your *sister!*"

Giles's quick grimace promised retribution to his sister. "Precisely because of *this*, Mummy! I knew you'd make a scene. At least I can be thankful you did it here, inside Simon's house and somewhat in private, rather than in front of everyone in the village!" He threw up his hands. "Now, just go home, Mummy, and stop worrying about what people will think. Most of them couldn't care less, I assure you. The whole village doesn't spend every waking moment wondering what you and I are doing every blasted minute of the day!"

"Well!" Lady Blitherington drew herself up, the very picture of outraged virtue. "I can see that I shall get precious little sympathy *here*. And, *you*, some public servant *you* are!" she said venomously to Detective Inspector Chase. He shrugged, and she wheeled around and marched out the door. Moments later, my gate rattled loudly in its frame.

"Simon, I must apologize for this," Giles said. "I would understand, believe me, if you decide that you want nothing further to do with me." He looked desolate at the possibility I might accept his offer.

I laughed, and his handsome face cleared of worry. "Giles, I haven't the slightest fear of your mother, I assure you. I understand her, believe it or not. So you're welcome to keep your job if you like."

"Thank you, Simon," Giles said, relieved, then he turned and went back into my office and to work.

Detective Inspector Chase cleared his throat. "I, too, must apologize, Dr. Kirby-Jones. I had no idea that Lady Blitherington meant to accuse you in such a dramatic way. She accosted me in the village and insisted that I accompany her. I wasn't quite clear on exactly what she wanted, but I kept trying to tell her that employing her son as a secretary was not an actionable offense."

I laughed again. His expression of dismayed contrition was so adorable. "There's no need to apologize, Detective Inspector. I know Lady Blitherington well enough by now to understand the situation. You have nothing for which to blame yourself."

"Thank you, Dr. Kirby-Jones," he said, proffering his hand. "And now, if you'll excuse me, I have further *real* business in the village."

I shook his hand and saw him out the front door, and off he went, down the lane to the village, whistling merrily. I stood in the doorway, enjoying the view, until he was out of sight. Giles startled me, clearing his throat behind me, as I was about to shut the door.

"Simon," he said when I turned to face him, "I'm going home to have some lunch and to have a talk with my mother. I can assure you that there will be no further such outbursts on her part."

"Thank you, Giles. I'd appreciate that very much," I said, trying to keep a straight face.

"Would you like me to come back this afternoon?" Giles asked. "I've made a lot of headway with getting your files in order, but there is still more than enough to keep me busy for several hours this afternoon."

"If you're that eager to work," I responded, smiling at him, "far be it from me to keep you away. Take as long as you like for lunch, then report back for duty. I have an engagement for teatime, but other than that, I'll probably be here working."

Giles raised an eyebrow interrogatively when I mentioned my engagement, but I didn't enlighten him. He didn't need to know everything I was doing, secretary or not. I shooed him out the door, then went upstairs to change into more comfortable clothes. I really cannot write, or even read long enough to do any research, unless I'm wearing the right clothes. In this case, "right" means shabby, worn, and comfortable.

Back at my desk, I turned on my computer, and when it had booted up, I clicked on my word-processing program and called up the most recent bits I had written. I read back over them to get myself into the proper mood, but for some reason, it wasn't working. The voice wasn't coming to me as it should. Frowning, I stared at the computer screen as if willing it to start talking.

Sighing, I turned away from the monitor and propped my head in my hands, leaning my elbows on the desk. I knew what the problem was. The scent of Giles's cologne, subtle, warm, and masculine, lingered in my office. Not to mention that the scene with Lady Blitherington was still echoing in my head.

Giles was disturbingly attractive, and in a very short time, he had taken to occupying too much time in my thoughts. I had little doubt as to my ability to withstand him physically. *That* organ I could easily control. It was another part of my anatomy that worried me. (And, yes, we do have them; that's why driving stakes through them can kill us.)

More than likely, as is occasionally the case with me, I was putting the horse several leagues ahead of the cart. Giles appeared sincere in his interest in me, but he could be just another gold digger. I had met a few of those already, ever since my books had begun attracting attention—and serious money. Time wounds all heels, they say, and that might be the case with Giles. I'd just have to watch myself and take things slowly.

If I didn't throttle his damned mother first, that is. I thought back over her reaction to the news that Giles was working for me. Ridiculous as it was, it proved one thing: If she reacted that strongly to her son's working as a secretary to someone like me, then she might truly kill to keep even more humiliating secrets as quiet as the grave.

Upon that conclusion, I decided I was once again in the mood to write a murder mystery, and I turned back to the computer monitor and keyboard with grim determination.

When Giles returned from lunch, I was so engrossed in what I was writing that I acknowledged his quiet greeting with a grunt, and then I was lost again in the story I was creating. Giles may have made noise as he worked, but I was so involved in my work that I didn't notice.

At some point, the haze lifted, and I came back to the present. I saved my document, expelled a long sigh, and turned to find Giles offering me a cold drink.

"Thank you, Giles," I said gratefully. "This is exactly what I needed." I glanced at my watch after I downed the drink. Oops! I had only a few minutes to get dressed, take my dose of medicine, and be at Jane Hardwick's door to accompany her to Colonel Clitheroe's cottage for tea.

I shouted an explanation over my shoulder as I moved quickly out from behind my desk, around Giles, out of the office, and up the stairs. I was back downstairs again in seven minutes flat, neatly attired in public clothes once again, not a hair out of place.

"Amazing," Giles commented, his eyes wide in surprise. "Are you entirely certain you're gay, Simon?" he asked with a laugh. "I've never known a gay man who dresses as well as you do who could dress that quickly and still look so good."

"Flattery will get you nowhere, Giles," I said, trying to appear stern, but pleased nevertheless. I couldn't tell him that, as a vampire, I could move more quickly than a human, but not at the speed of light like a comic-book superhero.

I gave him instructions on locking up, presenting him with a spare key. I forbore to admonish him about using it for nefarious purposes, hoping against hope that he wouldn't try anything like waiting in my bed for me again.

"See you tomorrow, Simon" was all he said as I left him.

Jane Hardwick was waiting impatiently outside the gate of her cottage. She took my proffered arm and hurried me along the lane and down the High Street to Colonel Clitheroe's cottage. As we trod the flagstones of his walk, approaching the front door, I admired his garden. It did look militarily precise, every flower, every bush, every tree exactly in place, nothing sticking out at an odd angle, all neatly arranged as if by a master clockmaker. The colors vibrated brilliantly in the hot summer air. If the colonel could help me achieve something similar, I might really have someone redesign my garden.

Colonel Clitheroe answered Jane's knock immediately, as if he had been waiting just the other side of the door. He stepped aside and motioned us inside. The cool dimness of the interior was a welcome change from the heat of the August afternoon.

The colonel steered us through a short, narrow hallway into his sitting room and gestured us into our seats. He had seated Jane beside a tea tray, and she took on the duties of playing mother with good grace. I let my eyes rove over the room while Jane chatted at the colonel, who as yet had very little to say.

I wasn't quite sure what I had expected. The decor was not at all reminiscent of service in India or Africa, as I had feared it might be. No elephant's-foot hat stands or grimacing native masks or life-size statues of the goddess Kali or anything at all pukka sahib. (I suppose I had read too many of a certain sort of English novel once upon a time.) Instead, the room was furnished in what I would call comfy English country. The colonel was either less of a caricature than he let on or he had had the sense to hire someone to decorate his cottage for him.

I tuned back in to Jane's flow of conversation.

". . . was such a shock to all of us who knew her, naturally. Don't you think?" Obviously, Jane was speaking of the murder, the number-one topic in Snupperton Mumsley these days.

"Didn't surprise me in the least," said the colonel, taking a sip of his tea. "Only surprised it hadn't happened years ago. Whoever did it deserves a medal, I'd say."

Chapter Twenty-three

"That seems to be the general opinion," I observed mildly to the colonel and Jane. "Not one person I've talked with since the murder happened has had anything very positive to say about the late, and definitely unlamented, Miss Abigail Winterton."

The colonel harrumphed into his tea, while Jane urged me on with one raised eyebrow.

"The question that pops into my mind," I continued, "quite naturally, I think, is *why* did everyone dislike the poor soul so much? What did she do that was so offensive?"

The colonel gave me rather a nasty look over his teacup. Perhaps he might not be terribly forthcoming with gardening tips, after all.

Clearing his throat, the colonel said in his surprisingly high voice, "She was a busybody, that's why. Damned, interfering snoop." He ducked his head briefly in Jane's direction. "Pardon the strong language, ma'am. The woman was a sight too interested in everyone else's affairs. Had this sly way of asking questions."

"Such as?" I prompted when the colonel fell silent.

In a rumble eerily reminiscent of the late, unlamented's

voice, he said, " 'So you're a widower, Colonel. I suppose your late wife probably succumbed to one of those nasty tropical fevers among those heathens out in India. Such a terrible waste, I'm sure.' "

"Oh, dear, Colonel," Jane said, "that *was* rather nasty, wasn't it?"

The colonel laughed grimly. "M'wife was run over by a lorry in Islington, which is what I told the damned idiot woman after she asked me that fool question." He snorted. "Exactly what she wanted all along. She'd say something outrageous, then tilt her head like a bird waiting for a bug, and you'd end up answering her question, whether you wanted to or not."

I set my tea aside for the moment. "I couldn't help but notice, Colonel, even in my brief time in the village, that Miss Winterton seemed inordinately interested in several people." I had done no such thing, of course, but the colonel didn't need to know I was lying. "She seemed quite fascinated by the vicar and Mrs. Butler-Melville, for example, not to mention Trevor Chase."

The colonel looked carefully down at his hands, which trembled slightly. He, too, set down his teacup. "Vicar and his wife are a happily married couple. Abigail Winterton envied that, always trying to wedge herself in somehow. No one had ever seen fit to marry *her*. Had to get her claws into anyone who was happily married."

"That doesn't surprise me," I said; then, struck by some sort of weird inspiration, I went on. "But the odd thing was that she kept going on and on about skiing holidays in one conversation I overheard." I affected a puzzled look while casting my eyes sideways at the colonel's face.

The skin seemed to have tightened all across the colonel's face. Otherwise he gave no sign that he knew what I was talking about. The man had iron control.

"I couldn't imagine what she was going on about, since

she didn't look like the skiing type to me, but you never know. She could have been quite the sportswoman, as far as I knew." I babbled on for a moment, waiting for further signs of reaction, but none came.

"I don't imagine that anyone would have called Abigail a sportswoman." Jane finally entered the conversation again. "I cannot imagine, either, why she would be so interested in skiing. But perhaps she was merely inquiring about someone's holidays."

"Certainly likely to do that," the colonel agreed. He held his cup out to Jane for more tea.

"And then one time," I went on mendaciously, "I heard her talking to Trevor Chase about his teaching experience. I of course hadn't known that he had been a teacher, but I suppose it should have been no great surprise to me."

This time the colonel didn't seem to react, or else he had schooled himself to hide any further reactions. I kept nattering on about various inconsequential things, slipping in teasers about Samantha Stevens and her husband and the Blitheringtons, but the colonel never batted an eyelash. He was not going to confide in Jane and me about his son's death, that seemed obvious. Jane and I would have to dig further for the truth of what happened.

The colonel had little to add to the conversation, so Jane and I did our best to fill the void with friendly chatter. At a signal from Jane, I asked the colonel if I might avail myself of his facilities, and rather curtly he directed me upstairs to the first-floor landing.

On the way up the stairs I glanced quickly around for any signs of family photographs, anything that might give a clue to the colonel's past. There had been nothing in his sitting room, not even a regimental photo. I opened the bathroom door, waited a second, then closed it with a bit of a bang. Then I tiptoed across the hall into what looked to be the colonel's bedroom, hoping that the floorboards wouldn't squeak and betray me.

For a moment, I thought this room, like downstairs, was totally devoid of any kind of memorabilia. Then I espied one small frame on the dressing table. I moved quickly and silently over to it and picked it up.

Two faces stared back at me, the colonel's and his son's. At least I presumed it was the son, but the young man in the photograph looked nothing like the colonel. Perhaps he favored his mother. I glanced around the room again. There were no other photographs in evidence. Odd. I would have thought that the colonel would display at least one photograph of his late wife.

Time was ticking by much too quickly. I needed to be back downstairs. I glanced at the photo again. The colonel looked much younger in this one. Most likely it was taken not long before the son's death. His clothes looked vintage for the early 1970s, at least. The face was not handsome but had at least enough character to keep it from being plain. His hair was cut so short, he looked almost bald. His nose was rather big and slightly hooked, I thought. If it weren't for that, he would have been almost good-looking.

I put the picture down and tiptoed back out onto the landing. I opened the bathroom door silently, shut it behind me, then flushed the toilet. I ran water in the basin for a moment, then opened the door again and clumped back downstairs.

Jane had the colonel safely on the subject of gardens, and I chimed in, offering several sincere compliments on his own garden. The colonel thawed enough actually to offer to come and give me some advice on my garden. He even said he could recommend someone to do the work for me if I wished.

I definitely wished. I didn't want to grub about in the dirt myself. There are times when a vampire wants to cover himself in soil, but this wasn't one of them.

Jane indicated that it was time to end our little visit. We thanked the colonel for the tea and for his advice, and he accompanied us to the front door. He pointed out several plants in the garden, and I praised their color and vitality.

Then Jane and I were walking down the High Street again toward her cottage.

"So?" Jane said when we were at her gate again. "Did you find anything upstairs?"

"One photograph of the colonel and his son, I assume." I described it to her. She agreed that it was most likely Lester Clitheroe in the picture.

"There was something familiar about him," I said. "I can't quite place it, but I think I've seen him somewhere before."

"But if he's dead, Simon, how could you have?" Jane asked reasonably.

"I don't know, Jane," I looked at her sharply. "But what if he's not dead?"

"What if he and Neville Butler-Melville faked the accident, you mean?" Jane said.

"Exactly! What if Lester Clitheroe is alive and well and living here in Snupperton Mumsley? Or somewhere nearby?"

"But why?" Jane said. "Why would he have wanted to pretend to die and then take on another identity?"

"That's what we have to discover," I said. "This could simply be some wild idea. I don't know, but it bears a bit of investigation."

"Yes," Jane said. "It's not any more far-fetched, I suppose, than anything else we've hit upon. I tell you what, Simon. I have a friend in Oxford who can help us. I'll ring her this evening, and if I can, I'll go to see her tomorrow and try to dig up some of the history of Lester Clitheroe and Neville Butler-Melville before the accident."

"Capital idea, Jane!" I said. "But before I forget, what happened with the detective inspector this afternoon?"

The self-satisfaction in Jane's smile befit a Wimbledon

champion. "Everything went according to plan, Simon. We went upstairs to look at Abigail's books, and I picked one up off the shelf. And for some odd reason, several pieces of paper fell out of them. The detective inspector gathered them up, and I can tell you, I wouldn't be in the shoes of the men who searched Abigail's house."

"Whew," I said in mock relief. "I'm glad the evidence is found. You're something else, Jane, you know that."

"Yes, Simon," Jane said, "I do." With that, she turned and went up the walk to her front door.

She definitely knew an exit line when she heard it, I mused as I wandered on to my own front door.

I was a bit disappointed, though I was loath to admit it, that Giles had gone. The scent of him lingered on, and once I was again dressed in my writing duds, I let it settle around me as I got back to writing.

I worked hard until sometime in the morning, pausing only briefly for a quick snack around midnight. Around three, I finally turned off the computer and went up to bed for a slightly extended nap. I was back downstairs, showered and perky, working away, by the the time Giles arrived a little after nine o'clock.

"Good morning, Giles," I greeted him from behind my desk, hands resting idly on the keyboard of my computer.

Giles dropped a small satchel down upon the table where he had been working yesterday. "Simon, you'll never believe this!"

He paused dramatically. "They've arrested Trevor Chase for the murder of Abigail Winterton!"

Chapter Twenty-four

"Has Trevor actually been arrested, Giles?" I asked. "Or is he simply 'helping the police with their inquiries'?"

Giles thought for a moment. "Probably the latter." He deflated visibly. "It's all over the village this morning that Detective Inspector Chase had Trevor taken in late last evening. And you know how tongues will wag and magnify." He grinned.

"Sit down, Giles," I told him a bit sternly. The time had come to get to the truth of certain matters.

Uncharacteristically solemn, Giles did as he was bid. Unsmiling, he stared at me from across the cluttered surface of my desk. I had managed to undo some of his diligent work of the day before, and Giles grimaced at my handiwork.

"What is it, Simon?" Giles asked me when I had sat and stared at him for a moment without saying anything.

"Do *you* think Trevor Chase could have murdered Abigail Winterton?"

Giles sat back in his chair, surprised by my question. "To be honest, no, I've never thought of Trevor as the murdering type." He waved his right hand in the air. "I know that probably anyone can, and will, commit murder under the proper circumstances. But Trevor, despite his penchant for obsessional behavior, has never impressed me as the homicidal type."

"Would he murder someone in order to spare himself great humiliation?"

"Because of his past, you mean?" Giles said, his face clouding momentarily.

"Yes," I answered, watching him closely.

"Look, Simon," Giles said, leaning forward in his chair. "Trevor did go to somewhat abnormal lengths to be near me, to no purpose, but I think basically he's harmless. He'd be rather upset if he were exposed to ridicule by the village, but it wouldn't be the end of his life. He could sell the bookshop or simply close it up and move away, and he wouldn't be in difficult financial straits. There isn't that much tying him to this village, actually, but he does seem to like it here. I don't think he would have had enough motive to kill Abigail Winterton."

"Not even if she were blackmailing him?" I asked, wanting to put it clearly to him.

"Not even then," Giles said, his voice firm with certainty.

"Then let me ask you this," I said. "The other day, when I met you in Trevor's shop, I overheard what Trevor said to you when I was coming down the stairs. What he said could easily have been construed as a threat to you. And to Abigail Winterton."

Giles thought for a moment, trying to recall the incident. Then his face cleared, and he laughed. "Oh, that! Simon, that's evidence more in Trevor's favor than against him. He had already told me that Abigail Winterton had been trying to get money out of him but that he refused to pay her anything. She had dug up something about him, something that happened when he was right out of university, in his first teaching post. Something scandalous, evidently, though Trevor wouldn't tell me just what it was. And apparently she kept trying to wheedle money out of him, but he told her where to get off." Giles eyed me speculatively, but I gave nothing away.

"Trevor flatly refused to give her any money," Giles repeated when I remained silent.

"And what was the context of his remark to you? It wouldn't get you anywhere, either, or words to that effect?"

Giles glanced away for a moment; then he faced me, turning on every ounce of his charm. "Well, Simon, there I have a confession to make. That play that I submitted to SMADS? Trevor helped me with it, but when I presented it to the group, I just happened to leave Trevor's name off the page."

"And Trevor was insisting that he get proper credit?" I asked. So Giles was something of a gold digger, after all.

"Yes," Giles said. He heard the sudden coolness in my voice, and he shrank back in his chair.

"I knew it was wrong of me, Simon, you have to believe that. But something just came over me when I told my mother about the play. She was so thrilled to know that I had actually written something. I tried to tell her that I had written it with Trevor, but she got so carried away with the notion that her darling son had written a play, she didn't give me much chance to explain. And then I let the misunderstanding continue." The self-mockery in his voice lessened my disappointment in him.

"I confessed to my mother that night, when we got home. She took it better than I expected, actually. Though she wasn't too keen on my having much to do with Trevor."

"I can understand your wanting to avoid a scene with your mother, Giles," I said dryly. "But you simply cannot go around taking credit for other people's work. At least not if you want to have anything to do with me." No matter how appealing he was, he had committed one of the cardinal sins of writing, and I wouldn't let him do that to me.

Either Giles was a consummate actor, a true loss to the on-going success of theater in the West End, or he was horribly stricken by the thought that I might cease to be his employer and putative mentor. He stood, eyes abjectly on the floor. "Please, Simon, if you'll give me another chance, I promise I won't do anything underhanded. I'll make it up to Trevor as well. You can trust me. I've learned my lesson, believe me. Please."

I invested my voice with every ounce of menace that I could muster. "If I *ever* discover that you have been dishonest with me over anything like this again, you will not enjoy the consequences."

Giles shivered where he stood. His eyes wide with surprise, he stared at me. Perhaps I had gone too far. I forget just how frightening I can be when I make the effort.

"No, Simon, I'm sure I won't." His voice held the slightest quaver. Then, quickly, his natural bouyance asserted itself. "But you won't have to doubt me, ever again. I swear it."

"Then you'd best get on with your work, hadn't you?" I smiled, and he happily gathered up several files from my desk and started putting them back into order.

I thought I had best clear out of the office for a while and let him have some time to himself. He needed a chance to ponder our conversation, and frankly, so did I. I needed some physical distance in order to think clearly.

"I almost forgot," Giles said, reaching for his satchel. "I stopped by the post office this morning and picked up your mail for you." He pulled his hand out of the satchel and brandished a fistful of envelopes of varying sizes. I hadn't the stomach to deal with correspondence just then, so I told him I'd look through it when I returned from my walk.

I chose a hat from the hall tree, put on my sunglasses, and headed out the door. I needed a good ramble to clear my head. Like the late Abigail Winterton, I generally preferred to take such walks during the middle of the night, when there was little chance of encountering anyone else. Instead of heading down the High Street into the main part of the village, I turned in the opposite direction, ambling past the few cottages on the other side of mine. My destination was just down the lane, a public footpath leading through the nearby countryside. I had walked it a couple of times in the dead of night (I do love unintentional puns, don't you?), and I might as well see what it looked like with the benefit of sun.

Clambering over the stile, I paused on the other side for a moment to get my bearings. The footpath meandered along the edge of a wood, through a field overgrown with grass and brightly colored wildflowers. Once upon a time it had been used as pasture for livestock, but now it stood quiet and empty of visible animal life. The sun dallied behind a light cover of clouds, so the light was muted, and the air was noticebly cooler than that of the day before. I sniffed at the wind. Perhaps we were in for some much-needed rain; this had been rather an unusually warm and dry summer. I was delighted to know that it wasn't typical. I had had more than enough of hot and humid back in Houston.

I moved slowly, savoring the fresh smells of the natural world around me, plodding down the footpath in the shade of trees on my left side. My mind emptied as I gazed around me. The tranquillity of the setting could have mesmerized me had my mind been capable of being still for more than a few seconds.

Sighing, I kept walking while my thoughts returned inexorably to the murder of Abigail Winterton. Pathetic though she may have been in some respects—I couldn't help thinking of what Jane and I had seen of her very private self in her bedroom—she nevertheless seemed to have been a veritable spider, gathering victims into her web and feeding on them over the course of many years.

Which victim had finally turned on her? Which one had

inevitably been pushed beyond endurance and reacted with violence?

If Everard Stevens had a good motive, I could easily imagine him killing Abigail Winterton. Or, at the very least, ordering his brutish manservant to do so for him. Samantha Stevens had impressed me as a woman not to be crossed lightly. She and her husband made a formidable team, in some ways, though I'd be willing to bet neither of them trusted the other very much. One of them was going to end up dead before too much longer, I'd be willing to bet.

The Stevenses were more than capable of murder. But what motive would have compelled them to commit such an irrevocable act? Samantha Stevens was obviously frustrated, thwarted by her husband from continuing in London the types of activities she seemed to thrive on, and evidently Lady Prunella Blitherington and Abigail Winterton, between them, had managed to keep her from gaining much power here in Snupperton Mumsley. Was she so frustrated by this that she had resorted to murder to remove one of the stumbling blocks in her way?

That was possible, I thought, but it seemed even more likely to me that Samantha Stevens was biding her time, waiting for the right opportunity to divest herself of her odious husband in an innocuous and apparently innocent manner. If Everard Stevens didn't die "accidentally" in the next year or so, I'd quit writing mysteries.

The Stevenses weren't the only viable suspects, of course. Lady Prunella herself could be standing at the head of the line. If it turned out that she had truly cuckolded old Sir Bosworth and presented him with a son and heir who wasn't truly his, she could have been horribly embarrassed by the ensuing scandal. But—I thought this one out further—surely if there had been any question about the identity of Giles's father, it would have surfaced when Giles was born? What would be the point of resurrecting it a quarter of a century after the fact? Bastardy was still potentially embarrassing, I supposed, but it was rather old news, wasn't it?

But if one had inherited an estate that one wasn't legally entitled to, then one might have a most excellent motive for murder. As much as I'd like to, I now admitted to myself, I couldn't take Giles's name off the list of suspects. Yet.

Then there was the vicar and his wife. A bit of a mystery lingered there, according to that clipping Abigail Winterton had, about the death of Lester Clitheroe. Had Neville Butler-Melville, in his youth, done something despicable? Had Miss Winterton somehow discovered proof of it and been using it to increase her hold gradually over the vicar and his wife? Letty Butler-Melville was so protective of her husband that I couldn't imagine her letting Miss Winterton get away with much unless the threat was rather serious. How far *would* Letty go to protect Neville? Would she murder for him?

I certainly couldn't imagine Neville exerting himself to save Letty. Though handsome and charismatic, he nevertheless was a bit of a wanker. He just didn't have the gumption, I suspected, to murder someone, no matter the reason. But he could always depend on Letty to do it for him.

How was Colonel Clitheroe connected? If he was indeed the father of the mysteriously dead Lester Clitheroe, how did that relationship connect him to the present crime? Did he, too, suspect Neville Butler-Melville of having murdered his son? Was that why the colonel had settled in Snupperton Mumsley around the same time as the Butler-Melvilles? But, again, there was the aspect of timing. Why wait twenty or so years? What had happened recently to bring the situation to a head?

Trevor Chase had been called into the police station. That was a fairly serious step, as far as I knew. Not actually an arrest but an indication of more than ordinary interest in a suspect on the part of the police. I considered the possible evidence against Trevor. If the story about his early teaching job were true and if the full story of his pursuit of Giles were told around the village, he would no doubt be a laughing-stock, if not worse. In my brief exposure to him, Trevor had proved more than a bit prickly, not as easygoing as he had seemed upon our first meeting. Would he remain in Snupperton Mumsley if his past were exposed to ridicule and censure by the locals?

Of all the people connected with the case, Trevor seemed to have the strongest motive. There could be another suspect lurking somewhere in the background. There was Giles, naturally, who might be motivated by the same reasons as his hideous mother, but I really preferred not to think of him as a potential murderer.

Besides Giles, the only other person of my current acquaintance in Snupperton Mumsley was Jane Hardwick. I laughed at the thought of Jane as the murderer.

Then I caught myself up short. Maybe the idea wasn't so ridiculous, after all. If I interpreted recent events in a certain way, I could see that Jane had stage-managed me (or maybe "manipulated" would be a better choice?) into following just the paths that she wanted me to. After all, Jane could easily have sneaked into Abigail Winterton's cottage with none in the village the wiser, and Abigail would probably have little reason to fear Jane. Jane, despite her small size, was strong enough to have throttled Abigail Winterton.

And it was certainly interesting, I thought abruptly, that Jane had known where to "find" evidence of Abigail's black-mailing activities. What if Jane herself were the blackmailer and had planted that evidence in Abigail Winterton's bed-room? Jane had led me there like a fatted calf to the slaughtering pen.

What could be the motive in that scenario? I thought disgustedly. Had Abigail Winterton somehow discovered Jane's true nature?

I was getting more and more twisted in my thoughts, and nothing was clear except that I was accomplishing nothing. Fat lot of good this walk was doing me, I thought sourly as I climbed back over the stile and marched down the lane to my cottage.

Inside, I hung up my hat and went back into my office. Giles looked up from his work to smile briefly in my direction, but a glance at my face warned him that I was in no mood for idle chatter. I plopped myself down behind my desk and pulled the pile of mail toward me. As long as I was grumpy anyway, I might as well deal with the mail.

Several of the envelopes obviously contained bills, and I set those aside for later. Giles could handle those as part of his duties as secretary. One large envelope bulged with what looked like a manuscript. Struck by a sudden thought, I picked it up and ripped it open. Surely it couldn't be?

The pages spilled out on the desk, and I snatched up the title page.

Here was Abigail Winterton's missing play.

Chapter Twenty-five

Staring down at the manuscript of the play, I made a quick decision. I put the manila envelope down on top of the title page to obscure it from view.

"Giles," I said casually, and he looked up from his work, his face cautious. I smiled, and he relaxed.

"Yes, Simon," he said. "Is there something you want me to do?"

I nodded. "I've been thinking that as long as I'm going to have an assistant, he should have his own computer. There will be work you'll need to do, and having a computer to yourself will make that work much easier." I grinned. "I really don't like sharing my computer with anyone."

Giles smiled broadly. "That makes sense, Simon. I have a computer at home, and I could bring it here if you like."

"No, Giles, you should keep that at home for your personal use," I said. "I thought you might go into Bedford and shop around for something." I glanced at my watch; it was nearly noon. "Why don't you go on now? Take your time, have lunch, look around. Chalk it up to expenses, and I'll reimburse you, since it will be a working lunch. Get the specs on what you think will be necessary and bring them back to me tomorrow. We'll go from there and get you set up with your own equipment."

Giles's face clouded momentarily as he eyed the stacks of papers that yet needed to be organized in my files.

"There'll be plenty of time for all that later," I assured him. "Besides, having the computer, not to mention your own printer, will help you get me organized that much more quickly."

He laughed at that. "True enough," he said, standing up and stretching, letting me have a long look at the muscular torso beneath his snugly fitting shirt. "So you want to get rid of me for the rest of the day. You're the boss."

"Cheeky!" I said, smiling.

Giles picked up his satchel and cast me one last grin as he headed out of the office. "See you tomorrow, then!"

As I heard the door close, I sat and contemplated the pile of papers in front of me. I picked up the envelope again and felt something still inside. I drew out a thick piece of heavily embossed notepaper. Abigail Winterton's name and address were emblazoned across the top in scarlet Gothic lettering, and the paper was an expensive, creamy stock. Miss Winterton had written me a letter in neat, crabbed handwriting. I squinted, deciphering it.

> *Dear Dr. Kirby-Jones:*
> *I beg you will pardon my forwardness in send-ing you this with no forewarning.* [Goodness, *I thought,* she sounds like the heroines in my histor-ical romances.] *Jealous and prying eyes surround me, and I am entrusting myself to your reputation as a scholar and to your status as a newcomer to Snupperton Mumsley. Having read your works and having chatted with an academic acquaintance who shares your specialty, I know that you have the bona fides of a true member of the literati, un-*

like some others in this village with pretensions far beyond their abilities, meager at best. Discretion being ever the better part of valor, I decided, after having announced to my fellow members of the SMADS the existence of this play, I would ask an impartial witness to read it and pass judgment before I shared it with the world at large. I do trust that you will give this work your undivided attention and discuss with me, at your earliest convenience, its suitability for production by the SMADS. I have little doubt that the enclosed work of fiction [and the word was heavily underscored] will pack the house, as the saying goes. If you agree, I will then share the manuscript with the rest of the committee. For the moment, they can wait, as do I, for your decision.

Yours most sincerely,
Abigail Winterton

I could picture the murder victim sitting at the desk in her bedroom while she penned this note with great self-satisfaction, drawing me into her web. In my mind, I saw her scurrying downstairs to the post office and placing the envelope in the appropriate bin or pile, then going on about her business. Happy with the turmoil she had created among the members of SMADS, she fed off the ensuing fear and anxiety until at some point, one person, pushed beyond endurance, had come and killed her. That person might have found any other existing copies of the play and taken them away to be destroyed, thinking he or she had gotten away with them all. Miss Winterton might yet have the last laugh.

I should have called Detective Inspector Chase immediately to report what I had received, but of course I was much too nosy to let this chance go by. I decided to exercise some self-restraint, however, by making a copy of the manuscript and not handling the original further before reading it. Rummaging around in the kitchen, I found a pair of very thin latex gloves, which allowed me, in a clumsy fashion, to handle the manuscript with some attempt at care. Once the copying was done, I put the pages back in the envelope and settled down for a quick scan of the copy before I called the police.

There wasn't much to the play, only about sixty pages, and since I read quickly, I was done with it in perhaps fifteen minutes. Abigail Winterton had been no stylist, but what she lacked in literary ability she made up in venom. The portraits of my acquaintances in Snupperton Mumsley within the pages of *Village Affairs: a Modern Morality Tale* contained vituperations of the nastiest kind.

One Lady Prudence Blister made a brief appearance, with her bastard son, Miles, in tow, happily announcing to the world that she and her son were to be at long last reunited with her one true love (and, incidentally, Miles's real father), a former gardener on her estate who was returning from Australia, having made a fortune in some unspecified fashion. Which helped, naturally, since Miles would be disinherited, the truth of his base birth now broadcast to one and all.

June Bartwick, however, was highly upset, because the police were in her garden, tearing apart her flower beds, looking for the bodies of several young men who had disappeared, in succession, shortly after dining with her. June apparently had a habit of consorting with men much younger than she, young men who seemed to vanish abruptly after having been seen entering her cottage a time or two late at night.

Everett Stewart and his blowsy, slatternly wife, Susie, were currently at the mercy of the Inland Revenue for various offenses that were never made quite clear.

Tristan Case wandered through, with a handsome, noticeably effeminate, young choirboy in tow, insisting loudly to anyone who would listen that he was just tutoring the boy for his A-levels, nothing more.

Finally, there was the vicar and her husband, Lottie and Greville Baker-Mandeville. (A most interesting switch, I thought, and perhaps the most telling one in all of the twisted portraits thus far.) The vicar went about minding everyone's business but her own, running the parish into the ground by ignoring the offers of assistance from those who knew better than she, while her husband remained at home, where he did little to help. Instead, he sat around all day, eating chocolates and devouring romance novels by the dozen. Greville was rumored to have a dark secret in his past, one that precluded his serving the church despite his degree in theology and his training for the priesthood. He was often observed wringing his hands in the manner of Lady Macbeth (Miss Winterton did not forbear to quote the Scottish play, sadly) when he thought no one could see him.

I put the pages aside and fought the urge to wash my hands. Instead, I picked up the phone, found the card that Detective Inspector Chase had given me, and dialed the number of his office in Bedford. When someone answered, I asked to speak to Detective Inspector Chase but was politely informed that he was unavailable at the moment. I identified myself and informed the person at the other end that I had just come into possession of important evidence in the Snupperton Mumsley murder case and asked if he would please let the Detective Inspector know I would be at home whenever he could come by. After receiving an assurance that the message would be forwarded to the detective inspector with all due speed, I rang off and sat back in my chair.

I was tempted to get a pair of tongs from the kitchen and transport my copy of the play (a sad misnomer) and deposit it in the garbage can. But putting aside my finer feelings for the moment, I instead forced myself to think about the implications of what Abigail Winterton had written.

How much of it was simply a spite-driven interpretation of innocuous fact? Was any of it based on at least a grain of truth? And had Abigail Winterton really believed the play would ever have been performed? What was she trying to do in forcing this on her neighbors?

In Trevor Chase's case, certainly, there was a bedrock of truth present in the play. Trevor had, at least once, become involved inappropriately with a minor, if Abigail Winterton's distant friend, Parthenope Foxwell, were to be believed. Trevor had also become obsessed with Giles Blitherington, although the obsession seemed to have faded. At least Giles no longer appeared troubled by Trevor's presence in the village, whereas in the beginning, he must have been uncomfortable.

What if Giles really were illegitimate? There did seem to be some sort of story there. Abigail Winterton could be making it up out of whole cloth. I thought back to the clipping in her collection, the one telling of Sir Bosworth Blitherington's antipodean trip. The timing was odd, given the date of Giles's birth, but there could be an innocent explanation. And certainly a DNA test could probably answer the question, should it ever come to that point. What would happen if I simply asked Giles point-blank? The idea made me uneasy. Perhaps there was another way to get at the information. At the moment, however, I couldn't think of one.

The charges against Jane Hardwick were far more serious. I had taken Jane at face value, delighted to find a fellow vampire in Snupperton Mumsley, someone with whom I could truly let my hair down. Had I been willing to take too much on trust? Tristan Lovelace had said not a word about her, and surely he would have warned me against her if there were something not quite cricket about her. I could easily see Jane having a taste for young, attractive men. I could even imagine her, in the days before our wonderful little pills were invented, satisfying her urges by feasting on such young men.

But the Jane I had met had not impressed me as reckless or stupid—both of which she'd have to be to behave in the manner imputed in the play. Abigail Winterton had intuited some of the truth about Jane, but I didn't think she had managed all of it.

The question now was, should I confront Jane with this? Simply show it to her and laugh it off? Or take a sterner stance and demand an explanation? To be honest, I wasn't all that keen on a showdown with her, because she frightened me. She had been a vampire a hell of a lot longer than I had, and she was correspondingly more knowledgeable and more dangerous. She hadn't survived over four hundred years as a vampire without being well able to take care of herself, and that made me nervous about trying to question her.

I put Jane aside for the moment and went on down my mental list. Abigail Winterton seemed to have included the Stevenses only as a matter of course. She obviously had a score to settle with them over her lost nest egg, but the vagueness of her portrayal of them in the play was telling. She didn't have enough on them to make them viable suspects in her murder. As attractive as Everard Stevens might be in the role of cold, conscienceless killer, this was one dog that wouldn't hunt, I concluded regretfully.

That left me with Neville and Letty Butler-Melville. The contempt in Abigail Winterton's characterizations of them was vicious. She had cast Letty as the strong partner in the marriage. Even I, who barely knew the Butler-Melvilles, could see the truth in that. But how much of the rest of her interpretation was sheer spite? Had Neville Butler-Melville really been responsible for the death of Lester Clitheroe all those years ago? Had his guilt been hanging over him all this time? And what would Letty Butler-Melville do to protect her husband? Would she have murdered Abigail Winterton to stop her from spreading such an ugly story?

For the life of me, I couldn't see what kind of evidence that

Abigail Winterton might have had in order to convince any-one that Neville Butler-Melville had a death, accidental or otherwise, on his hands. I supposed, however, that rumor might be enough to get him in serious trouble, especially combined with the fact that it was Letty who seemed to shoulder the burdens of the parish rather than Neville him-self. I wondered, suddenly struck with the idea, whether Letty even wrote his sermons for him. I had attended one ser-vice during a quick weekend trip to Snupperton Mumsley two months ago, and at the time, Neville had impressed me with the erudition and style of his sermon. Having been around him a bit more, though, I was now suspicious. He had an actor's ability to sell himself in a role, but did he also have the ability to write his own dialogue?

I checked the time. Getting close to one. Jane wouldn't be back from Oxford for a while yet, probably not until after teatime at least. I wondered whether she would forgive me readily for turning the play over to the police without letting her see it first. I wondered just what she *would* do once she was aware of the accusations against her in the play. Would the police be bound to search her garden? I couldn't help admit curiosity as to what they might find if they did.

Time for some tea, I thought, getting up abruptly from be-hind my desk. Surely Detective Inspector Chase would arrive soon, and I could turn this mess over to him. I had been in-trigued by the puzzle of Abigail Winterton's murder, but now that I knew more about all involved, I was disgusted by the sordidness of it all. Even if the remnants of an all-too-human curiosity were still lodged within my brain.

I was sipping at my tea some fifteen minutes later, staring blankly at the manuscript on my desk, when the doorbell rang. Setting down my teacup, I was all set to dash to the door, but then it occurred to me that I should put away my copy of the play. It wouldn't do to have Detective Inspector Chase spot the evidence of my illicit activity! Casting about for a hiding place, I decided to stuff it in the bottom drawer of my desk, where small mammals could disappear for months at a time.

The doorbell rang again, and I almost ran to the front door. Detective Inspector Chase was going to get a welcome he wouldn't soon forget, with me at my most innocently helpful.

I swung the door open, a huge smile of greeting blasting out at the handsome policeman.

Except that it was Colonel Clitheroe standing patiently on my doorstep.

Chapter Twenty-six

Poor Colonel Clitheroe took a step backward as my beaming smile morphed into a disappointed scowl.

"Apologies for calling on you like this," he squeaked.

"Not at all, Colonel," I said. Drat! Where was a good-looking policeman when you expected one? "Please pardon me. I've been wrestling with a thorny problem in my research, and I'm afraid I was lost in thought when I answered the door. Writers, you know."

Smiling uncertainly, the colonel said, "Quite."

I motioned him in. "What can I do for you, Colonel?"

"Been thinking about your garden," he said. "Came by to have a recce and see what might be done." He cleared his throat. "Might not be a good time, though. Could come back later, I suppose."

"Not at all, Colonel," I said, trying not to sound impatient. What if the detective inspector showed up while I was discussing perennials with the colonel? One had to observe the social conventions, nevertheless. "Would you like a spot of tea before we go out to the back garden?"

Colonel Clitheroe nodded. "Most kind of you, I'm sure."

Sighing inwardly, I invited him to make himself comfortable in the sitting room while I went to the kitchen to put more water on for tea.

My hearing is acute, as I believe I've already mentioned, and over the noise of the water from the tap, I could hear surreptitious footsteps leaving the sitting room. What was he doing?

Putting the kettle quickly on the stove, I tiptoed to the kitchen door and peeked down the hallway just in time to see Colonel Clitheroe's back disappearing into my office. What have we here?

I could have charged down the hallway right then to confront him, but I decided to give him a little line to see what might happen. I waited until the water boiled, busying myself with preparing the tea tray, then went back to the sitting room. Tray in hand, I discovered Colonel Clitheroe sitting innocently in my favorite chair, looking bored as if he had been waiting there for quite some time.

Scanning his clothing, I didn't spot any unusual bulges. For the moment, I couldn't think of a good reason to excuse myself to go into my office to check on the manuscript of the play. He couldn't have known it was there. What had he been after?

I served the tea and made idle chatter with the colonel about herbaceous borders and the hardiness of certain varieties of lilies. Since I knew nothing about either subject, the colonel did most of the talking, quite happily, I might add. Whatever sneakiness he might have been engaged in, he was still an enthusiastic gardener.

After a few minutes of this, I was pleased when the colonel decided it was time for a look at the back garden. I took him down the hall through the kitchen and out the back door. Excusing myself at the sound of the telephone, I left the colonel gazing in dismay at the undisciplined growth.

The caller was Detective Inspector Chase. "I just received your message a few minutes ago, Dr. Kirby-Jones," he told me. "I expect to be with you in about fifteen or twenty minutes." Judging by the static I could hear, he must be calling me from his car.

"Not a problem, Detective Inspector," I said. "I'll be waiting for you."

On the way back outside, I glanced quickly at my desk. From what I could see, the pages of the manuscript hadn't been disturbed, though the envelope in which they had arrived might have been shifted a bit on the desk. Had the colonel seen enough to satisfy his curiosity?

As I came out the back door, the colonel was slipping his hand into the pocket of his rather baggy pants. I hadn't paid much attention to them before, but they looked capacious enough to hold a cellular phone. Which is what I thought the colonel had been putting away.

"Sorry about that," I said. "Business call."

The colonel waved that away. "Over here," he said, pointing at the jumble of plants (some of which might have been weeds, for all I knew) lining the wall on the northern side of my property. "Lot of work needed there," he said. "Too much unrestrained growth." From his enthusiasm he might have been Margaret Thatcher going after cuts in old-age pensions.

For the next ten minutes I listened while the colonel outlined a plan for bringing my garden back under control. I simply nodded, wondering how much it would cost me if I were to follow through with any of this. All the while, I was wondering about his real motive in coming here today. Finally, the colonel told me he could recommend a man to do the job, and I suggested that we go back inside so that I could write down the man's address and phone number. As we were finishing in the hallway, my doorbell rang again.

This time it was, thankfully, Detective Inspector Chase.

"Good afternoon, Dr. Kirby-Jones," he said, smiling, though he looked more than a bit worn around the edges. I found out later that he had just come from attending the post-mortem on Abigail Winterton.

"Please, do come in, Detective Inspector," I said, standing aside to allow him in. "Colonel Clitheroe has very kindly been giving me advice on taming my back garden."

"Better be going," the colonel said, nodding stiffly at the policeman.

"Thank you again, Colonel," I said, ushering him out with relief.

"Not at all," he said, pausing for a moment on the doorstep. Then he turned and marched down the walk and out into the lane, having turned precisely on his heel at the gate.

"What is this new evidence you've got?" Detective Inspector Chase asked once he had explained his delay in responding to my call.

"Please come into my office," I said, "and I'll show you." With a flourish I waved him in, then stopped in surprise as I scanned the top of my desk. The play and the envelope in which it had arrived were gone.

I said something rather vulgar, and the detective inspector blinked in surprise. I motioned for him to sit while I did the same.

"What I *had* to show you," I said, "was Abigail Winterton's missing play. Which seems to have gone missing again!"

"What?" the detective inspector said, halfway coming up out of his chair. "How did you come to have it?" He sat tiredly back again.

"It came in the mail, along with a letter from Miss Winterton explaining that she wanted someone who was a professional, more or less, to look at it before she let anyone else read it. Something the killer probably didn't expect."

Sighing, thinking about the inevitable embarrassment, I opened the drawer where I had hidden my copy of the play and was relieved to find it just where I had put it, mixed into the jumble of junk. Somewhat reluctantly, I pulled it out, along with the copy I had made of Miss Winterton's letter to me. "This is a copy," I muttered.

Detective Inspector Chase struggled to hide a smile at the chagrin in my voice, but at least my nosiness may have foiled the plan the killer had to destroy all the evidence of the play's existence.

"Before you take that away," I said, "I'd better tell you about what just happened here." I sketched the details of Colonel Clitheroe's visit, including my notion that he had been putting away a cell phone when I came back outside.

"You think he alerted someone to the presence of the play and that person came and removed it while you were still talking in the back garden." More a statement than a question, really—Detective Inspector Chase beat me to the punch line. "Had you left the front door unlocked?"

I nodded ruefully. "Most of the time when I'm at home, unless it's late at night, I generally do. I've never seen the need to worry about it. After all, that's one of the reasons I came to Snupperton Mumsley. The low crime rate." I arched an eyebrow at him, and he grinned briefly.

"It's a lucky thing that you had the foresight to make a copy of the play, then," he said with a perfectly straight face.

"Amazing coincidence, isn't it?" I agreed, grateful that he was taking such a sensible attitude toward my indiscretion. Or my helpfulness, if you chose to look at it that way.

"And did you have time to read the play?" he asked.

"Yes, and it's altogether a nasty piece of work, as you'll discover."

He arched an eyebrow, and I took that as encouragement to comment further. "Though she changed their names, the more prominent citizens of Snupperton Mumsley figure prominently. Apparently, each of them has something to hide. Presumably something worth killing for. But there's one thing I still can't quite figure out."

"What's that?" the policeman asked after a moment.

"What she expected to gain by forcing them to put on this play!" I snorted in disbelief. "I can't imagine she thought she'd really make them do it. It would have been the ultimate humiliation for them all if it had gone ahead. If she were truly blackmailing them over what she was insinuating in this play, why did she suddenly try to bring it all into the open?"

Detective Inspector Chase examined his hands rather closely for a very long minute.

"I believe I can tell you this in all confidence," he said. "As I explained earlier, I have just come from attending the postmortem on Miss Winterton. The police surgeon discovered that she had a large tumor on the brain. Such a condition, as I expect you're aware, can cause someone to act erratically at times."

"Good grief," I said. "No wonder the poor woman was dotty."

"Exactly," Chase said. "And now, in view of what has happened," he said, "I had better take this straightaway to my office for safekeeping." He stood up. "In the meantime, I'll have one of my men start making discreet inquiries about anyone who might have come along in the last half hour and been seen entering your front door."

I followed him out into the hall and to the front door. "I wish you good luck," I said. "I hope this will be the break in the case that you've been needing. Though having quickly scanned the play, I'm not sure just what is going to turn out to be the key to the case."

"I'm sure if you'd had more time with it, you might have

come up with something." And with that ambiguous parting shot, the detective inspector took his leave.

So much for dazzling the fair Robin, I thought regretfully, closing the door. And bloody hell to whoever it was who'd had the nerve to sneak into my home in broad daylight and steal something from my desk! That made me quite angry. I had held the anger in check while the detective inspector was with me, but now I felt the urge to tighten my hands around the miscreant's neck. Vampires are even more protective of their personal space than all the crystal sniffers in California. For the sake of whoever had done it, I hoped the police got to him or her first.

I went back into my office and stared glumly at the blank computer screen. I felt disinclined to do much of anything except fume.

Whom had the colonel warned about the existence of the play?

I quickly ruled out Jane Hardwick, for she was probably still in Oxford or en route back to Snupperton Mumsley. The only person with whom I had seen the colonel in close contact was Letty Butler-Melville. I recalled that odd scene in the shadows of the churchyard. What had it meant? Had they been plotting something together even then? They seemed unlikely allies. But I really knew so little about them.

This could be one of those Orient Express–type cases. (If you haven't read the book, I won't spoil it for you.) But I thought that would require too much cooperation in certain quarters.

Besides Jane Hardwick, the only other suspects in the case who lived close enough to nip over, slip into my house, and steal the play were the Butler-Melvilles. It had to have been one of them.

If Neville Butler-Melville had had a hand in the death of the colonel's son, however, why was the colonel assisting him or his wife?

None of this made much sense, given what I knew about the case. There was obviously some crucial fact missing. Maybe Jane had unearthed it during her visit to Oxford.

I eyed my watch in irritation. Just a few minutes past two. When would Jane get back from Oxford?

Chapter Twenty-seven

Patience was never my long suit. Sitting at my desk, waiting for Jane to return from Oxford, I fumed over the theft of the manuscript from my desk—not an activity guaranteed to lighten my temper. I needed to be doing something, but I was in the wrong frame of mind to attempt any writing. Whatever I wrote now would surely have to be discarded later. I glanced out the window yet again, looking for signs of Jane's return, but to no avail. I did behold, however, the sight of Lady Prunella Blitherington sailing up the walk toward my front door. Just what I needed for the day to improve.

Sighing heavily, I got up from my desk and went into the hallway. I debated ignoring the insistent ringing of the bell, but I'd have to face her again at some point. Dealing with her might even prove diverting.

"Good afternoon, Dr. Kirby-Jones," she said stiffly. "I trust you will pardon this interruption, but I felt that I must speak with you."

"Certainly, Lady Blitherington," I said. "Please do come in." I ushered her into the sitting room, where she looked about uncertainly for a moment, as if trying to find somewhere clean enough to park her aristocratic posterior.

I gestured toward a chair, and she plopped down. I winced, hearing the protesting groans of the belabored chair.

"Now, what can I do for you, Lady Blitherington?" My tone was brisk but polite. Just.

"I have come to apologize, Dr. Kirby-Jones," she said, gazing down at her feet, "for that *most* unfortunate scene I enacted. You *will*, I trust, forgive the protectiveness of a creature who is a *mother* first above *all* things." Then she had the nerve to bat her eyelashes at me.

"My dear Lady Blitherington, I can well understand your maternal instincts, but frankly, I cannot see that offering your son a job—and one, moreover, at which he seems extremely capable thus far—can in any way demean him."

"I am endeavoring, Dr. Kirby-Jones, to keep in mind that you are an *American,* and however well educated you *might* be, nevertheless you are *still* unaware of the *nuances* of social position in our village. And, indeed, in our *society* as a whole."

I started to speak, but she held up her hand to stall me.

"Pray, let me continue, Dr. Kirby-Jones. You *will* have your say at the appropriate time." In other circumstances, her air of noblesse oblige might have been amusing. I simmered quietly. "Giles is destined for other work, something of *far* more importance than serving as secretary to an historian, no matter *how* distinguished." She sniffed. "One of our connections, my dear cousin Sir Horace Ragsbottom, is even now holding a place for Giles in one of his companies. I feel it *most* imperative that you should endeavor to *dissuade* Giles from this *foolish* notion of his becoming a *writer.* He belongs among men of *power* and influence in the City. It is his *birthright,* after all."

"Yes, Lady Blitherington, I do believe I had heard that your father was in *trade,*" I said. She blanched slightly. "But if such is Giles's birthright, why does he persist in calling himself simply "Giles" and eschewing his title?" Not waiting for a response, I asked, "Could it be that he has no right to that title?"

"Whatever do you *mean,* Dr. Kirby-Jones?" Lady Prunella's air of outrage almost had me fooled for a moment. "How *dare* you cast such aspersions!"

I shrugged. "From information I have recently encountered, I was of the impression that Giles's birth occurred at an *interesting* interval after your late husband had departed the country for a two-month visit to Kenya."

"*Where,* pray tell me, did you get such scandalous *misinformation?*" she demanded. "That is utterly, *utterly* ridiculous!"

I could see, however, that my accusation had badly rattled her. Despite her protests, she had heard this before. From Abigail Winterton, no doubt.

"Is it truly misinformation?" I asked.

"Giles's father was my late husband, Sir Bosworth Blitherington," she said in tones that would have chilled my blood if it weren't cold enough already, "and, if you *must* know, Giles was, like many first babies, a *late* arrival."

That had the ring of truth to it. In spite of myself, I was nearly convinced. But a little further probing seemed in order. I probably couldn't make her dislike me any more. "If someone, like our late postmistress, perhaps, were to have made such a *rumor* public, how would you have felt?"

Her eyes rolled back into her head, and for a moment I thought she was going to faint. I was relishing the notion of pouring cold water over her when she sat forward, eyes wide open and blazing fire. "Abigail Winterton would never have *dared.* She *knew* the truth about Giles's father, but she couldn't *resist* teasing me from time to time over the *lateness* of Giles's arrival after my *dear* Bozzie was sent off to Kenya on that mission!"

"Now, at least," I observed mildly, "Miss Winterton can

no longer taunt you—or spread the rumor throughout the village."

The implication finally hit her. She stood up. "I had *nothing* to do with the death of Abigail Winterton, I assure you. To think otherwise is *utterly* ridiculous. You are even more *common* than I thought, to harbor *such* ideas about someone of superior station!" She looked around for her handbag, which had fallen behind her chair. Retrieving it with a jerk, she faced me again. "Why Giles is infatuated with you, I'll *never* know! It's bad enough that he has these horrible *proclivities* in the first case—frankly I blame his public school—but if I have *anything* to say about it, he'll never darken *your* door again."

I stood up, towering over her. "That's *enough*. Now, sit *down!*" Startled, she complied, clutching her handbag to her bosom for protection. A bit like using a postage stamp to cover a football field, frankly.

"It might have escaped your notice, madam, but a woman was *murdered* in this village. And murdered in a particularly unpleasant way. From what I've seen, you had *just* as good a motive as anyone else in this village. You, with your notions about your place in society and your attitudes toward others who *you* seem to think are inferior because of an accident of birth." I snorted. "Have you so quickly forgotten your *own* origins, Miss Ragsbottom? *My* family owns one of the largest plantations in the southern United States and has done so since the early nineteenth century. They are as well educated and as well bred as anyone in *this* village. My family tree is full of senators and professors and philanthropists and high-powered businessmen. And if I want to hire your bloody *son* to be my *secretary*, then I damn well will! Anything *else* which might happen is up to him and me and is *none* of your business! Are we *clear* on that?"

The whole village was probably clear on that, because I

forget just how loud my voice can get. Lady Blitherington, eyes wide with fear, simply nodded. I stepped back, and we both subsided into our chairs.

In a gentler tone I continued: "I admire your wish to protect your son, Lady Blitherington, but he is an adult. An intelligent and capable young man. A little spoiled, but he'll grow out of that, given the proper direction. Working for me might just do that for him, and it certainly can't hurt. Shall we have a truce, then?"

I stood and held out my hand to her. Blinking, she regarded me for a long moment, then held out her hand. We shook on it.

In curiously harmonious silence, I escorted her to the front door. She hesitated for a moment on the doorstep, and I said, my voice firm, "Good day, Lady Blitherington."

"And to you, Dr. Kirby-Jones." She turned and marched away.

Shutting the door, I thought, *Well, Giles, you had bloody well better be worth it!* I could almost see the humor in the situation. Almost.

I went back into my office and looked out the window toward Jane's cottage. Signs of her return were still lacking; I pondered what to do next. Lady Blitherington's visit had unsettled me, but at least I thought I could safely rule one suspect off the list.

Just who was it, though, who had conspired with Colonel Clitheroe to steal the copy of Miss Winterton's play from my office? I still thought one of the Butler-Melvilles the best bet, but I decided that a quick visit to Trevor Chase wouldn't hurt. After all, he was close enough to have nipped down to my cottage, though I couldn't imagine his collaborating with the colonel on anything like this.

Grabbing up hat and sunglasses, I went out the door and down the lane toward the Book Chase. Inside the shop I found Trevor sitting glumly behind the counter, staring off into space.

"Good afternoon, Trevor," I said, bringing him out of his reverie. He hadn't even noticed the bell on the door clanging as I entered.

"Oh, Simon," he responded with a noticeable lack of enthusiasm. "Come to visit the village pariah, have you?"

"Whatever do you mean, Trevor?" I said lightly, pulling off hat and sunglasses and placing them atop the counter. "Why should you be a pariah all of a sudden?"

Trevor grimaced. "Surely you've heard that I was invited to the police station in Bedford to assist the police with their inquiries? Surely you know that I am the chief suspect in Abigail Winterton's murder?"

"I had heard the former, Trevor, but I have not heard anyone calling you the chief suspect." Other than Jane and me, I added silently.

Trevor laughed bitterly. "It doesn't take much in this village. You'll learn quickly enough, Simon, that everything you do, or even anything someone thinks you do, becomes a matter of public interest and debate."

"I grew up in a small town in the southern United States. It isn't much different there."

He sighed. "No, I suppose not."

"But you've not been charged with anything, have you?"

"No," Trevor said, his face brightening. "Because I have an alibi for the night of the murder!"

"Then why did you have to spend such a long time with the police?"

"Because I didn't feel that I could compromise the person who constituted my alibi," Trevor said, his face darkening.

"Why? Because he was underage?" I asked bluntly.

"Certainly not!" Trevor stood and glared at me from behind the counter. "After one unfortunate incident in my own youth, I have been careful to form *attachments* only with those of an appropriate age, I assure you." His eyes narrowed in suspicion. "Where might you have heard otherwise?"

I waved a hand vaguely in the air. "Oh, there was a rumor about something that happened during your first teaching post in the north of England."

Trevor sat down with a thump. His face lost all color. "Does the whole *village* know about that?"

I shook my head, and color started seeping back into his face. "Thank God," he whispered. Then he realized. "How did *you* find out about that?"

"It doesn't really matter, Trevor," I said gently. "I can promise you that it will go no further. Now, tell me about your alibi. Surely you have nothing to worry about now if someone can vouch for you during the time that Miss Winterton was murdered?"

"I suppose you're right, Simon." Trevor drew a long, calming breath. "The young man who provided my alibi could be placed in a rather dangerous position were it to become known that he spent the night in question with me. He's a mechanic, and his mates wouldn't take kindly to the fact that he prefers men."

"I'm sure the police will do what they can to respect his need for privacy, not to mention safety," I said sympathetically.

"I hesitated to involve him," Trevor said, "but he heard that I had been taken to police headquarters. He came there, on his own, in my behalf. He doesn't lack for courage." His face beamed with pride and affection, and something more besides, perhaps a sense of something new and wonderful discovered. For a brief moment I actually felt jealous.

"Good for him," I said. I picked up my hat and sunglasses from the counter. "I'm relieved to know that you're well and truly out of it, Trevor. As for the village, don't worry. As soon as the truth is out, they'll have forgotten that you were ever questioned at such length."

"I trust that you're right, Simon," Trevor said.

"Then I'll bid you good day."

Trevor's farewell echoing in my ears, I stepped outside. That was two suspects down. With Lady Blitherington and Trevor Chase out of the running, the circle had narrowed. Colonel Clitheroe, Neville Butler-Melville, and Lettie Butler-Melville. Which of them was the killer? And why?

Chapter Twenty-eight

As I perambulated down the lane, deep in thought, a black Volvo sped by me. Startled, I recognized Jane Hardwick at the wheel. Quickening my pace, I arrived at Jane's cottage as she was opening her front door, her arms laden with bags bearing the logo of Blackwells. I smiled briefly. In Oxford on a sleuthing mission, Jane couldn't pass up a visit to a bookstore.

Jane welcomed me with an excited grin, looking almost girlish, and I helped her with her parcels. "What did you find out?" I demanded, and she shushed me until we were safely inside.

Bags placed carefully on a table in the hall, Jane and I ensconced ourselves on the sofa in her sitting room. "I received some very interesting information. Nothing completely conclusive, mind you, but certainly very suggestive. I think we're nearing the end."

"Do tell!" I said. "And then I have some things to tell you as well!"

"I have a very dear friend, Araminta McClain, who is one of us, vintage 1801. (She actually knew Jane Austen, Simon!) Minta has been in Oxford for the past seventy years or so, and she knows all the decent gossip there is to know. And if she doesn't know it herself, she knows exactly the person from whom to extract it."

"Sounds like an important person to know," I said. "But if she is so much in the know, how does she keep herself camouflaged?"

Jane laughed. "To the mortal world, Minta looks seventy-odd, with a decided emphasis on the 'odd.' I suppose if anyone ever gave it much thought, they'd realize she's been there forever, but while others come and go, Minta's there, essentially the same, year after year. People tend to take her rather for granted, and she encourages that."

"Clever," I said, "Miss Marple in the flesh, so to speak."

"Yes, exactly. Anyway, I consulted Minta, and she supplied what we needed. She even remembered Neville and Lester Clitheroe vaguely from their days as undergraduates. One of her sources of information at the time was in the same college, and Minta got some rather juicy tidbits about Neville and Lester."

Jane paused teasingly, and I urged her to continue. "You'll love this bit, Simon! Apparently, Neville and Lester were *extremely* close. So close, in fact, that they often slept in the same bed." She paused again. "But they weren't doing a lot of sleeping."

I whistled. "And I thought dear Neville, handsome as he is, was unabashedly straight. Appearances *can* be deceiving!"

Jane laughed for a moment, then sobered. "The most interesting bit of information about *that* relationship that I gleaned was this: Apparently Lester very much enjoyed dressing up in women's clothes. Undergraduates get up to all sorts of rags, some of which involve cross-dressing, but from what Minta said, Lester's interest went far beyond that."

"What are you saying, Jane? Transvestism isn't all that unusual. Do you mean that Lester actually wanted to *be* a woman?"

"That's what Minta seemed to think." Jane shrugged. "Neville was allegedly heard to refer to Lester as 'Lettice' on occasion."

"My Gawd," I said. "Then what about the mysterious accident that befell poor Lester in the Swiss Alps? No more Lester/Lettice?"

Jane's eyebrows arched upward. "After bringing Minta up-to-date on what had been going on here and telling her what I knew of Neville and Letty Butler-Melville, Minta suggested that the authorities might want to dig a bit deeper into Letty's background."

"Because the death of Lester Clitheroe might have been staged so that he could assume the identity of Letty Clivering? Who in turn became Mrs. Neville Butler-Melville?"

Jane nodded.

"It makes a certain sense, given Letty's general appearance and some of her mannerisms," I said. "Or should I say *his?*"

"According to that clipping in Abigail's trove, Neville and Letty met in Denmark."

"Where she/he could very well have had gender reassignment surgery," I said.

"Exactly."

"But what's the big deal? So Lester became Letty? Who cares?" Then the answer hit me. "The Church of England would *never* go for a vicar with a transsexual wife. Good grief! Is such a marriage even *legal* in England?"

"I don't know about that, Simon, but you're certainly right about the church. That would be the end of Neville's career, such as it is, in the grand old C of E."

I stared at Jane for a long moment. Suddenly, various things were beginning to make a lot of sense. "Letty is the one who actually ministers to the needs of the parish, not Neville. And I'd be willing to bet the advance on my next book that she writes the sermons, and so on. She's the one who does the real work of the parish, while Neville sits there looking handsome and distinguished and vicarlike."

Jane sighed. "Yes. I had never given much thought to the situation because in my experience many clergy wives are much like Letty. Hardworking handmaidens of the Lord who do their best to further their husbands' careers, veritable mainstays of the parish. Neville is perhaps more of a figurehead than I had realized, but Letty is truly the vicar of this parish."

Jane and I sat quietly for a while. I thought with great sadness of an institution that had no place for someone such as Letty Butler-Melville. A woman in a man's body who had made the most drastic change possible for a human being to make, under a compulsion that even I could only dimly understand. The Church was only now, and very reluctantly, it seemed to me, accepting women into important pastoral roles, but twenty-five years ago those avenues were not available to women in England, as far as I knew. So I supposed that Letty had gone about it the only way she knew how, working through her husband, who was obviously complicit in her scheme.

Then Abigail Winterton had somehow got onto the situation and threatened to reveal their secret, thereby destroying both their lives. I frowned.

"But, Jane," I said at last, and Jane looked at me inquiringly. "There wasn't much in Abigail's cache of evidence that would indicate that she really knew the truth about this. Not even in the play."

"What do you mean, in the play?" Jane's tone was sharp with disbelief. "Has a copy of it turned up?"

I explained quickly how the play had come into my possession. I gave her an edited version of the play's contents and a recounting of my conversations with various and sundry during the day. I had omitted the bits about Jane in the play, and oddly enough, she didn't ask me whether she had figured in the play. I pondered the significance of that while we continued talking.

"There really wasn't anything in the play to indicate that she knew the complete truth about Letty Butler-Melville," I finally concluded.

"Abigail doesn't seem to have gotten close to the actual truth," Jane said. "But if she kept pressing the point about Lester Clitheroe's supposed death, they could have gotten the wind up sufficiently to take some drastic action."

"And the colonel is implicated as well, since he had to have called either Letty or Neville to come and remove the play from my office."

"Yes, the colonel is involved. He certainly knew that Letty was his, well, I suppose we'll have to say 'daughter,' won't we? But what is the extent of his involvement? Merely as an accomplice? Or could he have done it?"

"I don't know, Jane," I said. "Frankly, I'm sorry that we even got this far, to discover all this. It's appallingly sad, isn't it?"

"It is," Jane said softly. "There are times when death is the only answer no matter how distasteful one might find it as a solution. The urge for self-protection is an incredibly strong one." Her eyes had darkened, and she seemed to be looking somewhere within, dredging up old memories that might still be causing her pain. Her hands twitched in her lap. Then she came back to the present. "Though sometimes the circumstances might seem to warrant it." Her tone was firm, and she met my gaze with calm assurance.

"You're absolutely right, Jane. This has to be resolved, and justice somehow must be served. But what would the police think if we went to them with our bits of gossip and speculation? They already have the play. Maybe we should just leave them to it."

"They might well think that we're interfering busybodies with too much time on our hands," Jane said with obvious patience, "but if we take this information to them, Robin Chase might believe us." She tapped a finger against her temple. "But having something more concrete wouldn't hurt. I do think we should do our best to force the murderer's hand."

"With some sort of trap, I presume?" I began to see where all this might be leading as a certain pattern made itself evident in my thoughts. I groaned inwardly; I could never get away with this in one of my own mysteries, but in this case it might work. I thought quickly as an idea occurred to me. I filed it away for further thought.

"Okay, Simon," Jane said, "here's what we'll do." Nodding at suitable junctures, I agreed to her plan to trap Abigail Winterton's murderer. *Hercule Poirot, eat your little gray cells out,* I thought smugly.

Lights glowed in the downstairs windows of the vicarage as the evening faded gently into twilight. Darkness would come in another quarter hour, or so I reckoned as Jane and I walked toward the front door. The rest of Snupperton Mumsley was quiet around us, as if to underscore the seriousness of our task, and Jane seemed to make an unusual amount of noise as she banged the ornate knocker.

"Nervous?" Jane asked, smiling with cool confidence.

"No," I replied a bit testily. "Only anxious to get this over with." I had made a couple of telephone calls during the afternoon on my own initiative, and I was finally satisfied that I was doing the right thing in order to get this whole mess resolved. Jane might not agree with me, but there would be time enough to sort that out afterward.

The door swung open then, cutting off any further conversation between Jane and me. Here goes nothing, I thought, following Jane across the threshold. Neville Butler-Melville uttered no word of greeting as he opened the door. He simply waved us inside. His handsome face was scored with worry lines, Neville had aged since the last time I had seen him.

Jane and I paused at the door of the sitting room. Conversation ceased, and Lady Prunella Blitherington cut off her oration on the current state of British theater long enough to smile a welcome at us. This afternoon's confrontation seemed to have cleared the air between us. Samantha Stevens looked delighted at the respite occasioned by our arrival, and she motioned for Jane and me to join her on the lumpy sofa. Trevor Chase stood across the room, talking quietly to Giles Blitherington, and I smothered a momentary flare of emotion at seeing them, heads bent ever so slightly together.

Colonel Clitheroe came into the room trailing Letty Butler-Melville, who was wheeling a tea tray laden with cups and saucers and a teapot. I groaned inwardly. Just what the evening needed: some of Letty's truly dreadful tea.

The hum of conversation resumed as Letty served the tea. Jane had jumped up to offer assistance. I chatted idly with Samantha Stevens as Letty and Jane made the rounds, Letty pouring and Jane serving. I accepted a cup from Jane, raising it to my mouth almost without thinking. My nose caught a whiff of something odd about the tea. I froze. Then I did my best to pretend to take a sip. I set the cup down on the table in front of me and eyed it thoughtfully for a long moment.

Jane and Letty had by now completed serving everyone and had taken their places with the group. While I listened with half an ear to Jane's recital of her finds at Blackwells to Samantha Stevens, I thought some more.

After a few minutes, I cleared my throat. Expectant faces turned toward me.

"Thank you all for agreeing to meet on such short notice," I said, "but I couldn't wait to share my discovery with you."

"Yes, you did say when you called me that you had something exciting," Jane said. Then she addressed the group casually: "He gave me no hint about it, so I must admit to excruciating curiosity."

"Yes, do tell us, Dr. Kirby-Jones, about this *discovery* of yours," Lady Blitherington said, her eyes aglow. "It sounds *most* interesting."

"I do believe you will *all* find it of great interest," I said modestly. "You see, I received something in the mail today, something *utterly* fascinating." Pausing for effect, I then continued, "I received a copy of Abigail Winterton's *play!*"

I heard the hiss of several intakes of breath. This was bad news to more than one person in the room, but only one of them truly had reason to fear.

"A letter from the dead!" Giles exclaimed. "How morbidly fascinating!"

His mother shot him a pained look, which he patently ignored. "Surely you've read the play, Simon?" Giles asked. "Was it truly dreadful?"

The dear boy was playing along as if he had read my script. From the twinkle in his eyes, I knew he was on to at least part of the game that Jane and I were playing. I smiled inwardly.

"Oh, the play was *far* from dreadful," I said airily. "I'm sure you will all find it *most* amusing despite its deficiencies of style." With a flourish I pulled several copies out of the pocket of the bulkily unfashionable jacket I was wearing and started handing them around.

Giles and Jane had the only two faces in the group that retained a healthy amount of color at that moment. The room was deadly still for a long moment as shaky hands turned the pages. Gradually, faces resumed their normal colorations.

Letty Butler-Melville looked up from the copy she and Neville shared between them. "But this, this . . ." she sputtered.

I nodded, my expression grave. "Yes, I know. Rather sad, isn't it? I don't know *how* Miss Winterton thought she could get away with such a blatant rip-off of *The Cocktail Party*, but perhaps she presumed none of us was familiar with the works of T. S. Eliot."

Trevor Chase threw his pages down onto a table near his chair. "Then what the hell was she going on about (pardon me, I'm sure, Vicar) with that tripe about *moral decay* in a little village. This drivel is pathetic, but it's not anything about a village!"

Ah, the wonders of word processors, not to mention the ability to type quickly! It had taken me about three and a half hours to knock out this new version of Abigail Winterton's death warrant. In between phone calls, that is.

I clucked my tongue. "Rather appalling, isn't it? I don't know *what* she was going on about at that meeting. I thought it odd enough that she had sent *me* a copy of this through the mail. It quite gave me the shivers when I realized what it was, I can tell you." I paused to give them a suitably spooked look.

"Maybe the play she was talking about was another one that she had squirreled away somewhere," I said slowly. "Perhaps a copy of that play still exists somewhere." I looked straight at Letty and Neville Butler-Melville as I said it, and Letty blinked. "It would be *most* interesting if that other play were to surface after all this time, I should think." I shrugged. "But it *might* never happen." My eyes shot sideways at Jane. She sat very still on the sofa beside Samantha Stevens, who, in contrast, was squirming with delight.

Mrs. Stevens waved her copy of the play in the air. "This will certainly not do for our production." She shook her head. "I do wonder what on earth Abigail was thinking. I vote that we accept Giles's play for our fund-raiser and get on with the planning."

Amid the hearty concurrences, I sat back and watched Giles nervously explain to the group that he had actually written the play with Trevor's help and that Trevor deserved a great deal of the credit. Proud as I was of Giles's accepting responsibility in this fashion, I kept thinking about my cup of tea.

My cup of tea, which someone had poisoned.

Chapter Twenty-nine

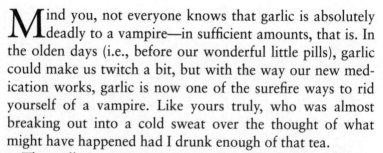

Mind you, not everyone knows that garlic is absolutely deadly to a vampire—in sufficient amounts, that is. In the olden days (i.e., before our wonderful little pills), garlic could make us twitch a bit, but with the way our new medication works, garlic is now one of the surefire ways to rid yourself of a vampire. Like yours truly, who was almost breaking out into a cold sweat over the thought of what might have happened had I drunk enough of that tea.

The really interesting question was: Who had put the garlic into my tea? It was a relatively simple thing to do, even in front of the group. Sprinkle quite a dash of garlic powder into the teacup, add Letty's supremely bitter hot tea, and you have yourself a handy dose of Raid for vampires. Unless Letty Butler-Melville had somehow sussed out the fact that I was a vampire, that left one person in the room who knew it for sure.

Jane Hardwick.

Why had Jane tried to poison me in front of all these folk?

The answer to that was all too easy. My earlier suspicions of Jane had been realized, though I had been inclined to dismiss them for a while. I nearly blushed right then and there when I thought back over how gullible I had been, how easily directed by Jane all along. But I had finally seen through what Jane was doing all along, and I had to consider her, along with Letty Butler-Melville, as the chief suspects in the murder. And now Jane was trying to get me out of the way so she could go on with her plan.

But Jane's little plan had been foiled because there was one thing she apparently didn't know. She had been a vampire for so long *before* the invention of those aforementioned little pills that she didn't know that someone like me, who had taken them from the very beginning, after making the transition, still retained most of his sense of smell. The same thing applied to taste buds. She hadn't expected me to be able to smell—or taste—the garlic in the tea. I should have taken one sip and then keeled over within about two minutes. Which would have left Jane completely free to continue with her own little Machiavellian scheme to frame Letty Butler-Melville for the murder of Abigail Winterton.

I tuned back in to the conversation. Time enough to serve Jane her comeuppance a bit later, now that she had confirmed my suspicions. The others were still discussing putting on Giles and Trevor's play.

"I think it's a marvelous idea," I broke in, "and you can certainly count on me to do what I can to assist." I looked directly at Jane. Jane knew I was on to her. She stared back as if daring me to say something publicly.

"Having settled in here," I continued, "I can't imagine wanting to live anywhere else. Nor can I imagine that anything could happen to convince me otherwise despite the rather unfortunate events of this past week. And, speaking of that, I wanted to tell you all that after speaking with Detective Inspector Chase this afternoon, I can assure you that the case is about to be brought to a conclusion. I can't say any more at the moment, but the detective inspector assured me that an arrest was imminent." I fixed Jane with a steely gaze. "The police are even now gathering more evidence nearby."

Amidst the cries of astonishment, Jane Hardwick eyed me coolly, and I met her glare for glare. "That is most welcome news, Simon," Jane said, standing up. "I'm sure the whole village will sleep more easily tonight knowing that poor Abigail's murderer will be brought to justice soon. But, if you will all excuse me, I have had a rather long and trying day, and I must get home. Good night, everyone." She moved quickly and gracefully through the group and was out the front door before anyone had much chance to return her farewell.

As the others stood in the wake of Jane's rather abrupt leave-taking, I made one further announcement. "I should correct something I said earlier." They all watched me carefully, Letty Butler-Melville with singular intent. "If Miss Winterton did indeed write another play, whatever it contained is lost to the public eye forever. Whatever nasty surprises she might have been planning will most likely remain unsprung."

Letty Butler-Melville mouthed the words "Thank you" to me, and I inclined my head very slightly. I had been convinced that she was the murderer, but my phone call to Tristan Lovelace during the afternoon had given me pause to think and to consider Jane Hardwick more seriously. Had it not been for Jane's attempt to poison me tonight, however, I might still have been inclined to see Letty as the chief suspect.

"Are the police waiting for Jane Hardwick?" Samantha Stevens interrupted my reflections with a cool assurance.

"Yes," I said. Though I didn't expect that they would actually be able to take her into custody. My money was on Jane to slip through their grasp. A vampire as old as she knew all the tricks for disappearing quickly and quietly. And I'd be willing to bet that she had spent part of her day making plans for an escape should it become necessary.

"Why did she murder Abigail?" Letty Butler-Melville asked. Her voice held sorrow tinged with relief. She probably realized what a narrow escape she'd had.

"Did any of you know that Miss Winterton wandered around the village late at night, poking about and peering into windows?" I asked.

Surprised, they all disclaimed any knowledge. Lady Prunella was startled; then the light of comprehension spread across her face. Her "stalker" had been Abigail Winterton.

"Well"—I sighed, continuing—"apparently at some point in her late-night rambles, Miss Winterton stumbled across the fact that Jane had a rather *interesting* way of ridding herself of, er, young men of her acquaintance."

"Oh, dear Lord," Neville Butler-Melville said, "all that work in her garden!"

Colonel Clitheroe looked positively ill, and I could sympathize. Every time I thought of how Jane had hoodwinked and manipulated me, I wanted to throw up.

At that point, I felt I had to get out and get some air. I made my farewells, which no one except Giles seemed to notice. I headed for the door with Giles at my heels. Lady Blitherington barely seemed to notice that Giles was leaving with me.

Walking in companionable silence, Giles and I made our way down the lane to my cottage. Numerous vehicles stood parked in the lane around Jane's cottage, and lights blazed all around. We paused for a moment to observe what we could. Sounds of digging and scraping echoed from the yard behind the cottage. Wouldn't be long now, I sighed, and the police would probably have the evidence they needed.

Giles waited until we were at the front door before saying anything to me. "I still can't believe that Jane Hardwick, of all people, murdered Abigail Winterton! Surely, Simon, you must know something *more* if you've been in such close contact with the police! How on earth did you figure it all out?"

I made Giles follow me into my office and sit down across from me before I said anything. I would feel more comfortable discussing this from behind my desk, as if I were consulting with a student about some research problem.

"I talked to an old friend today, Giles," I said slowly. "An old friend who happened to know a little something about Jane Hardwick's past. This old friend"—here Giles grinned knowingly, for it probably hadn't taken him long to figure out that I was talking about Tristan Lovelace, previous owner of my cottage—"told me that Jane had certain rather voracious appetites. Furthermore, that she was not always discreet in the way that she, er, terminated the relationships."

I had no doubt that the police would find, beneath the luxurious growth of Jane's garden, the bodies of several young men. Young men who had, once upon a time, been rather handsome. The autopsies would reveal certain fascinating peculiarities about the remains, and the word "vampire" might even be mentioned. But more than likely it would never make it into the official report. After all, no one really believes we exist. Right?

Giles sat and pondered what I had told him. Thankfully, he didn't seem to require any further explanation. "I suppose," he finally commented, "that explains why Jane Hardwick was always doing something to her garden. The rest of the village speculated on her spending money like that, but no one figured out that she might be doing it to hide bodies!" Alas, one of those little tidbits of village lore I hadn't known, but which might have gotten me to the correct solution much sooner.

"Everyone except Abigail Winterton, that is." And she had paid with her life. Jane, so incredibly strong, had broken the woman's neck. During our phone conversation this afternoon, Detective Inspector Chase had confided in me the full details of the manner of Miss Winterton's death. I could see the scene playing out in my head, and it made me sick to my stomach. To think that I was beginning to consider Jane a friend. Yet she had been pulling the strings from the moment I met her.

I thought back to my call to Tristan Lovelace this afternoon. When I finally got through to him, at the university in Houston where he teaches, he had just reached his office and was none too thrilled to hear from me. He hated having to talk to anyone before noon. I cut through his impatience with attitude of my own.

"What can you tell me about one of my neighbors, Tris? A woman called Jane Hardwick."

His snort of irritation echoed across the miles. "Really, Simon, have you called me just to natter on about your neighbors? Haven't you something better to do than indulge in idle village gossip? Like write one of those potboilers of yours?"

Taking a deep breath, I kept my temper. "Let's leave aside, for the moment, the fact that you know every bit of dirt ever uncovered about your whole department, not to mention the rest of the university, and that you willingly share it with anyone who will listen." I pretended not to hear the dig about my novels. "Instead, let's focus on what you have failed to tell me about the only other vampire—as far as I know—in Snupperton Mumsley!"

Tristan chuckled. "Ah, Simon, you haven't lost that bitchy quality which so endeared you to me. For a time, at least."

I was biting my tongue, and he knew it. Chuckling again, indulgently this time, he went on: "Dear Jane. Don't tell me she's up to her tricks again? She's worse than you or I ever dared to be, my dear boy. Can't seem to keep her hands off any handsome young bloke who takes her fancy. The only problem is, from what I've heard, she still has an old-fashioned way of ending the relationship. If one could dignify it by that word." He laughed. "That's what I've been told. I've not seen any of this firsthand, mind you."

"So while you were in Snupperton Mumsley, you never observed anything untoward?" I persisted.

"No, dear boy, I didn't," Tristan said a trifle testily. "Jane prefers to surround herself with those who are easily led"— well, *ouch!*—"and I was not one of those, as *you* well know."

I sighed into the phone. Tristan and Jane had been the proverbial oil and water, then, while Jane must have thought I was completely dense and suggestible. After all, I had been like an eager little puppy, so delighted was I to find a new "friend" ready-made in Snupperton Mumsley. I was still willing to give her the benefit of the doubt, nevertheless, because Letty Butler-Melville's motive was so compelling.

Quickly I sketched out the scenario for Tris, and he agreed, a bit reluctantly, that Jane could have killed Abigail Winterton in order to keep the postmistress from raising a stink. "I saw Abigail Winterton, late one night, wandering through the village. That must be how she got on to Jane."

Tristan laughed. "Yes, Simon, poor Abigail was a chronic insomniac, and many a night I looked out my window, when taking a break from work, to see her slinking about the village. At two and three in the morning. Since Jane usually confined her trysts to the wee hours of the morning in order to keep the villagers in the dark"—and he actually had the nerve to chuckle at his own atrocious pun—"Abigail Winterton was one of the few besides me who would have caught on to her dead-of-night dalliances."

I came back to the present. Giles had sat patiently while I was lost in my thoughts. He cleared his throat now and brought me back to the present. "What do you think will happen to Jane Hardwick now, Simon? I just can't imagine someone like her languishing in a prison cell."

I laughed bitterly. "That depends, Giles, on whether the police were able to catch her."

"What do you mean, Simon? Why wouldn't they have

caught her?" Giles stared at me, his eyes narrowing in suspicion. "Did you help her elude the police?"

I shook my head. "I planned all this with Detective Inspector Chase, Giles. Jane thought I was going along with *her* little scheme to frame someone else for the murder, but I had already suspected that she was the killer. So I set up a second plan to trap *her* with the help of the police if she turned out to be the murderer. Which she did."

Giles's face lightened. "Then how could she get away from the police? Surely they were watching for her?"

How could I explain this to him without revealing the complete truth? "You see, Giles, Jane is apparently somewhat experienced at this. Making a quick getaway, that is. When she left the vicarage tonight, she probably got out of the village as fast as she could and has gone to ground somewhere. The police should have been waiting for her outside the vicarage, but she could have gotten away from them. I don't know. But I'd be willing to bet she won't stand trial."

Giles didn't appear too pleased with that, but at least he no longer seemed to think I had helped Jane escape justice. Human justice, that is.

I couldn't tell him that Jane would be facing justice of another kind. Vampire justice. With the advent of our chemical alternative to bloodsucking, vampires had become increasingly wary of preying upon humans. So much so that there were vampire vigilantes who made sure that offenders like Jane didn't repeat their mistakes. When Giles left tonight, I had one final phone call to make. I felt a bit like Lord Peter Wimsey, meting out justice. But it had to be done.

And that was probably why Jane had attempted to kill me. Because she knew that, one way or another, I'd expose her. Neither human nor vampire justice would have had much appeal to Jane. Getting rid of me and framing Letty Butler-Melville for the murder provided her with the best way out of a sticky situation.

"If nothing else," Giles said, "I suppose we can get back to life as usual in Snupperton Mumsley." He grinned. "What a welcome you've had, Simon!"

I laughed again, less bitterly this time. "How right you are, Giles. How very right you are." I stood up. "Now, my dear boy, it's time you were on your way."

Giles stood and waited until I had come from behind my desk to stand beside him. He looked at me, his eyes full of longing. "Are you sure I must go home tonight, Simon?"

I searched his face for a moment. "Yes, Giles, for now, I think that would be best. We have plenty of time. Don't let's rush anything."

He smiled ruefully, and I accompanied him to the front door. He held out his hand, and I grasped it. "See you tomorrow, Giles. Don't forget, you have a job now!"

Laughing, Giles strode out the door and down the walk. In the glow of lights from Jane's cottage, I could see him as he turned and blew me a kiss. Smiling, I shut the door and went back to my desk and reached for the phone.